INTRIGUE IN CORONADO

Book 2
PICS Series
(Partners in Crime Solving)

℘

Donna Jeremiah
and
Peggy Leslie

PRESS

Intrigue in Coronado
by Donna Jeremiah and Peggy Leslie

Printed in the United States of America

ISBN 9781624194931

This book is a work of fiction. With the exception of known historical personages, all characters are the products of the authors' imaginations. *Intrigue in Coronado* is set on the island of Coronado, a suburb of San Diego, California. Most of the locales are real. A few, however, are figments of our imaginations.* We hope those of you who are familiar with the beautiful island will have fun distinguishing between the two.

*Notable imaginary location: Grant Lauder University. Coronado boasts no such school. But who says that will always be the case?

PICS (Partners in Crime Solving) Series

> *Storm over Coronado*
> *Intrigue in Coronado*

www.xulonpress.com

Donna Jeremiah
Ps. 27:1

Peggy Leslie
1 Cor. 2:7

ೞ

Dedicated to

OUR DAUGHTERS

Those we bore and those we happily inherited when they married our sons

DONNA'S GIRLS	PEGGY'S GIRLS
Janice Jeremiah Dodge	Karen Leslie Bayliss
Jennifer Jeremiah Sanchez	Kate Leslie Hagen
	April Jean Leslie
Cami Todd Jeremiah	Carolyn Tuohy Leslie
Merae Cox Jeremiah	Ann Kennedy Leslie

In loving memory of

ALICE JEANNE WILLIFORD McDONALD

Precious sister and dear friend of Peggy

February 20, 1943—January 17, 2012

Words in her own handwriting on the last birthday card
Jeannie sent to Peggy:

"We both know our destination and we know that
our almighty God will meet us there."

See you in heaven, Jeannie!

ACKNOWLEDGMENTS

❧

"How can I say thanks for the things You have done for me?" These words begin a song that expresses our gratitude to God for guiding and enabling us through the process of writing this book. All the true glory goes to Him.

At the same time, He has used many people to help and encourage us. Without them, our story would have been incomplete. Below are a few who were most helpful.

- Dave and Gene, we couldn't have done this without your love and support.
- Dear families, as usual you were with us every step of the way.
- Many, many thanks to our close friend and excellent local editor, Glenda Palmer of El Cajon, California. What would we have done without your tough and tender words of encouragement and critique?
- Thank you for your invaluable editing and comments...
    - ~ Carol Haynes, Oxford, Alabama
    - ~ Kate Hagen, Leucadia, California
    - ~ Ann Leslie, Poway, California.

- These friends allowed us to use their names:
    - ~ Linda Elfmon Fleishman and husband Joel, Greensboro, North Carolina Joel Fleishman succumbed to a brave battle with cancer on March 14, 2012. May the Lord keep His hand upon you, Linda.
    - ~ Durant Vick, Roanoke, Virginia
    - ~ Tim Volstad, Anchorage, Alaska

- We greatly appreciate those who helped us in various technical areas.
    ~ Don Stephenson: Guidance in legal issues in the story.
    ~ Scott Leslie, Eugene Scott Productions, San Diego, California: Expert film- production advice.
    ~ April Leslie: Professional musical suggestions.

If any details in these areas are incorrect, the mistakes are ours, not our advisors'.

- For our beautiful Cover design, we thank...
    ~ Paul Joiner (one of the most creative people we know), Director of Creative Service, Executive Producer, Turning Point Ministries
    ~ Martin Zambrano, Graphics Designer, Turning Point Ministries

- At Xulon Press, we especially thank...
    ~ José Medina, Production Representative
    ~ Melinda Howard, Typesetter
    ~ Sylvia Burleigh, Publishing Consultant

PROLOGUE

Friday evening, November 4

એ

"I...I have something to tell you," she said.

A quick, cold ocean breeze ruffled her shoulder-length ebony hair and lifted it from her slender neck. In one arm she clutched one long-stemmed Talisman rose. No fern, no tissue, simply the one exquisite gold and coral rose enclosed in a plastic sleeve. She shivered and led him a few steps away from the incoming surf.

Together they turned. At the horizon the moon cast a silvery ribbon of light across the dark, strangely still waters that spread gently over the sand. Even in the dark, sparkles of light shone like jewels from the sand.

Not sure what to expect, he asked, "Will I like it?"

She paused and stepped away so that her form was silhouetted against the moon's reflection. He saw how she hugged his rose to her bosom.

"Probably not." Her words held both dread and hope.

He moved close and encircled her waist from the back. She tensed, but didn't say more.

He waited, but she remained silent. At last he whispered, "What is it? You can tell me anything."

She turned and touched his face.

"I'm pregnant."

He pushed her away and stepped back. Jamming his hands into the pockets of his rolled-up jeans, he glared at her.

"You said you wouldn't let that happen."

She bent her head and spoke so softly he could barely hear her. "I know." She looked up, pleading with those luminous aqua eyes. "It could be a good thing, you know. A really good thing."

9

He snorted. "How can you say that? How could this possibly be a good thing?"

"Well..." She sounded so hesitant, so young and insecure, more like a scared teenager than a mature thirty-two-year-old. "Well, we could get married. We could—"

"Married! Are you crazy?" He grabbed her shoulders. "You know that's *not* going to happen!"

"But—"

He squeezed her shoulders until he could feel his fingers digging into her flesh beneath her quilted black jacket.

"An abortion." It came out like a command. "You've got to get an abortion."

She slapped him. Hard. Eyes snapping, she sneered. "I may not be the most moral woman in town, but I don't kill babies. How can you even suggest such a thing?"

"And how can you even think of anything else?"

"I told you. We can get married."

He grabbed her shoulders again and began to shake her. "And I told *you*. That's not going to happen!"

"Stop! You're hurting me!" Even as she struggled to free herself, she hung onto the rose. "And you don't think this will hurt *me*?" He let go of her shoulders and grasped her face in his hands, pressing hard and ignoring the fright in her face. "Have you thought about that? What this will do to me? You can't have this baby. You've got to get an abortion!"

"**No!**" Her scream tore the air as she pushed against his chest.

His hands moved from her face to her throat. "Shut up! You hear me? Shut up!" He squeezed her throat. Tighter. Tighter. Her eyes grew huge till they seemed about to pop out of her head. He kept squeezing.

With a long, rattling sigh, she quit struggling and went limp.

He released her. She fell to the sand, still gripping the lovely Talisman rose.

Chapter One

Four Days Earlier

ह

A late-afternoon chill touched the crisp, clear air above a lazy ocean as Cami Carrington and Kate Elfmon ambled out to the beach across the street from Cami's palatial Tudor-style home in Coronado, California, an upscale island suburb of San Diego. At the horizon, the sun cast a soft haze of coral, orange, pink, and purple that spread out over the water.

Cami, whose wardrobe was the envy of many a woman, stopped and tucked her hands into the back pockets of her jeans. Gazing at the brilliant sky, she said, "I'd love to have a dress in those colors."

"Me, too," Kate said, kicking at a stray piece of seaweed.

Cami nodded and pulled her warm jacket a bit closer.

Tall, slender, blue-eyed Cami and petite, brown-eyed, brunette Kate walked silently toward the water's edge, their long friendship not requiring continual conversation. By mutual consent, they stopped about half-way between the water's edge and the large rocks lining the street. The two had recently returned from a motorhome trip originally planned to last several months. However, after four weeks of flat tires, battery problems, and the unforeseen details of settling into various RV parks, they'd looked at each other over a split sewer connection in Albuquerque and said in unison, "Enough!"

A noise from the street caused them to turn and see a small silver motorhome pull up to the curb. It was similar in size and color to the one they'd traveled in. They watched as a young couple got out, followed by four small children. Cami and Kate looked at each other and shook their heads in wonder.

"At least there were only the two of us in ours," Kate said.

Cami's nineteen-year-old twins, Debra and Durant, had left for the University of Edinburgh a few weeks after their father's death, leaving Cami alone except for the couple who served as live-in housekeeper and gardener. She turned back toward the ocean, and her voice was unsteady as she said, "It was so hard to let them go, but it was what their father would have wanted."

The two friends became quiet, remembering the murder of Cami's husband, Braxton, in August. Since then, Braxton's brother, Victor, had run Carrington Investments, the family's multi-million dollar international business.

Cami broke the somber mood. She elbowed Kate and said, "I bet ol' Gunnar is biting his tongue to keep from saying, 'I told you so' after nixing your plan from the get-go." Gunnar Volstad was a big, blonde, Minnesota Norwegian. Like Kate, he was widowed and a dedicated Christian. He was the only man Kate had shown interest in since her husband Joel died four years ago, and he was madly in love with Kate.

"Who said he's bitten his tongue?" Kate laughed. "Still, the motorhome trip gave both of us time to sort some things out."

"Yes. It did. Me, trying to deal with all that surrounded Braxton's death, and you, working on your feelings about Gunnar. Any closer to a solution on that?"

"Let's just say that I miss him." Kate paused again. "I'm so happy I got that call from Grant Lauder University here in Coronado to fill in for the rest of the semester in the political science department."

"God does work in mysterious ways—," Cami began.

"—His wonders to perform," Kate finished, and both giggled at their old habit of finishing each other's thoughts.

Kate's cell phone pulsed in her jeans pocket. She got it out, looked at the caller ID, and smiled.

"Gunnar?" asked Cami.

Kate nodded, still smiling.

"I'll go back to the house and leave you two lovebirds to talk." Cami gave her friend a knowing look and walked away, but not too quickly to miss the lilt in Kate's voice when she answered her call.

Chapter Two

ॐ

The first "house" Mike Jenkins designed stretched across two thick limbs of an ancient, eighty-foot magnolia tree above a tumbledown shack in rural Mississippi. Mike's brother and sister helped him haul wood scraps, bits of tin and glass, and old shingles up into the tree. But it was Mike who conceived the design, rigged up a light from an old lamp and a long extension cord, and provided "running water" from a big plastic jug with a spigot. The house had a door, windows, shutters, and a tiny balcony. It fit so perfectly into the tree that it seemed to grow there. The local newspaper got wind of the children's project and featured it in a Saturday Extra edition. The reporter called Mike a "budding young architect."

Mike was ten years old.

Even before that, Mike knew he wanted to be an architect. Hard work, full-ride scholarships, and incredible talent had brought him to his present success in southern California. His firm, MelJen, Inc., was one of the largest architecture and construction outfits in San Diego County.

But Mike's true love, harking back to his tree house days, would always be the unique family residence. His own home, a 4,000-square-foot colonial-style marvel in the Mount Helix area of La Mesa, was his *pièce de résistance*. Forty-four-year-old Mike lived in it alone.

Mike had built the house twelve years ago for Melanie, the raven-haired childhood sweetheart he'd married the day after graduation from Mississippi State. She had stood by him during the struggling, tuna casserole days; she had supported him in his move away from her beloved

Mississippi and to California; and she'd been his most enthusiastic supporter as the business grew and grew. Ten months from the day they moved into the house, Melanie, in her fifth month of pregnancy, went into labor, hemorrhaged, and died. Within minutes, the premature baby boy joined her.

Six weeks after Melanie's death, in one of his frequent mind-numbing rages, Mike slung a shoebox across the bedroom. It fell open, scattering papers over the floor. His hand touched a bundle of letters tied in a lavender ribbon. At the bottom was an envelope, also lavender, Melanie's favorite color. It was addressed from her to him. Trembling he unfolded the three-page letter inside. Melanie had written it when Mike was in his junior year at Mississippi State School of Architecture.

The last paragraph stood alone on the third page.

> *I'll never forget the day when I was eight and you were ten and you showed me your tree house. I could hardly believe what you'd done. My little girl heart sensed something special in you. I was right. You made me proud way back then, and I know you will always make me proud.*

Mike crumpled the letter into a ball and threw it across the room. Then he stamped down the stairs, out the massive oak doors, past the soaring white columns, and to the front yard with its majestic view of the valley.

I know you will always make me proud. The words rang in Mike's head. Well, it may be too late to make her proud, but at least he could lay off the pity party. He spun around and strode back into the house, pulling his cell phone from his jeans pocket. In moments, the foreman of his latest construction project answered his call.

"Joe," Mike said, the confident sound of his voice sounding strange. "What's the latest on that condo in Mission Beach?"

A few minutes later, he went back to his bedroom and picked up the crumpled letter. He smoothed it out, returned it to the shoebox, and shoved the box to the back of a high shelf in Melanie's closet.

The heartbreak remained; the bitterness became a part of his being. But Mike was alive again, fully immersing himself in his already successful company, often spending weeks at a time in Europe on various company projects. As for female companionship, his somewhat rough-hewn good looks, his trace of Southern accent, not to mention his money, all made satisfying that need easy. He had his home and his business and no intention whatsoever of marrying again.

~~~

Mike's first glimpse of Lenae Maddox had come eleven years after Melanie's death. He was checking on some electrical issues at MelJen's newest completed project, twin twenty-five-story condominiums in downtown San Diego. He rarely handled such details himself anymore, but once in a while he liked to remind himself of how far he had come and "get his hands dirty." Besides he'd named these structures "The Melanies." He needed to go into the loft apartment to see if the electrical problem there had been resolved. The property manager had let the female occupant know it was all right to let Mike in. When the woman opened the door, she was talking on her cell phone. Her head down, she turned her back as she waved Mike in while she finished the call.

Mike felt paralyzed.

That shoulder-length black hair, that slender figure clothed in black pants topped by a pull-over sweater of lavender wool. The impression was so like Melanie that Mike had to force down a gasp. Then the woman turned, and the resemblance melted. Yes, this woman was near the thirty-one years of age Melanie was when she died and had the same thick, dark hair. But her eyes were an almost aqua blue, much more exotic than Melanie's soft brown ones. Also, the angular features were nothing like Melanie's gentler, rounder ones.

Still, he liked what he saw.

"Come on in." Even her throaty mid-western twang was nothing like Melanie's Southern tones. "You can't imagine how glad I am to get this electrical thing taken care of."

"We aim to please," Mike told her with a crooked grin.

Looking around, he took in the cozily untidy room with its clean-lined, comfortable seating, simple dining furniture near the galley-style kitchenette, and a long desk complete with computer and stacks of papers. Several paintings—impressionist pastoral scenes and floral renditions—graced the walls.

As Mike had envisioned when designing the building, right away the eye was drawn to the window spread across one entire wall. The stunning view encompassed sparkling San Diego Bay and the long, graceful curve of the bridge connecting downtown San Diego with the upscale island suburb of Coronado. Centered in front of the window was an artist's easel, flanked by small tables scattered with brushes, palettes, and several tubes of paints. The front of the easel, on which rested a medium-sized canvas, faced the window. Mike wondered about the painting.

As he moved from outlet to outlet in the loft, checking each one, he could feel her watching him. When he was done, he said, "Looks like everything is in order, Ms. Maddox."

"Thank you for your help." Her tone was formal, but her body language friendly.

Mike wasn't one to pass up an opportunity with an appealing woman. "Ms. Maddox," he said. "I've worked up an appetite. Care to join me for lunch?"

She hesitated, clearly unsure about accepting an invitation from a workman she'd just met.

Mike could have erased her doubts by telling her he was the contractor and, in this case, owner of the building. He felt uninclined to reveal that fact yet; and he knew his modest five-feet-ten height, rough-and-ready features, and general demeanor didn't immediately identify him as head of a multi-million-dollar corporation.

He had not gotten to where he was by giving in easily. He put up both hands and grinned. "I promise, I don't bite."

Studying him closely, she hesitated a few more seconds. Then she tilted her head to one side, and her lips spread into a wide smile.

"How about The Spaghetti Factory? It's nearby, and they do a mean antipasto."

~~~

That was six months ago. Since then Mike had seen Lenae at least once a week, and their relationship had quickly become physical. From the beginning she made no secret of the fact that he was not the only man in her life. Perfect. Especially in situations like now when he was on an extended business tour of Asia and Europe.

Tomorrow, in Paris, he'd have his last conference of a very successful trip that was winding up a few days earlier than he'd expected. He would be home Wednesday morning. He decided not to tell Lenae. Maybe he wouldn't even call her for a day or two after he got back. He didn't want her to think she was becoming too important to him.

Chapter Three

&

"**D**r. Elfmon?"

At the sound of the slightly husky voice, Kate Elfmon pushed back her dark hair and looked up from her desk at Grant Lauder University in Coronado. A slender brunette who looked to be in her early thirties—about ten years younger than Kate—stood at the open door. Kate was struck by the young woman's rather exotic look, especially the ultra-long lashes and the slightly tilted aqua eyes that nearly matched the top she wore with a charcoal pants suit.

"Yes," Kate replied. "And you're Ms. Maddox, Director of Human Resources, right?"

The woman pushed back a stray tendril of hair, then put out her hand. "Lenae," she said as Kate shook her hand.

"Glad to meet you in person, Lenae, after all those phone conversations we had before I got here."

"Me, too. Sorry I wasn't here when you first arrived. As you know, I was away for a few days." She pointed to one of Kate's two extra chairs. "May I?"

"Please do. I need a break from trying to get all the staff names and positions straight."

Lenae lowered herself into the chair and crossed one leg over the other. Swinging her leg slightly, she dangled a stylish black pump from her toes. She let out a pleasant laugh in that husky voice. "You pretty much have to do that on your own, but I'd be glad to help fill you in on most anything else."

"That would be great. As you know, I've only been here a few days."

"On sabbatical from Boston U, I understand. You wouldn't catch *me* working on a sabbatical."

"What would you be doing?"

"I'd be in Paris." Lenae stared up at the ceiling with a faraway look. "I'd be perched on a fold-up chair by the Seine with an easel and canvas in front of me and a palette latched onto my thumb." She grinned. "And I'd wear a painter's smock, spattered with paint." She touched her black hair. "And a little red beret."

Intrigued by the young woman's openness, Kate laughed. "I think I can picture you doing exactly that. As for me and my *working* sabbatical, the short version is that the plans I'd made for my year away changed. So when Grant Lauder contacted me about a need for a fill-in Poly Sci professor for a few months, I jumped at the chance—especially since it would put me here in Coronado, where I have a very good friend."

"Well, that was lucky, wasn't it?"

"More like God's perfect timing," Kate said, hoping her light tone would prevent her coming on like a preacher.

Lenae ignored the remark. "I thought I'd pop in and see if there's anything I can help you with."

"You're a lifesaver. Let me see, where shall I begin?"

For the next half hour, Lenae explained several policies and schedules and other tidbits about the university to Kate. Though their discussion was strictly professional, something about Lenae tugged at Kate. She couldn't put her finger on the reason, but something wasn't right. She'd learned not to ignore those kinds of feelings.

So, when Kate felt that Lenae had brought her up to speed about the school, she said, "Well, I think that does it, Lenae. You've been a jewel." She looked at the wall clock. "Hey, it's nearly noon, and I'm meeting the friend I told you about at the Burger Lounge for lunch. Why don't you join us?"

"Sounds great, but I don't want to intrude."

"Once you meet Cami Carrington, you'll know that's not a problem."

"Cami Carrington! Isn't she the rich, gorgeous blonde who—"

"Yes, Cami's the one whose husband was murdered at the Hotel del Coronado last summer." Kate had no desire to explain further. "Let's go. I'm hungry."

~~~

True to Kate's implication, Cami Carrington was not at all disturbed to have an extra person join them for lunch. Besides, Cami knew her friend well and guessed that Kate had sensed some need in the pretty co-worker whose friendly, confident air seemed tinged with vulnerability.

"This may be the best hamburger I've ever tasted," Lenae said, wiping her lips and snagging a French fry. "As long as I've worked on the island, I've never been here before. Sure beats McDonald's."

Cami leaned forward and whispered, "Don't even say McDonald's and Burger Lounge in the same breath. You may be put out." Grinning, she straightened and asked, "Where do you live, Lenae?" She may not have Kate's sense for a person's need, but she did have an insatiable curiosity about the people she met.

"Um, I live in a loft on Harbor Drive."

"A loft?" said Cami.

"I think Lenae may be an artist," Kate put in.

Lenae gave a deprecatory shrug. "I dabble a bit. The loft has a huge window with a great view of San Diego Bay and the bridge. The lighting is perfect for painting."

Cami let out an exaggerated sigh. "An artist's loft. How romantic."

"Yes, it is," Lenae said softly."My dream is to make enough money on my paintings—mostly watercolors—to give up the job at GLU." She frowned. "Only trouble is, lately that's seeming more and more unlikely."

Lenae took another bite of her burger and seemed to want to move on from that subject.

Kate spoke up again. "Anyone special in your life, Lenae?"

"You mean, like a man?"

Kate nodded.

"Two, actually."

Cami leaned forward again. "Two? Isn't that a little hard to balance?"

Lenae looked up, her expression troubled. "You could say that's an understatement."

Cami patted Lenae's hand. "I'm sorry. I didn't mean to upset you."

Lenae's lips formed a weak smile. "It's okay. It doesn't take much to upset me these days. Even getting flowers from those two men, as well as one of the law students, doesn't help."

Kate touched Lenae's arm. "Is there... Is there something Cami or I could help with?"

"Well..."

Just when Cami was sure Lenae would enlighten them further, Lenae said, "Do you think we could get back to the school, Kate? I have a lot of work waiting for me."

"Of course." Kate reached for her purse.

"Lenae's first burger at the Burger Lounge is on me," said Cami. "Y'all go ahead. I'm not quite finished. Oh, and Lenae, I'd love to see some of your paintings. A long time ago—in another lifetime, it seems—I thought I might like to be an artist. Maybe we can get together sometime."

"I'd like that, Cami. Very much."

After the good-byes, Cami watched Lenae and Kate walk away. She had been serious about wanting to see Lenae's paintings. For a moment, she indulged in memories of a young North Carolina girl with a small amount of artistic talent. Yes, those days seemed as though they occurred in another lifetime to another person.

~~~

On the short drive back to the university, though Lenae's manner was still friendly, Kate couldn't help noticing how her mood had become subdued.

"It was nice to meet Cami," Lenae said. "I saw her on the evening news and felt sorry for her about her husband's murder. I only thought of her as a beautiful, wealthy woman. But she's really down-to-earth and nice."

"And a good friend to boot," Kate added.

For the rest of the drive, Kate noticed that Lenae kept the conversation centered on the university. In the staff lot, Kate parked the red Audi TTS roadster that belonged to Cami's daughter. As they walked away from the car, Lenae placed her hand on her stomach.

"Are you okay?" Kate asked.

Lenae gave her a bright smile. "Too much of that delicious hamburger. Thanks so much for inviting me."

Before walking away, she dipped her head, but not in time to prevent Kate from seeing a hint of pain on her face.

Chapter Four

ॐ

Lenae moved a stack of papers from one side of her desk to the other, next to two other stacks. As usual, one group contained various inquiries and résumés from professors across the U.S., Canada, and several other countries, all hoping to find positions at the small but prestigious university. Lenae knew the draw was not simply the school's excellent academic reputation, but the hope to work and live in Coronado. To Lenae, "Coronado," the Spanish word for "crowned," perfectly fit this lovely little semi-tropical island across the bay from San Diego, self-acclaimed "America's Finest City."

A second stack of papers contained various applications for other positions at the university. The third group, much smaller than the others, involved various complaints against the school's personnel, mostly from parents who blamed their students' poor grades on professors. Glad not to have to deal with these, she would pass them on to the named professors. Several other miscellaneous items awaited Lenae's attention, but she shoved them to one side, stood up, and left her office. Soon she was outside the lovely Spanish-style admin building and approaching a nearly hidden sandy path to the beach.

Whatever possessed me, she wondered, *to say something to Kate Elfmon and her friend about the men in my life? But then, there's something about both of them that invites and inspires confidence.* Lenae reached down and removed her shoes.

Goodness knows I could use someone to unload on. Pretty sad that the only "friend" I have is a geeky twenty-year-old college student. Dexter Driscoll.

Dangling her shoes on her fingers, Lenae padded her way between low, scrubby bushes and a few palms to the end of the path. The waves beyond lapped at the shore gently, even peacefully. Lenae's thoughts were far from peaceful.

She had juggled two romantic relationships for weeks now, making sure that neither knew the identity of the other. And that didn't count the student she'd been fending off.

There had been a day when having three men attracted to her would have thrilled Lenae.

~~~

"Daddy, Daddy! Listen to me. I wanta tell you sumfin." Three-year-old Lenae tugged at her father's pants leg as he paced back and forth in the tiny living room in their house, the script of his latest show held before his face.

Kevin Maddox didn't even slow down as he said, "Not now, Lenae. Can't you see I'm practicing my lines?"

Lenae wasn't sure what "lines" were, but she fully understood her father didn't have time for her right now. Tiny shoulders slumped, she went off to find Cora, her middle-aged live-in nanny. Lenae had no clear memory of the woman who had borne her and walked out of the house a year later, never to return.

~~~

"Daddy, look at my drawing! Teacher says it's real good." Lenae, now a skinny seven-year-old with stick-straight black hair and aqua-colored eyes that seemed too big for her face, thrust a sheet of drawing paper under her father's nose.

Kevin looked up from the theater review page of the *Chicago Tribune* long enough to glance at the crayon rendition of a large dog and small kitten snuggled together. Paying no mind to the realism and attention to the detail unusual in a child his daughter's age, he patted her head. "Nice, honey. Real nice."

"There's an art show at school next week, Daddy. Thursday morning at ten. They're gonna show four of my drawings—more than anybody else's. Can you come? Please?"

"Um, maybe, baby."

"I know you won't be working, Daddy. You always work at night." By now Lenae understood that her handsome father's "lines" were for roles he performed for a major theater group in Chicago.

"Sure, baby. I'll try." He went back to the theater review.

Thursday morning Cora attended Lenae's art show while Kevin slept off a late-night rehearsal.

~~~

"Lenae, what happened to you in the second act? You really flubbed your lines." Kevin's black brows drew together, and his gaze swept her still-skinny, still-awkward body.

Tears stung the back of sixteen-year-old Lenae's eyelids. Though art was her passion, she had signed up for drama this year. As she'd hoped, her father was pleased and had even helped her memorize lines for her minor role in "Cheaper by the Dozen." But, as he'd said, she'd completely flubbed her lines in one scene.

"I'm sorry, Dad. I'm really sorry."

Kevin gave her a perfunctory pat on the back, but was silent all the way home. That night Lenae cried on Cora's shoulder. The next day she dropped out of drama and managed to get into the watercolor class she'd wanted all along.

~~~

"Whoo, whoo! Look at what's happened to the ugly duckling!"

Lenae spun around, ready to spit out a few choice words at the good-looking senior boy leaning against a wall in the high school hallway. But the open admiration she saw stopped her. Instead, she gave him a wink and sauntered off with a deliberate sway to her hips.

He was right. Over the summer, Lenae's thin body had filled out in all the right places. She got a new hairstyle, learned how to emphasize her unusual eyes, and acquired a new wardrobe that called attention to her new curves. Cora, now nearing sixty, had nixed the short skirt Lenae wanted to wear to school that day, so Lenae had left home in a more modest one, then changed in the Girls' Room.

She turned her head and winked again. That weekend, she lost her virginity to the boy, who spread the word to all his friends.

As for her father, his performances often took him on the road. When he was home, he rarely saw the daughter who had quit fighting for his attention, but had never stopped longing for it—and looking in all the wrong places.

~~~

Both Kevin Maddox and Cora died the year Lenae was a senior at the University of Chicago, where she had majored in Art and minored in Business. In a tragic accident, Kevin stumbled off the stage during a performance of Macbeth, and broke his neck in the fall. Three months later, dear Cora died of pancreatic cancer. Lenae was stoic at Kevin's funeral, which she attended with her current boyfriend. She attended Cora's funeral alone and fell to the ground sobbing at her graveside.

Two months later Lenae graduated with honors at a ceremony not even attended by the boyfriend. She didn't bother saying good-bye to him when, using part of the small inheritance her father had left her, she left Chicago and headed to southern California.

~~~

That was ten years ago. Though Lenae had sold a few of her exquisite floral watercolors, it hadn't been enough to support her. So she'd used her Business minor to obtain a series of office jobs that eventually led to her present position at Grant Lauder U. She'd come to recognize that her promiscuous lifestyle was a search for a father who didn't exist, but she hadn't been able to give up the search completely. At the moment she was seeing two men.

And, despite her usual precautions, she was pregnant.

Chapter Five

ಶಿ

From day one of his freshman year at Grant Lauder University, Dexter Driscoll knew that everyone at the small school considered him a nerd. Nothing new. The students at his high school back in Tucson had looked at him that way, too. Why wouldn't they? He bore all the physical trademarks. Thick glasses. Protruding ears. Short, wiry, blah-brown hair. Tall, lanky awkward frame. Cheap, ill-fitting clothing. Zits.

"Your mother must have had some premonition of how you'd turn out when she named you," Dexter's father often said. He'd made no secret of his disappointment in a son who preferred to keep his nose buried in a book rather than trying out for the football team.

Dexter had hoped moving away from Tucson to California would be a new beginning for him. Always an excellent pupil, he'd assumed his superior intelligence would be appreciated by university-level men and women. Possibly even admired. He'd pictured himself gaining confidence in the new environment. Most of all, he'd imagined being surrounded by a bevy of friends. Maybe even a few girls.

None of that had happened. First, a large percentage of the student body came from wealth. Many looked down on the work-scholarship students like Dexter. So, rather than gain confidence, he'd felt intimidated. Next, his attempts at making friends had failed as miserably as they had in high school. His only success was that his grades were outstanding, but at Grant Lauder that was not unusual. Little by little, Dexter became so achingly lonely that he fell into deep depression.

One day in mid-May, Dexter worked up the nerve to ask a girl for a date. Marsha Owens was quiet, shy and rather plain looking and seemingly as lonely as he. He had invited her to a movie.

Marsha had looked Dexter up and down and replied in an ultra-polite voice, "I don't think so, Dexter. I, uh, have other plans."

To Dexter, her words might as well have been, "I'm not that hard up for a date."

That night, embarrassing and humiliating incidents from his whole life played over and over in Dexter's mind. Marsha's rebuff was almost incidental, but it was the one that drove him over the edge. By three a.m., he knew he couldn't take it anymore.

He arose and put on his darkest, heaviest clothing, including a cap that came down over his ears. He quietly left the dorm and walked across the island to the Coronado Bridge. Dexter knew that the bridge was about two miles long and that at its highest point it soared two hundred feet above the waters of the bay. It was the third deadliest suicide bridge in the U.S. and was policed to prevent the very deed he planned. But this night was extra dark, the moon barely visible, and Dexter was wearing dark clothing. It could work.

It almost did. When Dexter got to the bridge, he tossed a rock onto the ground beyond the policeman on duty. While the cop went to check on the noise, Dexter managed to sneak past him. Keeping close to the rail, bending low, and ignoring posted signs that urged potential suicides to call a hotline number, he made his way to the highest point, about half-way across. There he crouched low until he saw the policeman look in the opposite direction.

Immediately, he stood and began to launch himself over the rail. It was higher than he realized, even for his long legs. But Dexter was determined. Between his focus on his goal and the cap pulled over his ears, he didn't hear a car pull up and stop.

He had one leg over the rail and was about to swing over the other one, when he felt someone grasp his ankle and jerk him back.

"Stop!" The husky voice spoke in a loud whisper.

The cop! was his first thought. No. A policeman would shout, not whisper.

Dexter struggled, but now he'd lost his hold on the rail. He fell back into the arms of his unwelcome rescuer. No! He'd almost made it. Nobody was going to stop him now. He jerked himself loose and turned, swinging his fist. His aim went wild.

When he saw that he'd nearly punched Lenae Maddox, head of

Human Resources at the university, surprise made him unable to speak.

Still whispering, Lenae said, "Get into my car, you fool, before that policeman sees you."

"No. No! Don't stop me. I want—"

"Shut up, Dexter. He'll hear you." She dragged him to her pale yellow VW Bug, opened the door, shoved him in, and ran to the other side.

Gloom darker than the black sky settled in on Dexter. He couldn't even succeed in trying to kill himself. Stopped by a woman, no less.

Without a word, Lenae drove him to her apartment. That night he paid little attention that it was a true artist's loft, complete with easel and painting paraphernalia. Without questioning him, she fixed him some chamomile tea.

"It'll help you sleep," she said when he made a face.

When he'd drunk the tea, Lenae opened her futon couch into a bed. He didn't even struggle when she pushed him down onto it and covered him up.

"Sleep, Dexter." she said softly.

He learned later that she'd spread out a sleeping bag on the floor for herself. When he'd asked what she was doing on Coronado Bridge at 3:30 in the morning, Lenae said she'd had to spend all afternoon and evening at the hospital with a student who fell down the stairs in the admin building and wound up with a broken leg. She'd waited in the crowded emergency room with the girl and during the wait for a doctor to be available to set the leg. Then she took her back to the dorm and even stayed until she was settled. Lenae didn't leave her until 3:30 a.m. Dexter felt a guilty twinge of pleasure when he learned that the student was none other than Marsha Owens.

From that day on, Dexter and Lenae, eight years his senior, developed an odd friendship. She was the only close friend he'd ever had. He shared thoughts and feelings with her in a way he'd never done with anyone else. In turn, she allowed him to peek into her heart.

So far, he was the only person she'd told she was pregnant. The one thing she hadn't told him was the names of the two men she'd been seeing.

Chapter Six

&

K ate wished she could shut out the bustle and chatter in the Grant Lauder University faculty cafeteria. She set her salad bowl aside and tried to concentrate on the paper spread on the two-person table she occupied alone. It didn't help that visions of Gunnar kept popping into her mind. Pushing her hair behind one ear, she continued reading an essay by one of her students. The assignment had been to write their opinions of the pros and cons of religion in politics. Without flaunting it, Kate had established her own Christian faith from the first day, yet had made it clear that her beliefs would not affect the students' scores.

This young man, Dexter Driscoll, apparently had decided to test her. First he had made a clear, well thought-out case for his view that religion had absolutely no place in the political arena. Then he had ended with: "Religious people should realize that mixing religion into politics dirties the waters."

Oh brother, Kate thought. Pen in air, she paused for a moment before making a note on the last page of the essay. "Excellent paper. Each point well worded and clear. Weak ending. You go from objective arguments that nicely support your opinion, to a stark judgment call. Work on that." She marked the paper with an A-minus rather than an A. In a way she hated doing that, as Dexter seemed to be practically friendless and lonely. Still, she knew she had to let him learn to deal with his problems.

Dexter's paper made her think back to some of the ones she had written in college and university. Like Dexter, she'd enjoyed taking her assignments to the very edge. That thought segued into memories of the serious student from Boston (herself, Kate Kelly) and the seemingly flighty, definitely flirty, and breathtakingly beautiful Southern Belle (Cami Stewart) who were roommates at Compton College, a Christian school near Raleigh, North Carolina, for two years. The two had clashed, settled into an uneasy truce, begun to understand and even like each other, and finally formed a friendship still strong more than twenty-two years later.

Kate let out a nostalgic chuckle as she picked up another essay, this one from Justin Rhodes, a rather desperate seeming law student whose writing had a tendency to be all over the place.

"Mind sharing the joke?" A deep masculine voice cut into Kate's reverie.

Kate looked up into the tawny brown eyes of a friendly face with a lock of wavy sun-streaked hair falling over a wide brow.

"Looks like all the other seats are taken," the man said. "Mind if I join you?" Though he held his heavily laden tray patiently, amusement colored his expression.

Kate looked around the room. The other chair at her table was the last one available, and her papers were spread across the surface. Embarrassed, she stammered, "Uh, sure." She moved the papers out of the way and nodded toward the empty chair.

As the good looking man...

Good looking? Where did that come from? She gave him a side-long closer look as he transferred several plates of food from tray to table. Tall—over six feet for sure. Muscular—triceps that bulged even beneath a long-sleeved shirt and rust-colored slipover sweater. Tanned complexion—accented by the fair hair that seemed to invite her to reach up and....

Stop!

Finally seated, the man focused on Kate. A grin twitched his firm lips. "Well?"

"Uh, well what?" Kate, who almost always spoke with assurance, heard herself stammering again.

"The joke. You said you'd share the joke."

"What joke?"

"Whatever you were chuckling about just now." He picked up a fork and pointed it at her. "I said, 'Mind sharing the joke?' and you said, 'Sure.'"

Kate kept her expression serious. "Maybe I meant 'Sure, I mind.'"

The man leaned back and let out a hearty laugh. Kate couldn't help joining him.

"Reese Sutherland." He extended his hand across the table. "Professor of Law."

Kate accepted his handshake, recognizing the name from the school catalogue. Dr. Sutherland wasn't simply *a* professor of law; he was the acting head of the Law Department. "Kate Elfmon," she said.

"...Interim Professor of Political Science," he finished for her. "Kate, for Katherine?"

"Yes, but I prefer Kate." She didn't tell Dr. Sutherland that the name Katherine reminded her of the formal, old-Boston parents who had had trouble knowing what to do with a lively, inquisitive daughter born when they were in their forties.

"Ahh. Kate Elfmon. The name suits you."

Kate liked that. When she had married Joel, she loved the sound of her new name. *Kate Elfmon*, she repeated in her mind. Kate Volstad simply didn't have the same ring.

Kate cleared her throat and said, "Thank you." She slipped her papers into a folder and started to pick up her lunch tray. "Well, I'm all done here. Nice to meet you, Dr. Sutherland."

"Make that Reese. *Doctor* sounds like the man who took out my appendix when I was thirteen." He scooped up a large forkful of spaghetti and meatballs and shook his head. "Never did like that man." When Kate started to rise, he spoke through a mouthful of spaghetti, "Unh uh. Not yet." He swallowed hard, making a gulping sound. "Please, don't leave. You haven't given me a chance to welcome you to the faculty of GLU—often referred to by students as The Glue."

"Only by students?"

He shot her a conspiratorial look and whispered, "And a few renegade faculty members." She glanced at her watch, then relaxed in her chair. "I guess I can stay a few more minutes—but only a few."

"Why? I happen to know that Dr. Howe—you are filling in for her, aren't you?"

"I am."

"I know." He grinned. "Susan—Dr. Howe—didn't have classes after lunch. They didn't change that schedule, did they?"

"Well, no."

Kate admitted to herself that she really didn't want to leave yet. It would be nice to make a few friends among the faculty. Some had been pleasant, others offhanded. She'd been too busy settling in to connect with anyone so far. Even Lenae Maddox, after a friendly beginning, was avoiding her now.

"Tell me about yourself," Reese Sutherland continued, unabashed.

"You'd find that a most uninteresting topic of conversation."

Pausing as he was about to bite into his toasted Italian roll, he studied her with an intensity Kate found disturbingly exciting. "I don't think so." When she didn't reply right away, he said, "Did I detect a New England accent?"

"You did. I'm from Boston—on sabbatical from Boston U's Poly-Sci Department."

"Thought I recognized it. I'm from Boston myself. I've been here almost a year and a half, filling in for Dr. Johanssen. Like you, he's on sabbatical. Gone to Sweden to work on a research project. He gets back at the beginning of the year."

"That's a long sabbatical."

"He asked for an extension at the end of a year. Hadn't completed his research. I sure hate to leave San Diego come January. I like it a lot better than Boston."

A flicker of overhead light caught his sun-streaked hair, and a sure realization struck Kate. "Better surfing? Golfing?"

"Hey, you're good. I used to surf a lot. Still love the sport. But these days, I do more golfing."

"As you know, working with college students sharpens your powers of observation."

"And my powers of observation tell me you're not wearing a wedding ring."

Kate looked down. "I was widowed four years ago." She heard her voice go sad, thinking of the horrendous moment she learned that Joel Elfmon, a photo-journalist with the *Boston Globe*, had been shot and killed while covering an uprising in Colombia. The following days and weeks had been the darkest of her life. That was the reason, she supposed, she was able to sympathize so readily with Cami's grief over her murdered husband, even though arrogant, controlling, wealthy Braxton Carrington had been nothing like her Joel.

"Calling Dr. Kate Elfmon," Reese Sutherland intoned in a robot-like voice. "Come in, Dr. Katherine Elfmon."

"Oh. Sorry. I'm afraid I wandered there for a moment."

"I'm the one who's sorry. I didn't mean to bring up unhappy memories." He placed one large, warm hand over hers.

Touched, Kate said, "It's okay. Really."

Again, reluctantly now, Kate started to reach for her things. "I really do have to go. It was good meeting you, Dr.—Reese. Thank you for your welcome to the coll—The Glue."

He clasped his hands around hers and gave them a quick squeeze. Just as quickly he released them, but not before Kate noticed that he, like she, wore no wedding band. "The pleasure was all mine."

Not all, Kate thought, glad for the pleasant and amusing interlude with a fellow faculty member. Make that an exceptionally good looking fellow faculty member.

Chapter Seven

&

"**M**r. Rhodes, *please* sit down."

Justin Rhodes shot a glare at Dr. Reese Sutherland's attractive grey-haired admin assistant. He ran thick, tanned fingers through his straight brown hair, then continued pacing about the small office. He stopped at a large painting on one side of the room. The artist had captured a breathtaking panoramic sunset view of a series of rugged cliffs above an emerald ocean. The land leading to the cliff was a lush, smooth green golf course, dotted here and there with trees. The focal point, small but definite, was a lone golfer, his body straight, his head bent, and his hands gripping a club that was touching a ball at the edge of a hole.

Recognizing the scene as the Torrey Pines Golf Course in La Jolla, Justin's lips tightened. At twenty-nine, his golfing days had been virtually over for a decade—since the day his father was convicted of fraud and embezzlement of the bank where he had been vice president. Justin Rhodes, Sr., had vehemently maintained his innocence, and Justin had believed him. All to no avail. The elder Rhodes was sentenced to twenty years in a federal prison.

For a moment Justin felt the old horrible clutching of his stomach every time he thought of what happened after the sentencing. Before morning, in the San Diego County jail cell from which he was to be transferred to federal prison, Justin, Sr., twisted together the sheets on his cot and hung himself.

That night a seed of bitterness dropped into the rich soil of shock and grief in Justin's young soul.

Justin paced back to the other side of the room, shaking his head to clear it of the morbid memory. He turned his thoughts to how the family

34

finances took a sudden dive, requiring moving from their fine Solana Beach home to a cheap duplex in a rundown area of Imperial Beach, the town at the end of the causeway that connected Coronado with the mainland. At the time, Justin had been a first-semester sophomore at San Diego State U.

Soon Justin found work with the landscaper who had once serviced his family's property. The man liked Justin and was willing to work around the devastated young man's school schedule. Justin soon learned to enjoy the work. It wasn't golfing, but it gave him time outside and helped him develop his five feet, eight inches into a physique his friends envied and co-eds drooled over—a fact he took full advantage of. His earnings helped his mother support the family, which included adolescent twin sisters. Meanwhile some State grants and scholarships carried him through to a degree in Business Administration. Still, his work and school commitments caused him to take an extra year to graduate.

Golfing had become a fading dream, but not long before completing his business degree, Justin became obsessed with another dream—going into criminal law.

He remembered the day he reluctantly approached his mother about the decision.

Chrissy Rhodes had come in from her job at a local Denny's restaurant, the only work she could find that would allow her to be at home when the twins, now fifteen, came in from school.

"Dorothea was in again," she said with a laugh, referring to the elderly woman who seemed to have made it her mission in life to complain about everything in the restaurant. Yet, she still came in several times a week. "I'm waiting for the day she's completely pleased. Well, maybe I'm not. I'd be too old to work by then."

Justin looked at the worry lines in his mother's pretty face, put there by their dire financial situation. Exasperated, he said, "I don't know how you can joke about it."

"What should I do, Justin?" She gave him a perky grin. "Cry all day? Besides, God is not going to allow me more trouble than I can deal with."

Justin chose not to comment on that statement. Instead he led her to an ancient sofa she had attempted to restore with cheap, bright blue fabric. "Sit here next to me. I want to tell you something."

Chrissy's expression became wary, but she simply said, "Okay."

Not looking her in the face, he fiddled with the darker blue piping on the arm of the couch. After several seconds of silent wondering how she'd take his news, he blurted it out. "I want to study law, Mom. I'm going to be a lawyer."

To Justin's amazement, his mother's eyes became both moist and shining at the same time. "Oh, Justin!" she cried as she leaned over and hugged him. "That's wonderful."

~~~

"Mr. Rhodes. Mr. Rhodes." Dr. Sutherland's assistant interrupted his thoughts.

"Oh, I'm sorry. My mind..."

"Was occupied." The woman smiled. "You can go in now."

Chapter Eight

ॐ

Reese Sutherland was thinking of Dr. Kate Elfmon when his trust-worthy admin assistant, Cecelia Hanson, buzzed and told him Justin Rhodes, one of his students, had been waiting for more than fifteen minutes to see him.

"I told him about your *conference call*," Cecelia said in a low voice, "but he's getting rather impatient."

Reese suspected Cecelia knew his "conference call" had been with a certain blonde, a would-be movie star in L.A. After hanging up from a rather inane but titillating conversation with the blonde, he had found himself comparing her superficial, if quite alluring, beauty to the simple, down-to-earth attractiveness of Dr. Elfmon. Kate Elfmon had clearly been deeply in love with her husband, but... Reese allowed himself a small smile.

I'm sure ol' Reesie can take her mind off a dead man, he thought, mentally calling himself by the name the starlet always used.

Then Cecelia had rung him about Justin Rhodes. She was always keeping him on track, even if he'd have preferred to keep on pursuing his pleasant thoughts.

He forced his mind to the issue at hand and spoke into the intercom. "Send Rhodes in." Reese leaned back in his swivel chair with its curved, tufted leather back and surveyed the student as he entered the office. In the two or three seconds before he greeted Justin Rhodes, he took in the muscular build, deep tan, and light brown eyes that crinkled slightly at the corners from exposure to the sun. Usually his expression combined determination with a chip-on-the-shoulder aura. Now it held a touch of desperation.

"Come in, Rhodes." Reese waved toward the chair in front of the large oak desk that he kept polished to a high sheen.

"Thank you, sir."

Reese noticed Rhodes look toward the antique leather golf bag propped in one corner of the room. The ancient clubs splayed out from the top of the bag were made of hickory and had cost a small fortune. Not that the price had been a problem to Reese.

Rhodes gave the bag and clubs a nod of admiration, then perched himself on the edge of the chair and gripped his work-scarred hands in his lap. "Thank you for seeing me, Dr. Sutherland," Rhodes said, his voice a little unsteady.

Reese looked down at the open file in front of him. He studied it for a few moments before speaking. "Had some trouble with that last thesis, I see." He looked up. "Failed it, in fact."

"Yes sir, but the file should show that up to now I've kept my grades up."

Reese turned over a sheet of paper. "Not way up, though."

"But, sir—"

Reese held up one hand. "I know, I know. You've got a decent ninety percent GPA."

His expression now smug, Justin relaxed a little. "Ninety-one, actually, sir."

Reese leaned back in his chair and regarded Justin without speaking. When the young man's grin disappeared and he began to squirm a little, Reese quirked a brow at him. "Do you know how many of our other last-year law students have ninety-five and above?"

Justin gulped. "Uh, no sir."

"Twenty-five percent."

Justin paled, as Reese had known he would. "I don't have to remind you, do I, Rhodes, that only the top twenty percent will graduate from Grant Lauder with law degrees?"

"B-but that's not fair!"

"Life is not always fair, is it?"

Justin let out a curse that ended with, "You said that right. But, sir, if you'll let me do that thesis over and I do well the rest of the school year, that will pull my grade up to that twenty- percentile group. You, see, this fall has been really busy. I have a full-time job and—"

"Where have I seen you before, Rhodes?"

Rhodes looked surprised. "Um, in class, of course."

Reese waved a dismissive hand. "Of course. But where else? Where is this full-time job of yours?"

"I work for Landers Landscaping, and with the heavy winds we had in September, we've been swamped with extra work. That's why—"

"Landers Landscaping. That's the company that services my town-house complex. Cerca de Costa in La Jolla. Must have seen you there."

A pitiful expression on his face, Rhodes leaned forward and curled his fingers over the edge of the polished desk. He removed them quickly when Reese frowned. "Please, sir. My outside work has slacked off some, and I'm already familiar with the subject matter for that thesis. I know I can do a good job if you let me do it over."

"Do you like landscaping, Rhodes?"

Rhodes frowned. "Yes sir, I do. But what's that got to do with—"

"What's your favorite part?"

Still frowning, Rhodes answered, "It may seem strange, sir, but I really like working with the flowers, especially the roses."

"So you're responsible for the roses on the grounds at my complex."

For the first time, Rhodes smiled. "I am," he said with a hint of pride.

"Why are you studying law, Mr. Rhodes?"

Clearly surprised at the sudden change of subject, the second in less than a minute, Rhodes said, "Because, well, because, well I want to see people get a fair—"

"Don't give me that, Rhodes. You think the law's your ticket to a bundle of money."

Placing both hands on the chair arms, Rhodes lifted himself and stood. "Sir!"

Reese folded his arms over his chest. "I can see by your expression that I'm right."

Rhodes' mouth turned down. "So what? What's wrong with that?" He walked over to the golf bag and ran one hand lovingly over its smooth leathery surface.

Reese stood. "Keep your hands off that." He hurried to Rhodes' side.

Rhodes gave the bag one last gentle touch, then squared his shoulders. "What's wrong with wanting to make money, Dr. Sutherland? What's wrong with being tired of doing without so your mother and siblings can have enough food and clothes? What's wrong with wanting the money to go back to golfing and sailing and traveling? I used to do all that, you know."

"Nothing's wrong with wanting to make money, Rhodes." Reese said in his most patronizing tone. "But you're going about it in the wrong way."

"What do you mean?"

"I mean you don't have what it takes for the law profession."

Rhodes' voice rose as he said, "Don't have what it takes? Whadda you mean I don't have what it takes?"

"I see from your transcripts from State that you have a real head for business and that you aced a couple of horticulture classes. Also, you like your landscaping work. What you should do, Rhodes, is use the money that would go to finishing law school to begin your own landscaping business."

"Wh-what!"

"You heard me."

"Does that mean you won't let me redo the thesis?"

"That's exactly what I mean, and you should thank me."

"*Thank* you? Thank you for trying to destroy everything I've worked for? I don't think so." Rhodes placed both hands on the desktop, ignoring Reese's glare. His whole face was so full of anger and hatred that Reese stepped back.

He was not quick enough to miss Justin's fist.

Fortunately the young man only landed a glancing blow on Reese's shoulder. Before Reese could react, Rhodes stomped out of the office, muttering curses and not bothering to close the door.

"You'll be sorry, Sutherland," Reese heard him mutter. "You'll be sorry."

A few seconds later, Cecelia Hanson stuck her sleek grey head in the office. "Are you okay, Dr. Sutherland?"

Shaken, Reese ran the back of one hand over his forehead, then shook it, as though shaking off perspiration. He gave his assistant a wry smile. "Yes, I'm okay, Cecelia." He had gained the sixtyish woman's undying devotion from the beginning by telling her that her young-sounding name suited her. "You heard all that, I guess? I noticed the door wasn't closed all the way."

Cecelia blushed, then lifted her chin and pressed her lips together. "I heard every word."

He got up and came around the desk to put his arm around her shoulder. Grinning again, he said, "You need to report this incident to Dean Simpson. This is grounds for dismissal. You are my witness to what went on here today."

~~~

Two people saw Justin Rhodes storm out of Reese Sutherland's office. Dr. Albert Bainbridge, short, slightly built professor of Corporate Law, had come out of his own office, next door to Reese's. He stopped to lean on his ornamental cane and glare at Reese's door. As he was about to continue down the hall, a burly student he recognized as the temperamental Justin Rhodes burst out of Reese's door. At the same time, a tall, lanky Poly-Sci student Bainbridge recognized as Dexter Driscoll came rushing down the hall and nearly ran into Rhodes.

"Hey, watch where you're going," Rhodes growled. "Get outta my way!" Coloring the air with curses, he shoved Driscoll out of his way and dashed outside.

Chapter Nine

Paris

ဆ

"Well, I think—as you Americans say—that does it." Pierre Barbeau, the portly, exquisitely dressed Frenchman put out a hand to Mike Jenkins. A large diamond sparkled from his pudgy ring finger, and a beam sparkled in his eye. "We at Barbeau Architectes look forward to working with MelJen. Ahh. A company named for yourself and your beloved wife. You must have a bit of French blood, Mssr. Jenkins."

Returning the handshake with firm pressure, Mike grinned. "None that I know of Mr. Barbeau. Pure Mississippi Anglo, I'm afraid."

The Frenchman jiggled his brows. "Hmmm. Maybe you should check your lineage. There must be a Frenchman hiding in there somewhere. At any rate, we here at Barbeau Architectes do look forward with pleasure to working with your excellent company on the new mall on the outskirts of the city. We expect it to be the finest Paris has seen to date."

"That's our plan. Shoppers from all over Europe will flock to it."

Barbeau kissed his fingertips with a distinctly French flourish. "Aha! C'est magnifique! How wonderful. Now, I must um, how do you say it? Extinguish a blaze?"

Mike let out a good natured chuckle. "Put out a fire."

"Ah, yes. I must put out a fire in our Berlin branch." Barbeau pressed a buzzer on his desk. "I'll leave you in Yvette's capable hands." He winked at Mike.

Yvette swayed her model-thin form into the room and gave Mike an unquestionably flirty look. Despite her thinness (except for obvious enhancements underneath a low, tight blouse) and ultra-short, ultra-black hair, she exuded provocative charm, and knew it. In the ten days Mike had been in Paris, Yvette had given him more "I'm available" looks than he could keep up with. He wasn't sure why he hadn't responded. All he knew was that her coy tactics left him cold.

With a slight bow and an "Adieu," Barbeau left.

Though Yvette tried to drag out the small amount of paperwork Mike needed to deal with, he managed to get away in fifteen minutes, leaving the French woman with a sultry pout.

Soon, he was outside, wrapped in a fur-lined trench coat with the collar turned up and striding toward one of his favorite venues in the city—the Seine. Even on this cold, cloudy November afternoon, tourists snapped pictures of the famous river and the Eiffel Tower in the background. Mingled among them, lovers walked hand in hand or with their arms encircling each other's waists, oblivious to the world around them. And all along the walkway, artists sat before their easels.

Mike zeroed in on a young woman earnestly applying oils to a Van Gogh-style painting of the medieval spires of Notre Dame Cathedral across the river. Her waist-length black hair fell across her face, and a red beret perched to one side of her head. She wore a paint-spattered purple smock over her jeans. He stopped and stared at her. She personified the word picture Lenae Maddox liked to paint of her dream of living the artist's life in Paris.

During the first couple of weeks after leaving San Diego, he'd called Lenae occasionally. Little by little the calls had increased, until he now rarely missed a day.

Why, Mike wondered, had Yvette—and all the other women who'd thrown themselves at him during this nearly six-week European business trip—held so little appeal? He was leaving Paris early tomorrow morning. Why was he spending his last day in the world's most romantic city alone? Why did he envision Lenae sitting across a tiny table from him at one of Paris's many outdoor cafés? Why did he imagine her lowering her chin and looking at him through her long, dark lashes? All at once, as though the sun had broken through the grey sky, Mike knew why.

He was in love with Lenae—and didn't want to share her with any other man.

Chapter Ten

&

Kate's cell phone was ringing when she stepped into the 1930s craftsman-style cottage that was her temporary Coronado home. The white clapboard house was not at all like Cami's Tudor beachfront mansion and in no way resembled Kate's tall, narrow three-story brick house in Boston. But she found the arched doorways, fireplace framed in Mexican tile, and all the unexpected nooks and crannies charming. She was grateful for Ben and Pat Nance, the adventuresome, seventyish couple who had needed a house sitter while they toured Australia. When Kate first accepted the interim position at Grant Lauder U—*The Glue,* she thought, inwardly chuckling at Reese Sutherland's explanation of the nickname—the assumption was she'd live with Cami and continue to help her work through her grief and anger over Braxton's murder and infidelity. The four-week motorhome tour had helped, but the young widow had a long way to go. Still, both women felt it was right for Kate to step in for the Nances.

Kate's phone rang again. She dropped her books onto the chintz-covered sofa and dug into her oversized purse.

I did better with a smaller purse, she thought. *Why did I let Cami talk me into this one? I can't find anything in it.*

That bothered Kate. She liked everything in order—home, office, life itself. And purse. On the fourth ring, she managed to extract the phone from the very bottom.

"Hello," she said, sounding out of breath.

"Have you been running on the beach or something?" a deep, familiar voice quipped.

"Gunnar!" Kate could feel a smile spread across her face. She settled her petite body into a corner of the couch, tucking her legs beneath her.

"Well, have you? Been running?"

"Not a chance. Not today. I just got in from school."

"Busy day?"

"You said it. I only have classes in the morning, but I stayed there to grade about a thousand essays."

"A thousand?"

"Okay, maybe a hundred. By the way, I had lunch with Cami today at Burger Lounge; and the woman who's head of HR, Lenae Maddox, joined us." Kate told Gunnar about the lunch and the two men in Lenae's life.

"Sounds a little hard to balance."

Kate laughed. "Cami's words exactly. But...somehow...I think Lenae is dealing with a bigger problem." She laughed again. "Maybe she hates being single."

"That's one thing I love about you Kate."

"What? That I'm single?"

Gunnar let out a guffaw. "You know better than that. It's that, inside that no-nonsense persona of yours is the most tenderhearted woman I know."

"I think you've got me mixed up with Cami."

"Oh no. I can almost hear the mental wheels spinning, wondering how the Lord is going to use you to help Ms. Maddox. But, speaking of Cami, how is she?" Genuine concern came from Gunnar's voice. Kate remembered how he had once assumed Cami was rather shallow. "Miss Bubbly," he had called her. He had changed his mind when he met her and found her to be light hearted, yes, but also intelligent.

"She's as well as can be expected, as the saying goes. No, she's better than that. You know how tragedy causes some people to blame God and turn away from Him?"

"And Cami? It sounded as if things were going fairly well last time I talked with you."

"Thankfully, Cami's been the opposite. During the first part of our road trip, she regularly dreamed about the night Braxton was murdered. Along the way we talked and cried and prayed, then talked and cried and prayed some more at least part of every day. Toward the end, there was less crying, but at times it's obvious the pain is still pretty raw."

"Well, it's only been three months."

"I know. The trip was good for her. I believe God really used it to help her start healing. Then the call from the school ended our travels." Kate paused. "And none too soon."

"Aha."

"I hate to admit it, Gunnar, but when you said I was out of my mind to even think of spending a year traveling in a motorhome—well..."

Gunnar chuckled. "Come on, Kate. You can say it: 'You were right, Gunnar.'"

Kate groaned and laughed in one breath. "Okay, okay. You were right, Gunnar."

"What about us, Kate?" Gunnar was serious now. "Did the trip help *you* start getting past some things, too?"

"Oh, Gunnar." With one forefinger, Kate traced around a large blue flower in the chintz sofa cover. She could picture big, ruggedly handsome Gunnar in his den back in Boston. Her mind saw his Norwegian-blonde hair, and her arms felt his around her. Suddenly she wanted to be there cuddled up next to him.

"Well?" Gunnar's voice was soft and gentle and a little insecure sounding.

Kate hated knowing she had made him feel that way, even if it was at least partly his own fault. If only he'd been up front with her about seeing a woman he had dated a few times after his wife Brita died. The situation had been mild and innocent on Gunnar's part, but Kate hadn't been able to quickly overlook his lack of total honesty. Now...

"I miss you," she whispered, stroking her smooth cheek as though it were his rough one.

"You can do something about that, you know," Gunnar said, raw emotion coming through the phone from all the way across the continent.

"Like what?" Kate knew what he meant, but wanted to hear him say it.

"Like get yourself back here to Boston. Back to me."

"If I could, I'd leave tomorrow. Tonight. In an hour. But I've committed to this job at the University for the next few weeks."

"And then?"

"And then, I'm packing my bags and turning my back on Coronado, beautiful as it is, and heading east. About 3,000 miles east."

A brief silence told Kate that Gunnar was too touched to speak.

"Will you be able to come out here before then?" she asked wistfully.

"I hope so. But work is pretty busy right now." Gunnar was a gas turbine software developer at Hub Digital Corporation, "The Hub" being a nickname for Boston.

"I'll pray hard that you— Oh, there's the doorbell." Kate unfolded her legs, rose from the sofa and smoothed her navy blue pants. "It's probably Cami here early. Hold on a minute."

"Cami early? Doesn't sound like the Cami we both know and love."

Kate chuckled. "Even Cami is early sometimes." When she opened the door, instead of Cami, a young woman stood there holding a long white box from the island's most exclusive flower shop. Kate took the box and stepped back to her purse for a tip for the delivery girl.

"What is it?" Gunnar asked.

"As if you didn't know!" Cradling the phone against her shoulder, she undid the silky coral colored ribbon and lifted the box lid. She gasped. A rose. One perfect coral and gold rose nestled in a bed of fern and baby's breath. Kate recognized it as a Talisman rose.

"It's fabulous!" Kate lifted the box to her face and took a deep breath. "And it smells heavenly."

"What's fabulous? What smells heavenly?"

"Don't play innocent, Gunnar." Kate lifted the flap of the tiny envelope tucked into the baby's breath. "I know it's you who sent me this rose."

"No, Kate...."

Kate wasn't listening. She slipped a card from the envelope and opened it just as Gunnar said, "Kate, I didn't—"

Kate gasped again, this time in utter shock. The note on the card read, "Thank you for brightening a small corner of my day."

It was signed with one letter: "R".

Reese Sutherland!

Chapter Eleven

∞

The dream was back. As usual, somehow Cami knew she was dreaming and, as usual, she couldn't make it stop. Once again she was in the Oceanfront Ballroom of the Hotel del Coronado. It was the night of the party where Braxton planned to announce his intention to run for mayor of the island town. She could see the guests as clearly as though they were standing by her bedside. Kate. The twins, Durant and Debra. Braxton's brother Victor and his wife Ashley. Rosita DeLuca, Braxton's long-time administrative assistant. Cosmetic surgeon Dr. Stanley Weston and his provocative wife Erika.

And Braxton. There was Braxton. Tall, dark haired, blue eyed, achingly handsome. Exuding charm with every word, every lift of his brows, every tilt of his head.

Cami saw herself drifting toward him, drawn to him, loving him, wanting to be near him, to touch him. Suddenly she was seated at Braxton's side at the head table. A waiter placed fresh flutes of pink champagne at their places, and Victor introduced his brother as the "next mayor of Coronado."

As a streak of lightning lit up the moonless sky beyond the oceanfront windows, Braxton smiled down at Cami. He reached for his flute of champagne and took a sip.

Something was wrong.

Braxton's face twisted to a painful grimace. He dropped his glass and clutched the tuxedo fabric over his heart with both hands. As one hand let go and reached out toward Cami, a crash of thunder shook the room and the lights went out. A moment later, as quickly as they'd gone off, the lights again flooded the room.

In her dream Cami felt a scream rising from her throat and melding with those of the guests. Beside her, Braxton lay motionless across the table. Rosy champagne trickled across the snowy white cloth like pale blood.

~~~

Cami awoke screaming and sobbing and crying out again and again, "No! No! No!"

"Cami! Cami, wake up!" Kate took hold of Cami's arms and shook her smartly. "You're dreaming again. Wake up."

Cami shook her head, but it took several seconds to stop sobbing and clear her mind of the awful pictures in her dream. Kate was silent while Cami took deep, shaky breaths and regained her composure. Cami looked at her bedside clock. Only nine-thirty. She had gone to bed early tonight, soon after returning from her and Kate's outing to the gym and a casual restaurant an hour ago. But her mind was so foggy, it seemed she had slept for days.

"That was a bad one," said Kate.

"Those are the very words you used the first time I had the dream." Cami forced a weak smile and sat up. She pressed her fingers against her forehead, thinking of how the dream had occurred several times during the early part of the RV trip, but had gradually tapered off. "That's the first time I've had it in the few days we've been back to Coronado. I'm so glad you were here." She looked at Kate more closely. "What are you doing here?"

"A few minutes ago I realized that when I was here yesterday I left a book I need for class tomorrow. You said you were going straight to bed, so I let myself in with the key you gave me. Didn't want to ring the bell and wake up you or the Sterns. I was about to leave when I heard you screaming."

Cami kicked back the covers from her blue silk pajama-clad legs and took the matching robe from the bedpost. Standing straight and lifting her chin, she said, "I'm going to be okay now. Want to join me in a cup of hot chocolate before you leave."

"Of course." Kate grinned. "Do you think Edith will let you into *her* kitchen?"

"Huh! You'd think it really was her kitchen the way she's so possessive about it. Growing up in a middle-class family like mine, I have a hard time getting used to the way some people let their hired help tell them what to do in their own houses. Mama shakes her head when she comes here from North Carolina. For nearly twenty-three years she's been afraid I'll forget how to cook."

"Well, next time I see her I'll tell her about all the great meals you put together for us on the road—and how we'd have starved if we'd had to depend on my cooking."

"Come on, Kate, let's get some hot chocolate. In *my* kitchen."

Chapter Twelve

ॐ

As Kate, laden with her lunch tray, left the cafeteria line in the Grant Lauder staff dining room, she saw Reese Sutherland on the other side of the room, also bearing a tray. Good. She was hoping to see him today to thank him for the rose. Last night, over hot chocolate at Cami's, Kate had told Cami about Gunnar's call and the rose from Reese.

"Kate! I never figured you for a woman dangling two men on the hook!" Cami teased.

"Don't be silly. No man is *on my hook*, as you so delicately put it."

"Mmm. I guess not," said Cami, pretending to be serious. "Gunnar is definitely off the hook and in your fishing basket. Then along comes Reese Sutherland to upset the applecart."

Kate rolled her eyes at Cami's mixed metaphors. Leave it to her to make a phone call and one rose into a full-blown love triangle.

She thought of that late-night conversation as she looked over to where Reese was talking with Dr. Albert Bainbridge, one of the professors in the Law Department. The thin, almost effeminate man with his neat gray mustache and goatee wore a three-piece suit and, though he didn't have a limp, always carried a brass-topped walking stick. Every time Kate saw him, the old-fashioned word "dapper" came to mind. He was doing most of the talking, and it didn't look like a pleasant conversation. Reese seemed to be impatient to be done with it. He made some comment to Bainbridge and started to step away.

Bainbridge spun around to leave. As he turned, his arm bumped against Reese's tray. Hot cheese soup and a large plate of barbecued ribs splashed Reese's long-sleeved shirt and sweater vest with blobs of orange and reddish brown. Some chocolate ice cream landed on his cheek. On the floor bits of lettuce drenched with creamy salad dressing mingled with everything else. Bainbridge, ignoring the mess he'd caused, headed toward the exit.

Kate dipped her napkin into her glass of water and rushed to Reese's side. Reese grinned and took the napkin and dabbed at his cheek. "I think this mess is going to take more than a wet napkin to clean up," he said, still grinning.

By this time, two white-jacketed students were cleaning up the mess on the floor.

"What I hate most is wasting all that barbecue," Reese joked. "I'm starving."

One of the students, a curly-haired blonde, giggled. When Kate looked at her in surprise, the girl said, "Professor Sutherland is always hungry."

"Careful there, Mindy," Reese said with mock sternness. "I still need to grade your latest essay, you know."

The girl rose with her handful of stained towels. As she walked away, she shot him a flirty look over one shoulder. "Be sure not to get sauce on my paper."

Now the other student, a male, rose.

Dexter Driscoll, Kate thought. *I didn't know he was on a work scholarship.* She felt a wave of sympathy for the young man.

Dexter paused, scowling at Reese, who seemed unaware of it. Dexter glanced toward Kate, seemed surprised to see her, opened his mouth, snapped it shut, and hurried off.

Kate shrugged. You never knew what might cause a college-aged student to dislike a professor. And dislike Reese the young man definitely did.

Kate turned her attention back to Reese. "Most of the sauce is on your vest. Looks like it missed your shirt. Why don't you run to the men's room and take off the vest while I get you another tray of food. The dining room line is closing soon, and...." Kate imitated the pretty coed's tone to say, "... we don't want you to go hungry."

Reese laughed. "I never do that."

"Besides, I was hoping to see you today," Kate said.

He grinned again. "Back in a minute."

~~~

Dexter Driscoll threw the dirty towels into a bin, reliving for a moment his wiping up food at the feet of Reese Sutherland. It had felt like groveling.

I think I'm gonna puke. And Dr. Elfmon. What was she doing, rushing to help him clean up? Sure, I've baited her about her religion, but I really respect her.

Dexter went to the large sink to wash his hands. As he dried them, he thought, *Somebody oughta clue her in about Sutherland.*

~~~

Reese was back in the dining room by the time Kate got a tray of food for him. Luckily there were plenty of ribs left, but she'd had to substitute strawberry ice cream for the chocolate.

Reese was holding a plastic bag, which Kate assumed held his soiled vest. Watching him, she felt confused. Her feelings for Gunnar had deepened and matured during the past weeks to the point she was nearly sure she wanted to marry him—and that this was God's will for them.

So... why this lifting of spirit at the sight of Reese Sutherland striding toward her? Why did she smile inwardly at the way a lock of sun-bleached hair fell across his forehead, inviting her to brush it back for him?

I'm staring at him! she thought. She looked down at the table and began to rearrange the dishes and flatware. Only when she felt his presence did she look up.

"Oh, there you are," she said.

His amused grin told her he knew she'd been watching him. She felt like kicking herself for letting him make her feel flustered.

Flustered? Why should this man make her feel that way? She loved Gunnar, she was sure of it. Perhaps that thought was what made her next words less friendly than they would have been otherwise. "I think I got most of what you had before. Hope you like ranch salad dressing and strawberry ice cream."

"Love both." Reese settled himself in the chair opposite her. "All of a sudden you sounded serious."

He was observant. Kate liked that.

"Anything wrong?"

He sounded so concerned that Kate relaxed, but wasn't completely honest when she said, "Oh, no."

"Whew!" Reese wiped at his brow. "For a minute I thought you were going to tell me I was out of line sending you the rose."

"I'll admit I was surprised, but I loved it. I put it in a vase right away. It's gorgeous on the coffee table, and the aroma is intoxicating."

Looking as pleased as a little boy with a new toy, Reese shoveled a huge bite of ribs into his mouth. After concentrating wholeheartedly on his food for several minutes, he leaned back, no sign of his usual grin on his face. "Guess you're wondering about that little confrontation with Bainbridge."

"Couldn't help but do so."

"I like that about you, Kate. I can tell you say exactly what you think."

"Usually," Kate said, thinking of how she hadn't been completely honest when he asked if anything was wrong.

"Anyway, the long and short of it is that Bainbridge simply doesn't like me. As you know, I'm here while Dr. Johanssen is on sabbatical—only eighteen months in all."

"I remember, but most sabbaticals are for only a year, like mine."

"Johanssen was originally going to be gone for only a year. I think I mentioned the research he's doing for a book and how it has taken much longer than he anticipated. To put it mildly, Bainbridge is having a hard time with my being here so long. He can't get over thinking of me strictly as a temp. He has a tendency to object to every idea I come up with." Reese's face darkened for a moment. "I will say I didn't expect him to confront me publicly. Pretty unprofessional."

"What will you do about it?"

"Nothing. No point in it. He's a good professor—if somewhat distant with the students. Teaches Corporate and Tax Law." Reese made a face. "Knows his stuff. We need him in the department." His expression relaxed. "Hey, let's move on to a more pleasant subject."

"Such as?"

"Having dinner with me at Peohe's Saturday night."

Kate was taken aback. She knew that Peohe's was one of the most upscale restaurants on the island. "I, I don't know," she said, thinking immediately of Gunnar. On the phone last night she'd been open with Gunnar about receiving a rose from a fellow professor. He had said something about getting back to San Diego and staking out his territory. It would have sounded like a joke if not for the strong strain of seriousness behind the words.

"Why don't you know?" Reese said, breaking into her thoughts. "Is Saturday a bad night?"

"Oh no, Saturday's perfect." Kate wanted to bite her tongue. Now she'd made him think she was willing to go out with him.

"Then I'll pick you up at seven. As you know, I already have your address."

"But..."

Reese's cell phone interrupted Kate's words. He looked at it and said, "I need to take this call." He rose. "See you Saturday night. Seven sharp." He walked away, leaving his dishes.

What have I done? Kate asked herself. *And what will I wear?*

Chapter Thirteen

ॐ

Justin Rhodes stabbed at the dirt around the roses he was fertilizing outside Cerca de Costa, the luxurious La Jolla townhouse complex where Dr. Reese Sutherland lived. Located on the ocean side of Neptune Place, the front of the Spanish-style homes featured lush lawns leading to a cliff that sloped gently down to a boulder-strewn beach. He'd often wondered how Sutherland could afford a place like this on a law professor's salary.

Reese Sutherland! He stabbed again, harder. *That—* His mind rattled off a string of crude epithets.

Ever since yesterday's confrontation, Justin had expected to be called into the dean's office and expelled from the school. He'd forced himself to attend Dr. Sutherland's class this morning, but he slipped in at the last second and sat in the back behind an extra large fellow student. Still, with an inscrutable expression, Sutherland looked straight at him. After that he'd ignored Justin. That had been worse than anything else he could have done. Justin hardly heard anything Sutherland taught that day, except that a paper was due by next Monday. Well, he'd get the information from someone else. He couldn't afford another failing grade.

Maybe Sutherland's playing me. Justin gave the soft, moist earth another stab, yet being careful not to damage the rose's roots. *Making me sweat before dropping the bomb. Or—*his face brightened for a moment. *Maybe he's going to let me redo that failed paper after all.* He dug more gently for a while, then, *No way. He's got it in for me.*

He stood and let his gaze travel over the meticulous grounds. He maintained the flower beds of this complex along with two others nearby. As he'd told Sutherland, he especially liked the roses. He had done a good bit of research and learned there were thirty-five types of roses, or to be more precise, thirty five categories. No other flower had a wider range of size, color, shape, and bloom form than the rose.

He touched a petal on a white American Beauty and bent to take in its delicate scent. A few steps over, he smiled at the sight of his favorite, a gold and coral masterpiece with the mysterious name of Talisman. Next he stopped by a red one called the Playboy. Gritting his teeth he looked toward the townhouses with their glistening white stucco walls that slanted down and outward from blue tile roofs. That one at the end was Reese Sutherland's.

He thought of the shapely blonde he'd recently seen the professor leading inside.

I planted this Playboy in the wrong spot. His mouth twisted in disdain. *Should've put it in front of Sutherland's digs.* His thoughts shifted again to Monday's confrontation. *What if he expels me? I can't let that happen.*

Justin gave the ground another vicious stab near one of the Talisman rose bushes. The force caused one long stem to break off and fall to the ground. Chagrined, he stared at it, mourning its demise.

Then a thought came to him. *Lenae! She'd love this. The way she loves beautiful things... It must be the artist in her.*

Justin had asked Lenae Maddox out several times over the past few months, but she'd reminded him that university staff members were prohibited from dating students. Still, he kept asking, calling, finding moments at the university to "happen" in her vicinity.

"Justin, are you stalking me?" she'd once teased.

"Wanting to go out with a beautiful woman isn't stalking," he replied in his ever-serious manner.

Several times Justin had given Lenae flowers. Usually they were rescued from his landscaping sites. But twice he'd eaten peanut butter sandwiches at lunch for a week and used the money saved to order florist arrangements for her. The first was a mixed bouquet. His latest offering was a large fall arrangement of orange day lilies, yellow asters, and dark red mums arranged in a low ceramic dish. Lenae had thanked him politely and told him they looked lovely on her dining table, but she still refused his pleas for a date.

Now he tenderly picked up the perfect flower and thought, *This is it. A showcase flower. No woman could resist.* Something else tickled at the back of his mind. Then he had it. *Talisman. The word for a good-luck charm. Perfect. I know where she lives. I'll surprise her. I'll take it to her tonight.*

A thrill of anticipation crowded out his anger at Reese Sutherland, for now. With great care—for the rose and for Lenae—he placed the rose atop the cuttings in his wheelbarrow.

Chapter Fourteen

ॐ

"You did *what*?"

Cami stopped dead still on the sidewalk on Orange Street, Coronado's wide tree-lined main thoroughfare. She and Kate were nearing the small Baptist church where Cami wanted to attend Wednesday night Bible study. Kate had told her about accepting Reese's invitation to dinner at Peohe's.

"Cami!" said Kate, not stopping, but glancing around at the passersby. "You don't need to tell the whole island."

Cami caught up with Kate. "But what about Gunnar?"

"What about him?"

"You know very well *what about him*. One day you imply you're about to marry him; the next you're googly-eyed over another man."

"I am not googly-eyed over Reese Sutherland. You do come up with the weirdest expressions."

"Don't try to change the subject. You are, too, googly-eyed."

"I am not."

"We're here," said Cami. Entering the wide door, she looked back at Kate and whispered, "We'll talk about this later."

~~~

Neither Cami nor Kate had noticed the short, plump, nearly bald man who had been walking behind them and hearing their conversation before they entered the church. Neither saw the scowl on his face.

Dr. Stan Weston was a cosmetic surgeon on the island. When he saw Cami and Kate walking together, he had deliberately held back. Cami was a charming, gracious woman. However, running into Stan, whose wife had been involved with Cami's husband, might test her graciousness beyond its limits. Though he had held back, he couldn't help overhearing a name that made his blood run cold.

Reese Sutherland.

Chapter Fifteen

ॐ

Clutching the rescued rose, now enclosed in a cone of newspaper, Justin rang the bell at Lenae's loft. Daring to hope her face would light up, he felt a thrill of pleasure and anticipation. Okay, much as he'd wanted to, he'd never been to her home before and she wasn't expecting him.

But maybe when she sees this rose...

After what seemed like several minutes, the door cracked open, but the chain latch stayed on. Lenae peeped through the narrow opening.

"Oh. Justin," she said. "Um, hello."

Not exactly a thrilling beginning, but Justin hoped that would change in a moment.

Lenae left the latch on the door. Not a good sign.

Justin hated the awkward feeling that came over him. He tamped it down and forced a cheery, "Hello yourself."

When she didn't respond, he blundered on, "I–I brought this for you." He thrust the newspaper cone through the door.

Lenae took the offering and folded back a corner of the paper so that the rose was visible.

"Justin!" Her tone suggested exasperation rather than pleasure.

"You don't like it?" Justin was genuinely puzzled and began to feel a sense of dread.

"Of course I like it." Her words were short and terse.

Justin sensed Lenae felt as awkward as he did. Ill at ease even. His dread grew.

"I'm sorry I can't invite you in, Justin," she said. "This isn't a good time. I wish you'd called."

A movement beyond Lenae caught Justin's eye, and understanding dawned on him.

"You have company, don't you?" He could hear the accusatory tone in his words.

Lenae lifted her chin. "Yes, I do. Now I really have to tell you good night, Justin. I'll see you at the university tomorrow."

She closed the door, but not before Justin caught a glimpse of a tall vase on Lenae's small round dining table. It held one Talisman rose.

Chapter Sixteen

ဢ

Cami was restless. And she knew why. Earlier, at tonight's Bible study, she had hardly been able to keep her mind on Pastor Oates' message. All she could think of was how enamored Kate seemed to be with her fellow professor, Dr. Reese Sutherland. When she'd joked about Kate having two men on the hook, she didn't dream Kate would accept a date with Professor Sutherland.

Steady, sensible Kate googly-eyed about a man she'd hardly knew.

Yes, she was googly-eyed, no matter what she says, Cami told herself now, grimacing. *But then, what's it to me? Am I so set on her marrying Gunnar that I'm blind to Kate's right to her own decision?* She looked upward. *What* is *it to me, Lord? Why do I feel so negative about this?*

Because Kate's your friend, Cami. Friends are concerned about friends.

Cami had heard no voice, but she felt the words in her spirit.

Still, she was restless. She wandered into the small room she used for a personal office. It was next to the large one Braxton had used and that Cami had not entered since his death. Now, for reasons she couldn't explain to herself, she knew it was time to face up to her dread of entering the room that had been her husband's sanctuary. Stiffening her spine, she sent up a prayer and stepped from her office to the door of his. Before she could change her mind, she pushed it open, went inside, and flipped on the overhead light.

She meandered from the huge oak desk to the matching book shelves, file cabinets, and credenza, touching each piece, running her fingers along the spines of the books, remembering Braxton's dark head bent over some paperwork. Her throat tightened, but she wouldn't allow herself to cry.

Instead, she went back to the desk. Braxton's computer monitor and keyboard still sat at an angle on one side, as though he may walk in at any minute and turn it on. Angled on the other side of the desk was a leather-framed photo of the Carrington family.

Cami pulled the big leather chair away from the desk and sat down. She picked up the photograph, remembering the day it was taken. It was summer, not long after the twins graduated from Coronado High School. It was Cami's favorite photo from that day. After the pictures in their elegant living room were done, she'd asked the photographer to give them a few minutes to change into casual clothing, then go out to the beach for more photos. To her surprise, Braxton humored her.

The beach photos were as carefree as the others were formal. To Cami's further surprise, for his desk Braxton chose one of the family holding hands, laughing, and running in the sand rather than a copy of the large formal one over the living room mantel.

Cami touched Braxton's face in the photo, allowing memories of that day and other pleasant moments over the years to rush in and flood over the hurtful ones of his unfaithfulness and his murder. After a few minutes, she put the photograph aside. A few tears crept over her cheeks. For the first time since Braxton's death, the tears were sweet rather than bitter.

Choosing to omit any references to the painful parts of her marriage, Cami prayed, *Thank You, Lord, for the husband You gave me.*

A few minutes later, she closed the door to the office, knowing she'd never again dread entering Braxton's domain.

~~~

As Cami left Braxton's office, her cell phone rang. Her heart quickened as she saw the caller ID. She punched Talk.

"Durant!" she said. "How are you, honey?"

"I'm... um... fine, Mom."

"No, you're not. Your voice is hoarse. You're not used to that cold Scottish weather. I bet you're not wearing warm enough clothing."

"Mom, I keep so wrapped up they think I'm an Eskimo. Are you and Aunt Kate staying out of trouble?"

"I am."

"You are, but not Aunt Kate? That sounds backwards."

"Well... oh, it's nothing. It's only that one of the professors asked her out and she said yes."

"What! What about Gunnar?"

"That's what I'm wondering. What about Gunnar?"

Chapter Seventeen

ε⊃

Mike Jenkins used the private elevator in the south building of The Melanies and was soon exiting at the twenty-fifth floor loft. He had slept little last night and arose at 5:00 a.m. even though MelJen's private jet couldn't get clearance to fly out of Paris till three in the afternoon. Though he'd learned to sleep well on long flights, this time thoughts of Lenae kept him awake most of the trip. He debated with himself about telling her that his business had concluded several days ahead of schedule.

No. He grinned to himself. *It'll be more fun to surprise her.*

Though exhausted and bleary eyed, he'd picked up his black Escalade from his hangar at Montgomery Field, a small non-commercial airport. Then instead of going home, he'd headed straight to Lenae's, stopping only long enough to buy a bouquet of fresh flowers from a roadside vendor. If she wasn't in, he'd leave them at her door. Maybe not calling her hadn't been such a good idea, after all. What if she had a date? Why hadn't he thought of that?

One thing was sure: he *had* to know about any other men in her life so he could take steps to eliminate the competition.

Now, leaving the elevator with his shoulders squared and his head down like a bull rushing a toreador, he didn't see the stocky young man barreling toward him. At the last second, the man cursed and jumped to one side. Mike stopped and started to offer a rough apology. Then he raised his head and saw that the man's mouth was curled down, his complexion blotched and angry red.

Without thinking, Mike grabbed the young man's arm. "What are you doing here?" Mike demanded.

The man jerked away and merely glared at Mike. "I could ask you the same, mister. But if you want to know, I came to see Lenae Maddox." Smirking, he pointed to the bouquet Mike clutched in one hand. "Maybe you've come for the same reason. If so, you're a bit late."

"Late? What do you mean?" He started to grab the man again, but stopped himself.

The man let out a mirthless laugh. "You'll find that she already has a visitor," he said as he headed toward the public elevator. Looking over his shoulder, he said. "By the way, you're late with the flowers, too."

Mike stood still for a moment. Then he strode to Lenae's loft, punched the bell, and hammered on the door.

After a few seconds that seemed like half an hour, Lenae cracked the door to the end of the chain and said, "Look, Justin, I told you—" She stopped. "Mike! I-I didn't expect you. You should have called."

"Well, I didn't." He gritted his teeth. "Thanks for the warm welcome."

"Lenae? What's going on?" The male voice came from inside the loft.

"Nothing," Lenae replied. "Everything's okay. Mike, I think you'd better leave. As you see, I have—"

"Company! Yes, I can see." Exhaustion and dread had made Mike reckless. With one quick movement, he slammed his shoulder against the door. The chain broke with a loud clang, and Lenae jumped to one side. Mike stormed in.

Before him stood a tall, thin young man, about twenty Mike guessed, with thick glasses, ill-fitting clothing, and a hangdog look. This was clearly no romantic encounter.

Her voice low but steely, Lenae said, "Mike, I'd like you to meet Dexter Driscoll. And now you may leave."

~~~

Mike didn't leave. Dexter did. A few quick words and he was gone. Lenae had longed to be alone with Mike, yet dreaded telling him about her pregnancy. But his storming in infuriated her.

She turned her back and went to the sink to wash the mugs she and Dexter had used. "I thought your trip was supposed to last until sometime next week."

"I'm sorry for barging in like that." Mike spoke quietly, the earlier forcefulness in his voice now gone. From the corner of her eye, Lenae could see him run his hand through his hair. She'd already noticed that the other hand held a bouquet of mixed flowers.

She rinsed one of the mugs and set it on a towel by the sink. "Barging in? I'd call it breaking in."

"Sorry. I was a little too forceful. I let jet lag and temper get the best of me. I'll see that your chain is replaced tomorrow."

"Make sure you do. Shouldn't be too difficult. I hear you have an *in* with the owner." Lenae rinsed the second mug and set it by its mate.

"I-I stopped and picked up some flowers for you. The roadside vendor didn't have much left, only a mixed bouquet."

Lenae had never before heard Mike sound unsure of himself. But she was still angry and didn't want him to know she was touched. "The flowers are beautiful. Lay them there on the table." She couldn't help adding, "With the other one."

She heard him lay down the flowers with some force. She hoped he couldn't see the note on the Talisman rose. As she was wiping one of the mugs dry, Mike stepped behind her and gripped her arms. He bent his head and, breath warm on her neck, he whispered, "I'm sorry, Lenae. Really sorry. Can we start the evening over?"

"Oh, Mike!" Lenae turned, took his face in her hands, gave his firm lips a passionate kiss, then laid her head on his chest and sobbed.

~~~

An hour later Mike sat in his Escalade, still stunned. It had taken Lenae a long time, but between sobs, she finally spat it out. She was pregnant, about five weeks along. Mike had been away for six weeks. The baby couldn't possibly be his. He'd hardly known how to react, so he had left her still sobbing.

As he left, he stopped and read the card attached to the one gorgeous gold and coral rose. It was signed simply "R".

~~~

When Dexter left Lenae's loft, he settled himself on the floor in a dark, narrow alcove near the end of the hall. From there he saw Mike Jenkins leave, disbelief etched on his face. As soon as Jenkins boarded the private elevator, Dexter went back to Lenae's. Near the breaking point, she wouldn't let him in. In mild-mannered Dexter, a cauldron of hatred boiled and steamed against her earlier visitor.

How dare he hurt the only real friend I've had ever had?

Chapter Eighteen

Boston

&

Gunnar Volstad stared out across the grey waters of Boston Harbor, made choppy by the brisk November wind. The long, high-pitched *tooot-tooot* of a tugboat joined with the screech of a seagull flapping its way down to settle on a wooden post.

Though he often missed the wide, clean openness and the Norwegian atmosphere of his native Minnesota, Gunnar loved Boston. An obsessive history buff, he reveled in living in this city founded on Shawmut Peninsula in 1630. He loved strolling through Boston Common, which dated back to 1634, making it the oldest public park in America; and he delighted in looking out over this harbor, home of the famous Boston Tea Party of 1773. He admired the tall, narrow houses—one of which belonged to Kate Elfmon—and the cobbled sidewalks on Beacon Hill. At the same time, he liked the skyscrapers that rose behind him, and he enjoyed the energetic bustle of a very modern city.

Also, Gunnar liked his work at Hub Digital; and being an upbeat, friendly "people person," he enjoyed his co-workers. Most of all, he loved the church where he fellowshipped regularly with other believers and led a week-night Bible study with a group of young adults, mostly single.

Yet, with all he loved about Boston, something was missing.

He didn't have to wonder what—or who.

Kate, he thought. *It's Kate. What's going on with her? I know we agreed to see other people, but when we talked two days ago, I thought our relationship had taken a definite, nearly permanent turn. Until the doorbell rang and she got a rose from that professor.*

Gunnar watched as the seagull rose from the wooden post and floated toward one of the islands in the harbor. He wished he could do the same, except fly in the opposite direction. To another island. To Coronado, California. To Kate.

They had talked again last night. Kate had called after she and Cami returned from Bible study. With the three-hour time difference, though only nine p.m. in Coronado, it was midnight in Boston. Kate rarely called that late.

The conversation had been a little strange, too. After some rambling small talk, Kate had said casually, too casually to Gunnar's thinking, "By the way, I'm having dinner at Peohe's Saturday night."

A chill had touched Gunnar. "Yes, I remember the place," he said, trying to match her casual tone. "We ate there the night before I left to come back to Boston."

They'd had a table that looked out over the blue waters of San Diego Bay to the tall buildings of the city skyline. It was late August, and the night air was balmy, barely rippling the bay. Though he'd been about to leave Coronado under stressful circumstances—an argument over his not telling Kate that the woman he'd dated after Brita's death had moved from Minnesota to Boston and that he'd seen her a few times—the evening had been romantic.

"I remember," Kate said, responding to his comment. "I'll always remember."

The words were right, even sincere, but something in her voice disturbed Gunnar. "You and Cami having a night out on Saturday, huh?"

"Well, no."

"No?"

"I'm not going with Cami."

There was a silence during which he felt she wanted him to ask, "Then who?" Instead, he waited.

Finally she said, "I'm meeting a fellow professor."

He had had to force a casual tone. "The one who sent you the rose?"

He knew the answer before Kate said, "Yes, him. His name is Reese Sutherland. He's head of the Law Department at GLU."

Gunnar hardly knew how to respond. Besides, a rage of jealousy had blindsided him into speechlessness.

"Gunnar?" Kate asked. "Are you there?"

"I'm here," was all he could get out.

"Are you upset with me?"

Gunnar hadn't been able to keep himself from saying, "Of course not. I'm thrilled that you're having dinner with another man."

The conversation had gone downhill after that and ended with cool good-byes.

Now, looking out over a different harbor on the opposite side of the country, Gunnar felt not only disturbed about Kate, but ashamed of his reactions. Why shouldn't Kate see someone else? Though she had seemed to be coming close, she wasn't engaged to Gunnar. And unlike him a few months ago, she had been completely upfront about her date.

But my meetings with Natalie in Boston weren't really dates, he told himself. *They were more like counseling sessions with a woman who expressed interest in spiritual things.*

Sure, his conscience replied. *"Counseling sessions" with the woman you had a brief fling with after your wife died.*

Well, he had paid for keeping the truth from Kate, and he had sought not only her forgiveness but the Lord's. He knew the Lord had forgiven him; he wasn't as sure about Kate.

Lord, he prayed, *am I over-reacting? Am I making too big a deal about a simple dinner date?*

The silence felt as cold and grey as the waters of Boston Harbor.

~~~

What Gunnar couldn't know was how Kate had felt after their telephone conversation last night. Her emotions had ranged from anger to frustration to annoyance to ... guilt.

But why should I feel guilty? I care deeply for Gunnar. In fact, I'm pretty sure I'm in love with him. But I'm not engaged to him. And we agreed we were free to see other people. So why shouldn't I enjoy a night out with another man? She thought for a few seconds. She knew she needed to be as honest with herself as she was with other people. *Why should it always be Cami who attracts the handsome men? Why shouldn't it be me once in a while?*

Her self-honesty came to an abrupt end. She ignored the tiny Voice trying to tell her, **Take care, Kate. Be careful..**

Chapter Nineteen

ಬಿ

Cami pulled her dark blue Mercedes into a visitor's parking slot at Grant Lauder U. Deliberately delaying her mission, she stayed in the car and admired the landscaping of this part of the campus. Towering eucalyptus trees edged the parking lot, while more eucalyptus and tall palms dotted the lawn. Scattered at random intervals and lining a walkway leading to a stucco, red-tile-roofed classroom building, a variety of colorful semi-tropical flowers caught the midday sun. A native of North Carolina, Cami never got over marveling how with water and care, flowers could be grown all year here in southern California. Only a few students were in sight, most of them wearing jeans and light-weight hoodies.

I overstepped my bounds with Kate last night, Cami thought, still hesitating. *She's a grown woman, and she's not engaged to Gunnar. There's no reason for her not to go out with Reese Sutherland. She said she was going to tell Gunnar. I'm sure she did. Kate is so open and truthful—and one of the best examples of true Christianity that I know. She's my friend and I want her to be happy. Besides maybe I exaggerated. Maybe she wasn't "googly eyed," just pleased.* Cami rested her head on the steering wheel. *Lord, please don't let me say or do anything to hurt our friendship.*

Raising her head, she reached for a paper sack on the seat beside her. It was emblazoned with the bright red logo of a Chinese restaurant and contained an undisguised peace offering. She knew she'd arrived about fifteen minutes before Kate's lunch break. The air was warm today with only a hint of the chill that would begin to deepen sharply by mid-afternoon, so maybe they could eat on that bench near the classroom building. Smiling at the thought, Cami got out of the car, clutched the lunch sack in one hand and an oversized Prada purse in the other. Balancing the two, she bumped the door closed with her hip.

Seconds before she reached the walkway, she felt herself lunging forward!

She let go of the purse and lunch sack, caught her hands and knees on the ground, and fell over on her side. Stunned, she lay still for a few seconds before cautiously raising herself to a sitting position. Looking back, she saw that she'd caught her toe on an exposed eucalyptus root.

Groaning, she grimaced at the grass stains on her winter-white jeans and pulled at the matching denim blazer she wore over a pink striped blouse. Then she spied the contents of the lunch sack scattered on the ground.

"Oh, no!" *So much for a nice reconciliation lunch.*

Groaning again and feeling disoriented, she pulled her purse to her and began to gather up the take-out cartons. *What a mess!* She looked around for a trash container.

"Miss! Are you hurt?" A deep male voice came from above her. Way above her.

"N-no. I think I'm okay. A bit stunned and embarrassed—and mad about losing the food."

"You're also bleeding." He pointed to the bright red seeping through one knee of her white jeans.

"Oh! I hadn't noticed."

"Here, let me help you up." The man hunkered down and tucked a strong hand under her elbow.

Cami nodded and allowed him to help her to her feet. "Thank you. I'll be fine now," she said, looking up into a pair of golden-brown eyes in a handsome, strong-featured face.

She stepped away from him—and stumbled again. He caught her arm and grasped her around the shoulder. Shaken, she didn't pull away at once, but relaxed against his chest.

"I see you've met." Kate's words came from behind her.

Though still shaken, Cami stepped away from the man.

"Careful," the man said, catching her arm again. "Oh hi, Kate. I was about to head to the dining room. Thought I'd run into you there, but here you are."

Puzzled, Cami looked from Kate to the good looking man.

Smiling, Kate said, "Cami, I'd like you to meet Dr. Reese Sutherland."

~~~

"Come on with me to the restroom, and we'll see about that bloody knee," Kate said after the three cleaned up the ruined Chinese lunch. "And then you can join us in the faculty dining room," said Reese.

"Oh no, I—"

"Of course, you're joining us, " Kate said. "You were so thoughtful to bring me lunch, and now it's ruined. Besides, after we eat, I want you to see my office and classroom."

That's exactly what I came here to do, Cami thought. *But suddenly I feel like a third wheel.* Still, not seeing a graceful way to refuse, she fell in step with Kate and Reese. She shook her head to rid it of doubts.

"Head hurt?" Reese asked, sounding genuinely concerned.

"Um, a little," she fibbed, seeing an opportunity to depart. "Look, I think I'd better head on back home. Edith will rustle me up some lunch."

"Let me drive you," Reese offered. "I think you're a little rattled." He placed his hand on Cami's arm as he spoke.

It was a simple gesture, but somehow the gentle, lingering pressure felt intimate to Cami. She was about to say no thanks when she saw Lenae Maddox approaching them.

"Oh, hello, Dr. Elfmon." Lenae's voice was not exactly unfriendly, but—

Dr. Elfmon, Cami thought, as Reese released her arm. *Not Kate. Hmm. Maybe she prefers to be less informal here on campus.* Cami studied Lenae's face and felt a moment of recognition. After Braxton's death, she had become an expert in covering traces of long hours of tears and distress with make-up. Instinctively, she knew that Lenae's perfectly applied foundation and concealer hid puffiness and dark shadows beneath her eyes.

"Hello, Mrs. Carrington," Lenae said now.

Mrs. Carrington?

"Is this your first time on the campus?" Lenae spoke politely, but somewhat coolly.

"Oh, no, I've been here several times over the years, but never to this part." Cami made a face. "Otherwise, maybe I'd have known to watch out for exposed roots." She held out her hands toward her dirty white jeans and blazer. "Thank goodness Dr. Sutherland and Kate came along when they did."

"Yes, that was fortunate, wasn't it?" Lenae turned to Reese. "I'm sorry to bother you, Dr. Sutherland, but an issue has come up in HR that requires your immediate attention."

Reese released Cami's arm. "Can it wait, Ms. Maddox?"

"No, Dr. Sutherland. It's very important."

Reese let out a deep, regretful sounding sigh. "Duty calls, ladies," he said to Kate and Cami. "Nice to meet you Cami. Saturday at seven, Kate?"

"Perfect," Kate told him.

Tucking a hand in his pants pocket, he strode away, the sun touching his sandy hair and giving it a gleam of gold. Cami couldn't help noticing how Kate watched him, so focused on Reese that she didn't seem to notice Lenae's stiff posture as she walked beside him.

~~~

In his pocket Reese's fingers met a crumpled-up piece of paper. A note. He wrapped his fingers around it, crumpling it more, then pulled his hand out of his pocket. He thought he'd shoved the note back firmly. He didn't realize it fell to the ground and fluttered back to the area where Cami Carrington had fallen earlier.

~~~

What was happening? Cami was so sure that Kate had finally decided to marry Gunnar. It seemed so... so right.

A thought occurred to her. "Kate, what do you know about Reese's spiritual life?"

Kate jerked her gaze away from Reese. "Well, nothing yet. I really haven't had time to find out. I only met him four days ago, you know."

Cami was surprised. In the past, that was one of the first things Kate would have found out about a man she planned to go out with. Besides, Cami thought Kate sounded defensive.

"Well, you'll find out tomorrow night, I'm sure."

"Oh, sure. You know I will." Yes, Kate definitely sounded defensive.

"I'm so sorry about lunch," Cami said.

"I am, too. It was a sweet thought. But you should get home and get out of these pants before the blood stain sets in. Better sterilize the scrape, too."

"Will do, but I can tell it's not bad."

"Okay. I'll see you sometime tomorrow."

Fighting uneasiness, Cami grinned. "You can fill me in on your plans for your hot date."

"You're too much, Cami." Kate laughed and left, shaking her head.

As Cami turned toward the parking lot, she noticed a crumpled ball of paper on the ground. *I guess we missed a bit of my lunch trash*, she thought, leaning over to retrieve it.

A muscle in her leg tensed as she stood. "Ow!" She touched her blood-stained pants leg. "That hurt!"

She stuffed the paper into her blazer pocket to dispose of later.

~~~

Kate was annoyed with Cami. *Why does she have to question me about what I know about Reese spiritually? And anyway, isn't this backwards?* Unwittingly, she had echoed Durant's opinion.

When the two had met at Compton College in North Carolina, Cami was already a Christian, but somewhat casual about her faith. But once Kate came to know Christ, she was deeply committed from the beginning. In no time, she became the spiritual leader of the two. And now, here was Cami practically rebuking her. It put a damper on her plans for Saturday evening.

Saturday evening. Peohe's. Reese Sutherland. All thoughts of Cami Carrington flew from Kate's mind.

~~~

A man paused to watch Cami Carrington walk to her car. A few minutes earlier, Albert Bainbridge had pulled on his gloves and left through the back door of his office in the administration building when he saw a beautiful woman dressed in pink and white stumble over a eucalyptus root. He started to go help her, but as he leaned his ornamental cane against the wall, he saw someone else rushing toward her. Someone bigger, stronger, better looking.

Reese Sutherland.

A tight-lipped Albert watched as Reese worked his charm on the woman who fell. He'd apparently already captivated that new Political Science professor. The only one who seemed unimpressed was Ms. Maddox.

Albert gripped the head of his cane and walked down the steps to his car.

Chapter Twenty

ଚ୬

Reese resisted the temptation to look back over his shoulder at Cami as he and Lenae walked away. Now there was a real knockout—with that golden blonde hair, creamy complexion, perfect features, and slender but well-proportioned figure. And those eyes. He had never seen eyes quite that shade of smoky blue. Very alluring, though less exotic than Lenae's aqua ones. He was sure he wasn't the first to consider Cami Carrington one of the most beautiful women he'd ever seen.

Rich, too, he thought, recognizing the Carrington name. *Too bad I didn't meet her before Kate.* He put aside that thought, replacing it with, *Still, Kate's going to be a peculiarly exciting challenge.*

Lenae interrupted his musing. "So, you're going out with Dr. Elfmon Saturday night."

"Business meeting," he answered with a little smirk.

"Sure. The acting head of the Law Department and a fill-in Poly-Sci professor."

"Don't get huffy, Lenae. You and I agreed from the get-go that our relationship was strictly *no-strings*."

"Sure," she repeated. "I remember. Both of us seeing whoever we wanted to. Acting as if we barely know each other here on campus. We've done well, haven't we? I'm sure Dr. Elfmon doesn't suspect."

He caught her arm and stopped. "And you won't tell her." It was a command.

She pulled loose and kept walking. "Never planned to."

In two long strides, Reese caught up with her. "So what was so important?"

Lenae looked down as she continued walking. "Look, I've changed my mind. Good luck Saturday night. You may need it even more than you think. Dr. Elfmon doesn't strike me as an easy mark." She sped up and walked away.

Reese was tempted to say, "We'll see," but he wasn't one to close the door on a relationship he hadn't yet tired of. "Wait!" He caught up with Lenae and touched the smooth curve of the back of her waist.

When Lenae stopped, he gave her the easy grin he knew most women found hard to resist. Looking back to see that no one, especially Kate, was in sight, he tilted Lenae's chin. Seeing the pain and vulnerability in her countenance, he felt a small, unfamiliar pang of guilt.

"Hey, I'm sorry," he said softly.

Reese had never had a problem offering an apology to a woman. He knew those two words made him seem vulnerable and "sweet" and were almost as effective as declarations of love—which he also had little trouble making.

"Are you free tomorrow night?"

Lenae jerked her head to one side and casually lifted one shoulder.

Reese wasn't fooled. "How about a casual evening? Maybe a bite to eat at a cozy corner of The Jackal, here in Coronado, and a walk on the beach."

"Okay," she said. "But I have something to do earlier in the evening. How about I meet you at The Jackal about nine?"

"Sounds like a plan." Reese gave Lenae a mock salute and sauntered away, quite pleased with himself. But then...

He slipped his hand into his pants pocket. The note was gone.

~~~

At home in her bedroom, Cami Carrington tossed her blazer onto the elegant chaise lounge covered in gold, white, and black damask and headed straight to the shower.

Chapter Twenty-One

ৰে

D r. Stan Weston had closed his cosmetic surgery office last evening when he happened to be walking behind Cami Carrington and her friend Kate Elfmon. Overhearing them mention Reese Sutherland's name had been a chilling reminder of how shocked he was when Sutherland moved to Coronado about a year after Stan arrived there. So far he'd been able to avoid contact with the man.

This morning Stan was pacing back and forth in his Weston Clinic office. After a while he stopped to glance at his appointments. Good. Three surgeries this week: rhinoplasty, otoplasty, and abdominoplasty, procedures the public usually referred to as nose job, pinning back the ears, and tummy tuck. All were elective surgeries, and all would cost the clients a bundle.

Stan thought of the sign in front of his clinic. The low Spanish-style cottage could have been just another home on the pleasant, tree-lined street. The only indication of the transformations that took place inside was a small brass plaque on the door. The top line read "Weston Clinic." Below, in much smaller letters were the words "Cosmetic Surgery." Stan had known from the beginning of his career that discretion was nearly as important as successful surgery in this business—even with the recent spate of Hollywood stars flaunting their "fixes."

Stan went to his desk, sat down before his computer, and went online to the faculty page of the subtly elegant Grant Lauder University website. He already knew that it was a small private school near the North Island Naval Station on Coronado and that it catered to an eclectic mix of wealthy and scholarship students. Photos showed an exquisite campus done in true southern California style with white stucco buildings and red tile roofs. One photo mesmerized and terrified Stan: the one of the interim head of the Law Department, one Dr. Reese Sutherland. Thinking of his last encounter with Reese, Stan could feel perspiration break out on his forehead.

It had been in Boston, not long after Stan first saw Erika at an elegant restaurant that provided its patrons a fashion show to accompany their meals. His horribly obese wife, Margo Cramer, only daughter of steel magnate Wilson Cramer, was shoveling down thick slices of chocolate torte and cherry cheesecake. She didn't even look up when the tall model with flaming red hair and dressed in a ridiculous orange lounging pajama set sauntered by.

The model had not spoken as she gracefully turned and paused, turned and paused, her slender curves displaying the slinky outfit to its best advantage. Every time she turned and looked over one shoulder, her emerald green eyes sent Stan an open invitation. Before leaving the restaurant, Stan got her phone number from a male server.

Within days of his first clandestine date with Erika Morgan, Stan knew he wanted to be free of the corpulent—in size and bank account—Margo and marry the model who was only twenty-one at the time to Stan's forty-seven. By "being free," he had simply meant finding a way to divorce Margo without being cut off from her huge inheritance. He hadn't meant to...

Stan pushed away from his desk and went to stand before a diploma on the wall. It was from a school in Boston and proclaimed Stanley Richard Weston certified to perform cosmetic surgery. Only one person knew that said Stanley Richard Weston had never been inside the school. He had actually gotten his training in an unheard-of and unrecognized school in Tijuana, Mexico. He paid a young attorney working for the Boston school to doctor the records in case anyone ever checked, which was easy to do these days, thanks to the Internet.

That same attorney—Reese Sutherland—now not so young, was also the only one who knew what had happened to Stan's first wife, Margo. Stan stood staring at the diploma. After a few moments he banged his fist on the wall next to the framed document, then walked wearily back to his desk and slumped into the chair. The scene from nearly four years ago had planted itself in his mind.

~~~

Stan had been seeing Erika for three months and hadn't yet approached Margo about a divorce. By then he was so enamored with Erika, he'd decided happiness was more important than money. Besides, he was making plenty with his surgeries. One afternoon when he had finished work early, he walked into his Beacon Hill home and went in search of his wife. He would ask for a divorce today.

"Search" was an overstatement. He knew exactly where Margo would be—in a recliner in the den watching a soap opera and munching on a box of French chocolates. Though it was only mid-afternoon, she was still dressed in a tent-like neon green nightgown and matching peignoir. The sight of the triple chins jiggling as she chewed on the candy repulsed Stan as never before. Without bothering to cut off the disgust he felt spreading over his face, he snatched the remote control away from Margo and turned off the TV.

"Hey!" Chocolate dribbled from one side of her mouth as she grabbed for the device. "What do you think you're doing? I was watching that! Bill and Brenda's wedding starts in a few minutes."

Stan gave Margo a blank look. "Bill and Brenda?"

"Yes," she said with a tilt to her chins. "Bill Sanford and Brenda Martin are getting married at her parents' villa in Italy. They've been planning it for months, but they had to postpone it when Brenda's father was kidnapped by—"

"Pirates?" Stan sneered, understanding now that Margo was talking about characters on the soap opera.

"Of course not, idiot! He was captured by— Don't make fun of me. Give me back my remote!"

"Not right now. You and I need to talk."

"Well, make it quick. I want to get back to my show."

"Okay. I'll do that. I'll make it quick. Margo, I want a divorce."

She lowered the recliner footrest and laboriously stood to her feet. Her face turning almost purple, she sneered. "That will never happen. Never! I paid for you and I'm keeping you. Go ahead and have your fling with that little redheaded hussy, but don't think you'll get away from me."

Enraged, Stan shoved his wife. He had only meant to push her back into the recliner. He hadn't planned for her to stumble and hit her head on a table with the full force of her great weight.

Stan stumbled back from the mound of flesh that lay still on the floor. For a moment he stood paralyzed. Then he bent over and held his fingers to Margo's wrist. No pulse. Stupefied, he stepped to the telephone and dialed a number he knew well.

"Reese Sutherland," a deep voice answered.

"Reese. It's Stan. I'm in big trouble. Get over here right away."

Twenty minutes later, Reese Sutherland stood by Stan, hands on hips and looking down at the large, still form on the floor.

"I heard about that sweet young thing you've been seeing, Stan, but I didn't realize your little fling had gone this far."

Pointing at Margo, Stan groaned. "I only pushed her. I didn't mean to hurt her."

"Tell that to the police, Doctor."

"The police! No! Can't you think of something I can do, Reese?"

"There may be something. But it would cost you."

"Anything! Just tell me what to do."

"I have a certain medical doctor in my pocket, so to speak. I'll get him over here to sign a certificate that your wife suffered a massive heart attack brought on by her excessive weight. It will be tricky, but I think it will work."

Stan shook his head slowly and groaned again. Then he nodded. "There's one thing. Whatever this costs me, it will be a one-time thing."

"Of course," Reese said.

"And when this is over, I never want to see you again."

"Believe me, the feeling is mutual." Reese pulled out his cell phone.

~~~

Less than two years after marrying Erika, Stan had left Boston and its memories far behind by moving all the way across the country and setting up shop in Coronado, California. At least, that had been his desire.

Chapter Twenty-Two

❧

Lenae had felt Cami Carrington's appraisal of her yesterday. She sensed that some people thought of Cami as a rich, blonde airhead. Though she'd met the woman only once before yesterday, she instinctively knew that assessment to be wrong.

She saw right through my "cool" exterior. And I'm sure she noticed my attempts to cover up my swollen eyes from crying all night. Maybe the grief over her husband's death has made her tuned in to other people's problems. Lenae thought for a moment. *Or maybe Cami is simply an insightful, caring person.*

Lenae thought of how both Kate Elfmon and Cami had bowed their heads in a blessing before lunch at the Burger Lounge. She had a feeling that both of them were what dear old Cora would have called "godly women" during those years when she'd made sure Lenae attended Sunday School. Cora had been deeply distressed when Lenae plunged into a "worldly lifestyle" during high school. She had kept prodding Lenae to find some more uplifting friends. She'd have been horrified if she'd known the full extent of how far Lenae had strayed.

Her thoughts shifted again. Cora would have approved of Cami Carrington and Kate Elfmon. She'd have urged Lenae to confide in one of them. But which one? Kate seemed to be the more spiritual of the two. Or was she? If she was willing to go out with Reese Sutherland, she was either less spiritual than she seemed or she was blind—as Lenae had once been.

No, if Lenae ever wanted to confide in either of the two women, it couldn't be Kate. It would have to be Cami.

Cami seemed interested in my art work. I think she was sincere. One day next week I'll call and invite her to the loft to see my paintings.

The idea brought a measure of comfort Lenae hadn't felt in years.

Chapter Twenty-Three

ॐ

Justin Rhodes took an envelope from his Grant Lauder mail slot. Seeing the dean of the law school's name in the corner, he froze.

It had been three days since his confrontation with Dr. Sutherland. He had redone the disputed paper and put it in Sutherland's box, in case the professor would accept it after all. He'd made sure the most recently assigned paper was turned in the day before it was due. He had kept out of Sutherland's way as much as possible and had exchanged no more words with him. Having heard nothing more about the blowup in his office, Justin had begun to relax. Maybe Sutherland had a soft spot after all. Maybe he was going to let the incident slide.

And now this. In no hurry to read the message inside and glad that no other students were in the mail room, Justin went to a window and opened the envelope slowly. It contained a single sheet of paper with a single-sentence message:

Mr. Rhodes, please see me in my office this afternoon at three o'clock. Dean Simpson.

Justin's heart sank at the words. He leaned his head against the window and pounded his fist on the thick glass. Life wasn't fair! *Pound, pound.* His father's arrest. *Pound, pound.* His family's forced move from a nice home to a cheap duplex. *Pound, pound.* His eternal financial problems, constantly saving and scraping and never having enough. *Pound, pound.* His—

"You're going to break the window if you keep that up."

Justin lowered his hand and looked over his shoulder. *Who...*

"Oh, it's you, Dexter." Turning around, he rubbed his fist. "Guess I was making a fool of myself. Sorry you saw that."

"Looks like you got some bad news," said Dexter. He peered into his mail slot, patted his hand around inside, and pulled it out empty. Shrugging, he went on, "Wouldn't have anything to do with your run-in with Dr. Sutherland, would it?"

Justin pounded his fist again, this time into his other hand. "I guess the word's all over the campus."

"A small school's like a small town. Nobody's business is private. There's even been a few bets going around about how long it would be before you get the boot. Most have already lost out because they bet it would happen before now."

Justin's face darkened. "To tell the truth, I thought the same." He held out the note. "This is a summons to Dean Simpson's office this afternoon. You can guess what it's about."

"'Fraid so. Look, you wanta get a cup of java?" Dexter motioned his head in the direction of the campus coffee shop.

Justin shrugged. Dexter Driscoll wouldn't have been his choice for a companion right now, but hey, why not? At the moment any sympathetic ear was welcome.

Ten minutes later the two students—one thin, lanky and very young; one stocky, muscular, and older than most of the other students—wrapped their hands around cups of hot mocha. Justin watched the steam rise from his cup and breathed in the fragrance of coffee married to chocolate before taking a sip. He felt Dexter observing him.

After several seconds of silence, Dexter said, "I'm the visitor Lenae Maddox had when you came by Wednesday night."

Justin's head jerked up. "You? What were you doing there?" To say he was incredulous was an understatement.

"Last year Lenae saved my life—stopped me from jumping off the Coronado Bridge."

"What!"

"And we've been friends ever since. She invites me over now and then."

"I don't believe you. You're making that up. Why would a classy dame like Lenae Maddox be friends with—"

"—a loser like Dexter Driscoll?

"Don't put words in my mouth."

"It's okay. Doesn't bother me. I've always been a solitary geek. As for

Lenae, I think that when she rescued me, it made her feel responsible for me. That's how it started out. Eventually we became true friends."

"Nothing more?" Justin barely kept a sneer from his question.

"Nothing more." Dexter made a rueful face. "That's never going to happen."

Justin studied Dexter silently for a few moments, feeling an unwelcome tug of empathy for him. In different ways, Lenae had rejected both of them. A thought occurred to him. He sat back and gave Dexter a tight-lipped glare.

"If you were at Lenae's when I arrived, that means you were still there when that other guy arrived."

Dexter nodded, looking solemn. "She told him to leave, but he forced his way in. I left instead."

Justin leaned forward, his forearms and palms flat against the table. "Who is he?"

"Let's just say he's not the only man in her life. There's one who regularly sends her one Talisman rose. Always only one. Never more. He had sent one earlier that day."

Justin's mouth turned down. "I got a glimpse of it through the doorway. I was bringing her a rose that night. One. Same as that other guy. I feel like the worst kind of fool." He lifted his head. "Why are you telling me this? If you and Lenae are such good friends, why are you telling me about her personal life?"

"You won't like this, but I feel kind of sorry for you. I know you tried to get her to go out with you."

Angry and embarrassed that Dexter Driscoll of all people knew about his unsuccessful efforts to date Lenae, he scraped his chair back against the tile floor with a loud grating sound. He stood abruptly and leaned toward Dexter. "I don't need your sympathy!" he snarled. "Yours or anybody else's."

He stalked away, muttering curses against Dexter Driscoll, Reese Sutherland, Dean Simpson, and Lenae Maddox.

~~~

Four hours later, Justin walked out of Dean Simpson's office. It was official. He had been expelled from Grant Lauder University. Looking down at the letter of dismissal he held, he spoke aloud, "Reese Sutherland, you will pay for this!"

He didn't see Dexter Driscoll loitering in the shadows.

~~~

Next door in his office, Dr. Albert Bainbridge tried to suppress his excitement. Instead of tearing into the letter from the editor of the *California Law Review*, he took his time tucking the point of a black letter opener under the flap. He wanted to draw out the delight he anticipated a few seconds longer. Allowing himself a smile, he carefully removed the single sheet of paper, unfolded it, and began to read. His smile disappeared.

Dear Dr. Bainbridge,

Your essay on legal terminology is well researched and informative. However, we had already chosen a similar article by your fellow professor, Dr. Reese Sutherland, who...

Albert ripped the letter in half, then shoved it into his shredder. The machine jammed.

Chapter Twenty-Four

It had been a long day at Grant Lauder; Kate had been glad to get home. Now, as she started to pull Debra Carrington's Audi out of the garage behind the cottage, Kate thought of the Volkswagen she'd sold before leaving Boston nearly four months ago. Sometimes she missed it, but she had to admit she was enjoying the sporty red car much more than she'd have thought, especially when it was warm enough to put the top down. But not tonight, not with that cold wind blowing in from the Pacific.

Though Kate and Cami spent a lot of time together, they'd determined early on that living on the same island didn't mean they had to—as Cami put it—"live in each other's pockets"—as they had during their motorhome adventure. Each felt free to follow her own pursuits. Going to the gym was a prime example. Cami preferred to go early in the morning, while Kate went after work. Tonight, Cami was out with her friend Robin Byrd.

Kate looked at the clock on the dashboard. Five-ten. Plenty of time to run a couple of quick errands and then go to the gym before dinner.

Kate's phone rang. She looked at it before backing into the narrow lane that was typical of those behind most of the island's homes.

She felt a little tingle when she saw the name on the screen. She had turned the phone to silent mode this morning at the start of her first class and only turned the sound back on as she got in the car. She turned off the motor.

"Hello." She heard the lift in her voice.

"Hello, yourself," said Reese Sutherland. "You're a hard one to catch up with."

Kate felt a small, guilty thrill at knowing Reese had had to make an effort to get in touch with her. It reminded her of how a young Cami used to say, "You can't make it too easy for the guys. They appreciate a girl more when they have to work a little for her."

"What do you mean?" Kate asked Reese, smiling.

"I looked for you in the cafeteria today and also went by your office and even left several messages on your phone. And you had already gone when I checked by your office after my classes. Have you been hiding out?" His voice now held a teasing tone, but also sounded slightly demanding. Kate wasn't sure whether to be flattered or annoyed.

Cami would say if there's a question, take it as a compliment, she thought, deciding Cami was sometimes right. Kate let a flirtatious tone come into her words. "Now, why in the world would I be hidin' out from you?"

"No reason, I hope. Look, I was hoping you'd like to go out for a bite to eat. I have some Glue business to attend to later tonight, but..."

"I wouldn't have pegged you as a workaholic."

Reese chuckled. "Let me assure you I wouldn't be working tonight if it were not a, uh, kind of emergency. Anyway, since I'm going to be on the island, I thought I might as well get a bite to eat out there. Then I thought, hey, maybe Kate would like to join me."

"I'd love to," said Kate, disregarding Cami's long-ago advice. That was college, and Reese Sutherland was a college professor, no green undergrad. Besides, Kate had never been one to play games. "Only thing is," she said, "I'm heading out to the gym right now. I'm already in the car."

"Oh, that's too bad."

He sounded so disappointed that Kate, who rarely acted impulsively, blurted out, "Why don't you join me? I have some guest passes to the gym, and I've got a couple of things to do beforehand. That would give you time to get out here."

"Great! Give me the address, and I'll see you in an hour."

~~~

Reese came from the men's dressing room of the gym, where he'd changed into shorts and a muscle-revealing T-shirt. Kate hadn't yet come out from the ladies' dressing room. Oh well, women always took longer, and Kate was worth waiting for. She was intelligent, easy to talk to, and attractive, especially when a smile lit up the brown eyes that were her major beauty asset. Still, he usually preferred more glamorous women. With more obvious curves.

He happened to look up. *Like that one!* He took in a view of a head of glorious red hair bent over the water fountain. She stood. Five nine if she was an inch. Young. No more than mid-twenties. And, judging from her snug gym shirt and shorts, not afraid to emphasize her voluptuous curves. If he were not with Kate, he'd strike up a conversation with her.

He shrugged and looked away—right toward a short, plump balding man still in gym shorts and carrying a towel over one shoulder.

Stan Weston! He knew Stan had set up his cosmetic surgery in Coronado after all that mess in Boston a couple of years ago. Reese also knew Stan had married that model he was dating while still married to his first wife, wealthy but obese Margo Cramer, now conveniently dead. Despite all his and Stan's "dealings," Reese had never met the new wife. She was supposed to be a real knockout. Had to have married Stan for his money.

Reese stepped into a shadow by the wall and watched as Stan, perspiring profusely and wiping his bald pate with the towel, headed toward the water fountain where the provocative redhead seemed to be waiting for someone.

Stan leaned over to get some water. When he rose, he swiped at his sweaty forehead again and wrapped the towel around his neck. Playfully grumbling, he said, "Nobody but you could talk me into this. Ready to go?"

Stan was addressing the redhead. That was Stan's wife! Reese couldn't help himself. He'd made a point of avoiding personal contact with the man since both came to Coronado, but now he couldn't resist having a bit of fun with the good doctor. He glanced toward the dressing room. Kate was still in there. He strode to the water fountain and bent over as though to get a drink, then abruptly straightened.

"Stan Weston!"

The horror on Stan's face when he looked up into Reese's was worth the price of three Golden Putter clubs. Reese was impressed how quickly the shorter man recovered, though his voice was tight when he said, "Reese. I heard you were in San Diego."

Reese didn't correct him.

"Come on, Erika," Stan barked. "We need to get home."

"Stan," said Reese. Then sounding as innocent as he could, he asked,

"Aren't you going to introduce me? I heard you got *re*married." He made sure his emphasis on the "re" in remarried was subtle. "This must be your lovely *new* wife." Again, he made the emphasis subtle.

Reese almost felt sorry for poor, trapped Stan, who cleared his throat and said, "Yes. This is my wife. Erika, this is Reese."

Erika turned sultry green eyes with thick black lashes to Reese and looked him over from the top of his sandy blonde hair to the muscular arms to the tip of his sneakers. She held out a red-nailed hand and said, "I'm so glad to meet you, Mr...?"

"Reese." Reese took the soft hand and gave it a subtle pressure. "I'd heard Stan had married a beautiful woman, but I have to say the reports were highly understated."

Erika batted the long lashes and opened her luscious red lips to reply, but Stan cut her off with a terse, "Come on, Erika. We need to go."

"But Stan, I want to invite Reese to my birthday party tomorrow night." She glanced back at Reese. "Coronado Boathouse," she said in her sultry voice. "Drinks at seven."

Reese didn't miss the fact that Erika had made sure he knew basic details about her birthday party at The Boathouse with its architecture that echoed that of the elegant, Victorian-style Hotel del Coronado.

Stan caught Erika's arm and led her toward the exit. "I said we need to go. Good-bye, Reese." Reese would have liked to extend the fun if he hadn't seen the ladies' dressing room door open and caught a glimpse of Kate.

"Oh, there you are," Reese said.

"Sorry I took so long." Kate pointed to her feet. "One of my sneaker laces got tied into a horrendous knot. Thought I'd never get it out."

"No problem." Then, *One more bit of fun*, he thought. "I want you to meet an old friend. Wait up, Stan." Reese motioned toward Stan and Erika, who turned as he spoke.

"This is Stan Weston, and this beautiful—"

"I've met Dr. Weston and his wife," Kate said somewhat coolly.

Reese was taken aback at Kate's coolness, but he went on, "Ol' Stan and I were real buddies back in Boston." He cocked his head. "Right, Stan?"

Instead of answering Reese's question, Stan said, "It's good to see you again Ms. Elfmon. I hope all is well with your friend Cami Carrington."

"Cami is doing well, thank you."

Reese noticed that Kate didn't tell Stan it was good to see him, too.

"Um, that's, uh, good." Stan gave Kate a curt nod. "Erika, we need to go." Still gripping his wife's arm, he began walking away.

"So good to meet you, Erika," Reese said as Erika looked back over her shoulder. "Maybe I'll see you at your party."

"Oh, I'd love that," she purred.

Stan pulled his wife out the door.

"What was that all about?" Reese asked Kate when Stan and Erika had left.

"What do you mean?" Kate looked uncomfortable.

"You were downright unfriendly to them."

"You're right. I probably shouldn't have been that way. But I have a hard time being comfortable in the presence of a woman who— Never mind. I shouldn't have said anything."

"But now you've piqued my curiosity."

"Well, I guess it'll have to stay piqued." Kate gave Reese a playful poke in the chest. "Come on, let's see who can work up the most sweat."

~~~

As Kate and Reese headed toward the exercise area, Kate felt out of sorts. She was sorry she'd said anything at all about Erika to Reese. She wasn't given to gossip, but she'd allowed herself to be caught off guard. And that wasn't all. Kate couldn't help noticing the way Reese had devoured Erika with his eyes.

Well, why not? Erika would attract any red-blooded man's attention.

Still... Apparently Erika had invited Reese to her birthday party, and he'd indicated he might attend. *Again, why not?*

And why did Stan Weston seem so eager to get away if he and Reese had once been "good buddies"? Something was off there.

Kate pushed down a tiny seed of doubt.

~~~

"That was great, but it took longer than I'd anticipated," Reese said as he and Kate exited the gym. "It's nearly 8:30, and I need to get to The

Glue if I don't want to be there all night. I always keep some snacks in a small fridge at the office. Do you mind..." He took Kate's hand and gave her a pleading look.

"You get on over there. I need to get home, too. I'll look forward to seeing you tomorrow night."

"Not as much as I will." He squeezed her hand—much the same way he'd squeezed Erika Weston's earlier. Half an hour later, he entered a door, not to Grant Lauder University, but to The Jackal. In his arms, he carried the long-stemmed Talisman rose he'd ordered that afternoon.

Chapter Twenty-Five

એ

Erika could see that Stan was furious. Not only had he pulled out of the gym parking lot so fast he almost hit a man, but now—though he usually kept to the speed limit—he was driving twenty miles per hour too fast toward their home in Coronado Cays. She breathed in a sigh of relief when they pulled into the Cays entrance and past the guard shack. She'd been sure Stan would get a speeding ticket. His driving wasn't the only clue to Stan's fury. Even more telling was his total silence all the way home—that and the tight set to his mouth.

Erika felt a little afraid. Though Stan was generally easy going and non-violent, she couldn't help remembering the way he'd slapped her when he learned about her affair with Braxton Carrington. When they got to their Tuscan-style house facing one of the Cays' many marinas, she decided to try to lighten the atmosphere. Inside, she merrily tossed her gym bag onto an ornate couch and said, "Well, that was a great workout tonight. You really put yourself into it. Aren't you glad I talked you into going?"

Stan glared at her as if she'd lost her mind. Without answering, he stomped up the curving staircase. Though he was overweight and his legs were much shorter than Erika's, she had trouble keeping up.

In their elaborate bedroom, with its sleek furnishings and over-abundance of wall art and knick knacks, Stan slung his own gym bag onto the black-and-white bedspread. Irrelevantly, Erika noticed that it landed right in the middle of one of the many large concentric circles and knocked one of several black pillows to the floor. Before he turned around, she stepped behind him and placed her long, slender fingers on his shoulders. In a slow, sensuous rhythm, she began to massage them.

"You feel as tense as a spring," she said. "Why don't you get a shower then let me give you a good massage?"

"Take your hands off me, you, you... " Stan whirled around so fast he nearly knocked Erika over. His face was a frightening mottled red, so angry looking that Erika stepped back.

He moved toward her, and she continued backing up until her hand touched the glass-topped dressing table. Frightened, she moved back as far as possible.

"Wh-what's wrong, Stan? Wh-why are you so angry?"

"As if you didn't know," he snarled. "Why did I believe you when you said you wanted to try to make it work with us?" He moved closer again, his face nearly even with hers. "Barely three months later and you're already sending out signals to other men."

Though Erika knew exactly what Stan referred to, she asked, "S-signals? Wh-what signals?"

He grabbed her wrists. "Don't play innocent with me, Erika. You think I didn't pick up on how you looked at Reese Sutherland?"

"I-I was being friendly with him, Stan, that's all," Erika whimpered. "You know me, honey. I'm friendly with everybody."

"Not only that, you made a point to let him know about your birthday party. You even made sure he knew the day and location!" He tightened his hold on her wrists.

Erika felt her stomach grow tight. What would Stan do to her? How far would he go? Suddenly she knew what to do. She deliberately widened her eyes still further and took in a deep shuddering breath. Then she went completely limp, pretending to swoon. As she'd expected, Stan loosened his hold on her wrists and caught her as she fell.

"Erika! Erika!" Stan's concern became as deep as his anger had been moments before. "What have I done?" Though short and stout, Stan was strong, and he soon had her stretched out on the bed. "Sweetheart, wake up. I'm so sorry. I'm sorry."

Erika let her eyes flicker open. "I'm the one who's sorry, Stan," she whispered. "I didn't think... Well, I just didn't think." Shaking her head as if to clear it, she slowly sat up and let her legs drape over the side of the bed. "W-we can call off the birthday party if you want to. It's not too late to let everyone know."

Stan sat beside her and pulled her to him. He began to stroke her luxurious red hair. "No, no. I know how important it is to you. I doubt

Sutherland would really attend anyway—and if he does..." Stan's voice hardened. "We'll deal with that."

Something about Stan's tone made Erika ask, "What is it about Reese Sutherland that has you so upset? It seems like it's more than him flirting with me."

Stan became still. Eerily still. Then he turned Erika's face to him. Before he kissed her, he said, "There are some things you're better off not knowing, sweetheart."

Chapter Twenty-Six

ॐ

Mike Jenkins sat on a stool before his home drafting table about eight o'clock Friday evening. He created his best architectural designs there, and no matter how many divisions he added to MelJen, his true love was designing homes. He also did some of his best work in the evening when the phone was not ringing and no one was after him to un-gnarl some knotty company problem.

The present design was a jewel of a project in his opinion, and he wanted to finish it before immersing himself into the Paris mall venture. The founder of a home for state-confiscated children in the mid-sized town of Temecula, about an hour north of San Diego, had bought a large piece of property where another children's home had existed several years ago. When Mike saw the depressing institution-style block buildings where the children had lived, he wondered if any of them had gone on to success in life.

The new owner, whose resources were limited, wanted a genuine home-like atmosphere for the children, one with space and color and a cheerful atmosphere. The project had excited Mike from the beginning, and he had presented a ridiculously low bid for it. He wouldn't make a penny, would probably lose money, in fact. For once that didn't matter.

Still, tonight he was having trouble concentrating. He added a thick black line to his design and found himself thinking of Lenae Maddox's black hair. He drew in an oval window and pictured her mesmerizing eyes. He put a whimsical curved frame around a window and thought of her shapely form. He laid his pencil aside and picked up another, planning to shade in the area between window edge and frame. As the pencil touched the paper, he stopped. It was no use. He simply couldn't get

Lenae and the conversation they'd had two nights ago out of his mind.

Ironic, Mike thought. *Just when I realize that I want Lenae for myself and not share her with anyone else, I find out she's pregnant with another man's child. She might as well have kicked me in the gut when she told me that. No wonder I can't concentrate on my work.*

He tossed the pencil onto the drafting table, swung himself off the high stool, and wandered upstairs to his bedroom—the one he had shared with Melanie. There he tried to analyze his thoughts and feelings, much the way he analyzed the details of an architectural design.

Why had he steered away from permanent commitments since Melanie's death? It had been twelve years, for Pete's sake. *Am I still subconsciously clinging to Melanie? Do I feel guilty for having strong feelings about another woman?*

Mike knew his feelings for someone else could never match the tenderly passionate, even innocent emotions he once felt for Melanie. Still, he answered his own question aloud with a loud "No!"

Then am I afraid of commitment?

"No!"

He simply hadn't had a desire for a serious romantic relationship in all the years since Melanie's death. Until now. Putting aside thoughts of Lenae's pregnancy, Mike asked himself, *What is it that appeals to me about Lenae? Is it her resemblance to Melanie?*

"No." The resemblance between the two women was superficial beyond the hair color and general body shape. Also, Lenae wasn't exceptionally beautiful; Melanie had been much prettier. Besides, Mike had dated more raving beauties than he could count or name.

He paced around the room, finally slipping on a jacket and heading downstairs and outside. A million stars sparkled against the black sky. From his palm-studded hill, they seemed close enough to touch. He and Melanie had often stared at the heavens in awe in this very spot. At such times, he could almost join her in her belief in a Creator. Tonight thoughts of Lenae, not memories of his beloved wife, filled his thoughts.

What is *it about Lenae?* he asked himself again. Forcing himself to set aside his emotions and think analytically, he finally boiled his attraction down to three inescapable components.

One: The vulnerability lurking behind the independent spirit she liked to display touched a sense of protection he'd thought had died in him.

Two: She seemed to be genuinely interested in him, and not simply for the wealth he hadn't revealed to her until several weeks after they met. She'd asked about his parents, his siblings, his school friends, even Melanie. She knew his favorite color was blue. She had laughed that such a "tough guy" would prefer that rather conservative color.

Three? He simply enjoyed her company and wanted more of it—possibly to the extent of a permanent arrangement. Maybe even marriage.

Wait! What about the baby?

Lenae had admitted that the child's father would probably not want to marry her. She herself seemed ambivalent about the idea except for the sake of the child. She was determined to broach the subject to him.

Sobbing with every word, she had said, "He at least deserves to know."

Mike had demanded that she tell him the father's name. When she'd refused, Mike had stormed out, slowing down only long enough to look at the card with the rose on the table and see the initial "R", which meant nothing to him.

Could I accept another man's child? he asked himself now. It was a reasonable question that Mike couldn't honestly answer. *Probably not,* he thought. All he knew for certain was that he *had* to see Lenae.

Mike Jenkins was not a man to waste time. He looked at his watch. Nine o'clock. Not too late to call. He took his phone from his jacket pocket and, looking up at the twinkling night sky, punched in Lenae's number. After five rings, her voice came on with a simple, "This is Lenae Maddox. Leave me a message."

Mike tried the number three more times. Same result.

Where was she? Why wasn't she answering? She'd recognize his number on her caller ID. Was something wrong? Was she ignoring him?

Was she out with her baby's father?

The thought clenched at Mike's gut. He suddenly realized he'd made a definite decision. He would call Lenae tomorrow morning. If she didn't answer, he would go to her loft. He wanted to marry Lenae Maddox, and he would let nothing—or no one—stand in his way.

Chapter Twenty-Seven

&

From her table in the corner of The Jackal, Lenae waited for Reese. She'd arrived an hour early, and her emotions were roiling inside her, as they'd done for several weeks now. Seeing Mike Wednesday night hadn't helped. Why had she told him about her pregnancy? He'd known there was no possibility the baby could be his. What was he thinking now? She hadn't heard from him for two days. Probably never would again. With an inexplicable surge of hope, she got out her cell phone. Maybe he had called. The blank screen told her she'd forgotten to charge the battery. A sense of grief, similar to when Cora died, enveloped her. She was afraid to analyze the feeling.

She forced her thoughts back to the moment. *Why did I agree to this public place to meet with Reese? What was I thinking?*

She looked toward the door. There he was, striding toward her, a broad smile on his handsome face. A smile that had once mesmerized her, but now touched only a tiny chord inside. He was carrying one Talisman rose—no extra fern or baby's breath, only a plastic sleeve for protection from the thorns. How she loved receiving the beautiful flowers.

"Their colors are muted, not bold. They don't shout their beauty, they whisper," Reese had once said, dropping his own voice on that last word.

Matching his seductive tone, she'd said. "And what do they whisper?"

"Memories." He had taken her into his arms and brought his face down to hers. "They whisper memories."

Deciding to take the rose as a good sign—and forcing down the unexpected, futile wish that Mike was the father of her baby—Lenae rose and walked quickly to Reese. She could tell he was surprised.

"What—"

She took the rose, folded back the plastic sleeve far enough to caress one petal, then looked up. "Come on, let's get out of here," she whispered.

~~~

"What's going on, Lenae?"

Reese had difficulty hiding the irritation he felt. He shivered as a cold breeze from the ocean swept in to the shore. At The Jackal, after taking the rose from him, Lenae had rushed out and kept up a fast, silent walk that led them to the beach.

Reese had enjoyed his fling with Lenae over these past few months, but he'd begun to feel some pressure from her. He was ready to move on. Almost. He never liked to close the door on a romantic relationship until he was absolutely certain he was ready to end it. That's why he'd ordered the Talisman rose to bring to her tonight. It didn't seem incongruous at all to him that while he was out with Kate at the gym earlier, a flower for another woman rested in the back seat of his car.

"What is it?" He made his tone gentle, persuasive sounding.

When Lenae didn't reply, he found it impossible to push down his irritation any longer. "First you make a big deal about meeting with you, then you clam up on me when I arrive—after I interrupt a pleasant evening, by the way—and you drag me out here to the beach. We've been here for five minutes and you haven't said a word."

Lenae looked out to the dark water. She raised her shoulders and let out a long sigh, but still didn't reply.

"Look, this is getting ridiculous. I'm outta here." He turned to go.

"Wait, please." She turned to him. "I...I have something to tell you."

A quick, cold breeze ruffled her shoulder-length ebony hair and lifted it from her slender neck. In one arm she clutched his rose. She shivered and led him a few steps away from the incoming surf.

Together they turned. At the horizon the moon cast a silvery ribbon of light across the dark, strangely still waters that spread gently over the sand. Even in the dark, sparkles of light shone like jewels from the sand.

Not sure what to expect, he asked, "Will I like it?" He knew he sounded sarcastic.

She paused and stepped away so that her form was silhouetted against the moon's reflection. He saw how she hugged the rose to her bosom.

"Probably not." Her words held both dread and hope.

He moved close and encircled her waist from the back. She tensed, but didn't say more.

He waited, but she remained silent. At last he whispered, "What is it? You can tell me anything." He knew that was what she would want to hear.

She turned and touched his face.

"I'm pregnant."

Appalled, he pushed her away and stepped back. He jammed his hands into the pockets of his rolled-up jeans and glared at her.

"You said you wouldn't let that happen."

She bent her head and spoke so softly he could barely hear her. "I know." She looked up, pleading with those luminous aqua eyes. "It could be a good thing, you know. A really good thing."

He snorted and raised his voice. "How can you say that? How could this possibly be a good thing?"

"Well..." She sounded so hesitant, so young and insecure, more like a scared teenager than a mature thirty-two-year-old. "Well, we could get married. We could—"

"Married! Are you crazy?" He grabbed her shoulders. "You know that's *not* going to happen!"

"But—"

He squeezed her shoulders until he could feel his fingers digging into her flesh beneath her quilted black jacket.

"An abortion." It came out like a command. "You've got to get an abortion."

She slapped him. Hard. Eyes snapping, she sneered. "I may not be the most moral woman in town, but I don't kill babies. How can you even suggest such a thing?"

"And how can you even think of anything else?"

"I told you. We can be married."

He grabbed her shoulders again and began to shake her. "And I told *you*. That's not going to happen!"

"Stop! You're hurting me!" Even as she struggled to free herself, she hung onto the rose. "And you don't think this will hurt *me*?" He let go of her shoulders and grasped her face in his gloved hands, pressing hard and ignoring the fright in her face. "Have you thought about that? What this will do to me? You can't have this baby. You've got to get an abortion!"

"**No!**" Her scream tore the air as she pushed against his chest.

His hands moved from her face to her throat. "Shut up! You hear me? Shut up!" He squeezed her throat. Tighter. Tighter. Her eyes grew huge till they seemed about to pop out of her head. He kept squeezing.

With a long rattling sigh, she quit struggling and went limp.

He released her. She fell to the sand, still gripping the lovely Talisman rose.

Chapter Twenty-Eight

&

The fog was taking a long time to lift this morning, still folding itself around Cami like a blanket. The often roaring sound of the surf's steady ebb and flow seemed muted. Cami had awakened out of sorts and had thought a walk on the beach would cheer her up. Instead, she felt as eerily still and grey as the landscape. It wasn't really depression, she realized, but emptiness. She almost missed the raging grief she'd felt after Braxton's death and all that surrounded it. The motorhome trip had helped in that respect, but now...

She turned her face upward. *Maybe it's because the twins are so far away, Lord. Maybe I should have let them stay with me.*

You made the right decision sending them to Edinburgh, Cami. Don't look back and question what I led you to do. And be grateful for how Kate has helped you.

I am grateful, Lord, but I still feel empty. She allowed herself a wry smile. *Maybe I'm jealous of Kate and how she's had one godly husband and will probably soon have another one. But, Lord, You know that for all his faults, I loved Braxton.*

Cami stared out at the unusually still ocean, it waters lapping softly and steadily against the wet sand.

Be still and know that I am God, her heart seemed to hear. ***Let Me fill your empty cup.***

A sense of peace began to flow into her spirit, and she lifted her face upward again. *Thank You, Lord. I needed that.*

Cami wanted to hold onto that peace, to hug it to herself, to grasp the inner stillness that no longer felt empty. She wasn't ready to go back to the house and plunge into the activity of the day. Not yet. Pulling her jacket closer as if also pulling closer the welcome uplifting of her spirit, she headed down the beach.

A minute or two later, beside a low rock, she saw a small sand dollar at her feet. Thinking of her daughter Debra's curio cabinet full of sand dollars, Cami stooped and picked it up. She settled herself on the rock and studied the simple but elegant design in the sand dollar. She traced her fingers around the star in the center, and the five-petaled "flower" surrounding the star. She touched the small openings around the edge and wondered what caused them.

I'll add this to Debra's collection, she thought, wrapping her fingers around the lovely piece of art. Maybe there were more. She leaned to the other side of the rock and looked down.

What she saw was no sand dollar.

A woman lay just beyond the edge of the water. Ebony hair swept across her face and onto the white sand. In her hands the woman clutched the kind of plastic sleeve that florists used for flowers. Only a bit of stem was left in the sleeve. Cami looked closer.

Lenae Maddox!

Cami's scream split the peaceful silence of the morning.

Chapter Twenty-Nine

അ

Detective Carlos Lopez stood in Lenae Maddox's one-room loft in downtown San Diego. Hands on hips, casual jacket unbuttoned, tie loosened, he looked around the sparsely furnished room. With the San Diego Police Department being on overload at the moment, Lopez was on loan from Coronado. SDPD officers had done their usual routine—dusting for fingerprints, searching the room for clues, etc. They had also given him Lenae's computer. He hoped something in her email account or documents would yield some useful information.

Amazingly, the woman was still alive, though barely.

Lopez took a slow, deliberate walk around the loft, hoping to find something, anything that would add to the small store of information gathered from the scene. When he'd arrived at the Coronado beach this morning, the young woman lying in the sand looked even younger than the thirty-two years indicated by the California driver's license Lopez had found on her. With her even features, full lips and black hair, she was very attractive—even considering the effects of a night on the sand, with the water flowing over her when the tides rushed in. When Cami Carrington found her, the woman wore a long-sleeved red blouse, black quilted jacket, black jeans, and sneakers over socks embellished with multi-colored artist pallets.

Lopez wandered across the room to the huge window that looked out over downtown San Diego, with a view of the sweeping curve of the Coronado Bridge. In front of the window stood an artist's easel and a small table scattered with watercolor paint tubes, brushes, and a palette pad smeared with streaks of gold, coral, green, and brown. Against the easel rested a small painting—no larger than 8 x 12 inches—of one long-stemmed rose reflecting the colors on the palette. Because of his artsy wife, Lopez knew enough about art to recognize true talent.

A number of items in the room had confirmed Cami Carrington's and Kate Elfmon's statements that Lenae Maddox worked at Grant Lauder University, a small school near Coronado's North Island Naval Station. Her passion, they'd told him, was painting, and her job at Grant Lauder barely covered the rent at this "artist's loft" in the heart of the city.

Seeing nothing more and feeling frustrated, Lopez dropped the painting into a plastic zipper bag. He was about to leave when something caught his attention. On the brown and beige throw rug below the kitchen sink lay a small dark strip of something that almost completely blended in with the rug. Easy to miss. He got down on his haunches and carefully picked it up from the ends. It was the end of a stem, about three inches long. A rose stem.

Chapter Thirty

છ

"Cami, you're shaking all over. You need to lie down."

Kate had responded to her friend's beachside call early this morning. Cami had phoned her after calling 911. Kate was at her side seconds before the police and Detective Lopez arrived. Like Cami, she was horrified to see Lenae Maddox lying so still in the sand. Kate had also accompanied Cami to the CPD station, where both women were questioned only briefly since they could provide so little information, then sent home. Now the two were in Cami's den, Cami stretched out in a burgundy leather recliner and Kate sitting sideways on the arm.

"I'm all right," Cami said. "I just can't get it all out of my mind."

"I understand. It was bad enough for me, but at least you'd prepared me for what I would see. I can only imagine how horrible it was to come up on Lenae the way you did."

"Horrible. That doesn't even describe it." Cami shuddered. "You know that day we both first met Lenae, she said she'd invite me to her loft sometime to see her paintings?" She gave Kate a sad, bleak look. "Now I may never see them. Or her."

"That's not necessarily so. She's still alive, you know."

"Right." Cami's voice held a small note of hope. "Let's pray for her right now."

Kate felt a stab of remorse that Cami had thought of that before she did. She bowed her head as Cami offered up a prayer for healing for Lenae Maddox.

After a soft "Amen," Cami grasped the recliner's handle and sat straight up. "Enough. At this rate, I'll have you in a real state of depression for your date with Reese Sutherland tonight."

"Are you kidding? I couldn't possibly keep that date. I was going to call him in a few minutes and cancel."

"You'll do no such thing. I want you to go on and have a good time. You don't need to babysit me." Cami paused. "By the way, have you called Gunnar yet about ... about Lenae?"

"Not yet." For a moment, Kate wished it were Gunnar rather than Reese she'd be seeing tonight. She was more shaken about Lenae's attack than she'd let on to Cami. What a comfort it would be to fall into Gunnar's big arms and lay her head on his shoulder. Then she thought of Reese—those mesmerizing eyes and charming smile.

She looked upward. *I haven't stopped caring for Gunnar, Lord. But I can't help looking forward to tonight. There's nothing wrong with that. Is there?* Not waiting for her spirit to hear an answer, she told Cami, "Well, if you're sure you'll be okay, I'll go ahead and keep the date."

Chapter Thirty-One

ɞ

Detective Lopez had gone from Lenae Maddox's loft to her room in the intensive care unit of Sharp Coronado Hospital. Beside him stood Dr. Joseph Feldman, the Carringtons' family physician and Lenae Maddox's attending physician since he was on-call when she was brought in.

Lenae was hooked up to a tangle of tubes and wires that Lopez couldn't identify, as well as an oxygen unit.

"She was fully dressed," said Feldman. "Rules out sexual assault."

Lopez nodded. He was glad for that. Somehow that type of crime disturbed him more than most others.

Cami Carrington, was Lopez's next thought. Having served on CPD for twenty years, he was fully aware of the Carringtons, one of Coronado's most prominent and wealthy families. Yet he had never had occasion for contact with them until Cami's husband, Braxton, was murdered at a huge gala at the Hotel del Coronado on the very night he planned to announce his bid for mayor of the island. During that investigation, Lopez met and came to admire and respect Braxton's beautiful wife Cami. Now, here she was again, involved, though only as a bystander, in another crime Lopez was investigating.

"You want to know about Ms. Maddox's condition?" Dr. Feldman's voice interrupted Lopez's musings.

Lopez looked from the barely moving body to the slight, sixtyish man with tight, greying curls topped by a yarmulke.

"Sorry. My mind wandered for a minute there. What did you find?"

"I'm sure you saw these." Dr. Feldman pointed to some marks on the woman's slender neck. I found hemorrhaging in her throat, and whoever caused those bruises also fractured her hyoid bone. It's a miracle of God that she's alive. It'll be another miracle if she makes it."

Lopez had done enough investigations to know the hyoid was a horseshoe-shaped bone in the front, middle part of the neck right below the chin. He also knew that fracture of that bone was extremely rare, usually caused by a fall—or by the pressure of thumb and fingers.

"Attempted strangulation," said Lopez. "She was choked."

"Uh-huh. The fracture seems to indicate the attacker pressed her throat hard and fast."

Lopez looked away from Lenae. "A crime of immediacy," he said. "Passion of the moment. Anger probably. Or fear."

"Uh-huh." Feldman's words seemed significant.

"There's more?"

"She was pregnant. The baby didn't make it."

Lopez brought his fist down on the examination table. "Two lives snuffed out if Ms. Maddox dies." He pressed his lips together. "The pregnancy is probably directly related to the attack."

"I'd be surprised if it isn't."

"Were you able to determine a time frame?"

"Looks to be between ten and eleven last night."

"When the beach was pretty much deserted, especially on a cold night." Lopez stepped away from the table.

"What have you learned about her?" Feldman asked.

"As you know, Cami Carrington and her friend Kate Elfmon had already identified her as Lenae Maddox. Head of HR at Grant Lauder University. Lives in one of those artist-type lofts overlooking Coronado Bridge."

"Pricey."

"Yeah. Even though she had only herself to support, it would take a big bite out of her paycheck to cover the rent." His cell phone vibrated in its holder on his belt.

"Headquarters," he told Dr. Feldman. He put the phone to his ear. "What's up?" He listened a few seconds, then said, "I'll be there ASAP."

Feldman lifted his brows in question.

"San Diego PD had a couple of men stationed outside Ms. Maddox's apartment—or loft, I think they call it. A man showed up wanting to get in. Says he owns the building."

Feldman's brows lifted higher.

"Also says he's been dating her. Had been trying to call her since last night, but the phone kept going straight to voice mail, so he came over to check up on her. Tried to run off when they told him she was attacked and at the hospital, but they detained him. Thanks for your help, Dr. Feldman. I know you'll let me know if Ms. Maddox wakes up. I gotta run."

Chapter Thirty-Two

❧

Stan Weston had heard a TV report about the young woman who was attacked on the Coronado beach this morning, found by Cami Carrington, no less. He felt a stab of pity for the attacked woman—who probably wouldn't survive—and a slightly deeper stab for Cami. Her own daughter had nearly died on that very beach three months ago on the very night Cami's husband Braxton was murdered (a fact Stan had never mourned).

Right now Stan's thoughts were elsewhere as he stood by the window in his and Erika's upstairs bedroom. Behind him were the elaborate black-and-white furnishings and decor of the room. Ahead and below was one of Coronado Cay's many marinas. Steps led down from the houses to the docks where various types of pleasure boats floated idly on the sparkling blue water. When Stan and Erika had decided to buy a house on the Cays, Erika had insisted on one that faced a marina, even though Stan didn't own a boat. If Erika had her way, that would soon change.

For the most part, Stan didn't mind Erika's expenditures. Heaven knew she had had few enough nice things before she met him, her only chance for beautiful, expensive clothes being those she modeled for no more than a few minutes at a time. Though he considered her tastes to be on the gaudy side, he felt a kind of paternal indulgence toward her.

In other areas, his feelings for Erika were anything but paternal. He had been mesmerized by her flamboyant, red-haired beauty from the moment he saw her. And he was well aware that on her part, the attraction of a short, balding man twice her age was purely mercenary. She had married him for his money. Period.

Still, except for that sickening episode with Braxton Carrington, Erika had tried to be a good wife to Stan. He was sorry he'd lost his temper with her last night. Sure, he hated how friendly she'd been with Reese Sutherland. Then again, as she'd pointed out, she was friendly with nearly everyone. Also, she knew nothing of Stan's connection to him. She probably assumed Reese was an old friend, so why shouldn't she invite him to tonight's party? When she'd swooned in Stan's arms while he was berating her, his remorse had been immediate and complete.

She thought I was going to hit her. Stan gripped the window ledge. *Would I have? I did once, after I had proof of her affair with Carrington. What if I had hit her last night? What if I had hurt her like... I'll make it up to her. I'll buy that boat for her. I'll tell her as soon as she gets home.*

The doorbell interrupted his thoughts. On his way downstairs to answer the bell, he smiled, imagining Erika's childlike elation when he told her he'd be buying her a boat.

With the inheritance from Margo and the way so many San Diego women want a bit of plastic surgery, I can well afford it.

At the door stood a young woman from an island florist shop. She held a long white box, wrapped in gold ribbon.

Immediately suspicious, Stan was barely civil to the woman as he took the box and got out his billfold to give her a tip. A minute later, he laid the box on the dining room table and stood staring at it.

In the two years they'd been at Coronado, Erika hadn't made many female friends, despite her outgoing personality. He suspected most were either jealous or suspicious of her. Also, she had a tendency to go overboard at times. The birthday party, though expensive and elaborate and to be held at The Boathouse would be small. Most of the guests would be Stan's business associates and their wives. Only two of the other women guests lived on the Cays. Anyway, women didn't usually send flowers to other women.

So who were the flowers from? Uneasiness spread through Stan's mind and tightened his chest. He put out his hand to the golden ribbon on the box, then drew it back.

They're hers. She should be the one to open them.

He stood still and stared at the box. *I have to know who sent them! I have to.*

Putting aside his qualms, he jerked the ribbon off the box and lifted the lid. Inside lay one perfect long-stemmed Talisman rose. A small white envelope nestled in the blooms. Stan picked it up and hesitated only a moment before removing the card inside. Dreading what he knew he'd see, he focused on the bold black writing:

> *Erika, sorry I can't make it to your birthday bash. I hope the evening will be as beautiful as you are. Maybe we can get together some time.*
>
> R

"R". Reese Sutherland, of course. Blinding jealousy. Raging anger. Paralyzing fear. All fought for control in Stan. For a moment, he couldn't move. Then, he swept up the long, narrow box and stomped to the back door. Outside, he lifted the lid of the large garbage can and stuffed the box inside. Looking around, he saw a stack of newspapers intended for the recycle bin. He picked them up and tossed them on top of the flower box.

Chapter Thirty-Three

ও

"I wouldn't leave town for the next few days if I were you, Jenkins," Mike heard Detective Lopez say.

When Mike had arrived at Lenae's loft, the two police guards outside her door wouldn't let him in to see for himself that she was not there. They detained him and called for the detective in charge. Detective Lopez, who he was told was at Coronado Hospital when he got the call, arrived so soon that Mike pictured him flying over the Coronado Bridge. His questions were fast and furious, beginning with....

"Why are you here?"

"I came to see Ms. Maddox, to see if she was all right."

"Why would you think she wasn't all right?"

"She wasn't answering her phone. I got worried. You can check my phone records."

"Oh, we will. Where were you last night between nine and midnight?"

"At my home in La Mesa."

"Can anyone vouch for you?"

"No. I live alone, and my only servants are a gardener and a house-keeper-slash-cook. Both come in twice a week, but neither one was there yesterday."

"Did you know Ms. Maddox was pregnant?"

"Yes. She told me a couple of days ago."

"Your baby?"

"No."

"You sound pretty certain."

"I was out of the country at the time she would have become pregnant."

"How did you feel about that?"

"Angry at first."

"Angry enough to try to kill her?"

"No! After mulling it over I realized I'm in love with Lenae. I went to her loft not only to check on her, but to ask her to marry me."

"Even though she was expecting another man's child?"

"Yes."

"Pretty noble of you, Jenkins."

"As I said, I realized I'm in love with her."

Mike's answers to a few more questions told Lopez that Mike had seen the initial "R" on a florist's card attached to a gold and coral rose and that two other men had been at Lenae's loft Wednesday night.

"One was a goofy-looking young man about twenty," Mike said. "Lenae introduced him as Dexter something. The other one was leaving mad as I got there. No idea who he was."

After listening to a few useless questions about the two men, Mike stepped as close to Lopez as he dared and gave him a steely look. "Are you arresting me, Detective?"

"No." Lopez took what looked like an involuntary step backwards. That's when Mike heard, "I wouldn't leave town for the next few days if I were you, Jenkins."

As if I would! Mike thought.

"By the way," Lopez continued, "I also wouldn't expect to be allowed into Ms. Maddox's room at the hospital."

"But—"

"Don't even try it."

Chapter Thirty-Four

ℰↃ

"Oh, Stan! Do you mean it?" Erika could hardly believe she'd heard her husband correctly. "We can really go ahead and buy a boat?"

"That's what I said. I thought you might like a catamaran. Take it or leave it."

Erika was touched by the slightly sheepish grin on Stan's round face. She may not be romantically in love with him, but she did care for him and was trying to be a good wife. She was sorry she'd flirted with Reese Sutherland at the gym and had almost forgiven Stan for the anger he'd displayed over that. Now, here he was offering to buy her the boat she'd dreamed of ever since they moved to Coronado Cays.

Bending down a little from her four-inch heels worn with a short, form-fitting skirt, she kissed the top of his balding head. "I'll take it. I'll take it!" She kissed his head twice more, then stepped back and put on a deliberately coy expression. "Is the boat my birthday present?"

"One of them. You'll get the other one tonight at the party. I decided on the catamaran while you were out."

Mention of the party made Erika think of an accidental meeting with Reese Sutherland at a gas station a few minutes earlier. She remembered how Reese had told her, "Sorry, I doubt if I'll be able to make it to your twenty-first birthday party."

"It's my twenty-fifth," she'd replied, pleased even though she knew he was exaggerating.

"Well, you could pass for seventeen." He swept her form with eyes gleaming with appreciation, and Erika hadn't been able to help the flutter of excitement, despite her determination to be a good wife to Stan.

No, she now told herself again. *Stan couldn't possibly know.*

Having convinced herself, she felt relieved until Stan said, "Oh, I know more about you than you think, dear heart."

"Oh really?" Erika said, dropping her chin demurely to hide the panic that must be in her face. Once she was sure her facial expression was under control, she caught Stan's hand and pulled him over to the couch. There she sat in his lap and tried to tease him into telling her what he bought her for her other birthday gift. He refused, saying she'd have to wait till the party. She wasn't sorry. She preferred to be surprised.

An hour later, Erika went into the tiny backyard to toss some leftovers into the garbage bin. When she lifted the lid, she saw a pile of newspapers inside.

"Those should go with the recyclables," she said aloud to herself. "Stan should know that." She reached in and pulled out the newspapers. Underneath was a long, white florist box. Puzzled, she set the papers aside. She took out the box and opened it.

Erika caught her breath at the sight of the gorgeous coral rose inside. Then she saw the card. It had been removed from its envelope. With trembling fingers, she read the note from "R". Reese Sutherland.

Maybe we can get together sometime, he had written.

Regret and excitement ran alongside dread as Erika stuffed the beautiful rose and the newspapers—but not the note—back into the bin. Suddenly she was angry with Stan. What right did he have to destroy one of the most beautiful flowers she'd ever seen? It was *hers*!

She reread the card. *Reese had said he* probably *couldn't make it to my party.* What had begun as a simple reveling in attention from an appreciative male became something else. When she'd invited Reese to the party, the invitation was lighthearted, as was their accidental encounter at the boatyard. Now she hoped with all her heart that she would see him tonight.

She hid Reese's note in her low-cut blouse and went inside to get ready for her party. She was too angry to notice her husband slip away from the kitchen window that looked out onto the backyard.

Chapter Thirty-Five

რა

Justin had to get out of the house. Added to his fury over Lenae's treatment of him, was his mother's reaction to his getting expelled from school. Reeling, he'd stomped out and sped away in his rusty twelve-year-old Honda Accord. The little car lurched through the rundown neighborhood and almost hit a child who'd dashed into the street for a ball. Miraculously reaching Interstate 5 without an accident or a ticket, he headed south, having no clear destination in mind.

An hour later he gulped down cheap tequila in Señor Frogs, a crowded bar on Avenida Revolucion in downtown Tijuana. Outside on the sidewalk, a band of mariachis wearing broad-brimmed sombreros and black native suits trimmed in brilliant colors belted out "Cielito Lindo."

"*Ay-yi-yi-yi. Canta y no llore.*" The plaintive Spanish words and tune floated through the open door of the bar.

Justin translated the words in his mind. *Sing and don't cry.* He tossed back a shot glass of the strong liquor. Coughing and sputtering, he thought, *Well, your own mother didn't cry today, did she, Rhodes? I've never dreaded anything more than telling Mom that her only son had been expelled from law school.* Imagining Chrissy Rhodes' disillusionment, Justin had put off telling her until this afternoon. *And what did she do? She practically sang with joy!*

"Oh, Justin!" Her face had actually lit up. "I know what an awful disappointment this is for you, but it could be the best thing that ever happened."

"Mom!" Justin's shock immobilized him for a moment. Then he dug his fingers into her shoulders. "How can you say that? This is what I've dreamed of, sacrificed for all these years. I was almost at the end, where I could take the bar exam and get on at a good law firm. Then I could start paying off my bills and have a little more money for you and the girls."

Chrissy gently removed his hands from her shoulders, then held them in her own. "Justin, I've watched you nearly kill yourself working fulltime while carrying a load of schoolwork. Half the time, you're worn to a frazzle from burning the candle at both ends."

Justin jerked away from her. "Of course, I have. That's what it takes."

"When you first decided to study law, I was really pleased. But now..."

"Now what?" Justin snapped.

"Now the only time I see real joy in you is when..." She stopped.

"When what, Mom?" He glared at her. "Don't stop now."

"When you complete a landscaping project, that's when I see satisfaction, even a kind of excitement." When Justin started to interrupt, his mother held up one hand. "Or when you add a new plant to our own yard. Look what you've done to it, including the part that belongs to the other half of the duplex. On this shabby street, it looks like the Garden of Eden in the middle of a desert."

Justin stared at his mother. "What are you saying?"

"I'm saying that this could be your opportunity to do something you really enjoy, not chase after a career that you chose more for the money than anything else."

"I'm not following you," he said, though he strongly suspected where she was going.

She tilted her chin and looked him straight in the eye. "You could get into landscaping fulltime. Maybe even start your own business."

His own mother had echoed the words of Reese Sutherland.

Chapter Thirty-Six

ॐ

The first woman Reese Sutherland charmed with Talisman roses was his mother. Widowed when Reese was two and having no other children, Joan Sutherland doted on and put almost all her energies into her son. It didn't hurt that Reese steadily progressed from adorable blond haired, tawny-eyed infant to cute toddler to precocious teenager to handsome young man. Joan made no secret of her adoration of him, and Reese quickly learned how to manipulate her.

The only activity that occasionally shifted Joan's attention away from her son was her garden. She was especially proud of her prize-winning roses. Early on, Reese saw that on the rare occasions his mother disciplined him—if you could call shaking a finger at him and saying, "Now, Reese" discipline—he could get quickly back in her good graces by bragging on her garden.

He only remembered one time she ever became downright angry with him.

At sixteen he had already developed the charm that along with his good looks got him almost anything he wanted. Females of all ages were drawn to him, including five-year-old Kendy, next door. Any time Reese was in the yard, she followed on his footsteps, clutching her black-furred, white-pawed kitten Bootsie in one arm and sucking the thumb of her other hand. Then, one Saturday afternoon...

"Hey, Kendy, can I play with Bootsie?" Reese bent down eye level with the child, his forearms resting on his thighs.

Kendy hesitated a moment. She never let anyone other than her parents hold her kitten. But after a few seconds, Kendy gave Reese a shy, trusting smile and handed over her beloved pet. When Reese took a cord from his jeans pocket and tied it around the squirming, yowling kitten's neck, she cried out, "No, Reese! Bootsie doesn't like that."

"It'll be fine. You'll see. We'll teach Bootsie to follow you on a leash like a puppy," Reese said, hardly able to hold onto the wiggling kitten.

"But Reese, I don't want—"

"Quit whining and watch!"

Her lips trembling, Kendy sucked hard on her thumb as Reese placed Bootsie on the ground and tried to lead him across the yard. The kitten was having none of it. He fought like a tiger, jumping every which way in an effort to free himself of the cord. The harder the kitten fought, the angrier Reese became. Finally, ignoring Kendy's screaming pleas, he seized Bootsie by the scruff of the neck and began to shake him. The little cat retaliated by dragging its tiny claws across his captor's arm, leaving a long, jagged stream of blood behind.

Reese yowled and tossed the kitten onto the ground. He started to grab the cord again, but Kendy's escalating screams had brought Reese's mother out to the yard.

"Reese! What's going on?" She rushed to the side of the child, who was holding her pet and sobbing.

"He killed Bootsie!" Kendy wailed.

Reese covered his inward fury with an apologetic expression and joined Joan at Kendy's side.

"I'm so sorry, sweetie," he said, putting his arm around the child's shoulder and biting back a curse when she jerked away from him. He twisted his face into a contortion of sadness. "I didn't mean to hurt Bootsie. And look! He's coming around. He's going to be fine."

Sure enough, the kitten began to stir in Kendy's embrace. Little by little, her sobs settled into soft hiccups until, with a look of utter contempt at Reese, she ran off to her own home.

Joan was furious. "You could have killed the kitten, Reese!"

Inwardly fuming, Reese replied, "Aw, Mom, I was just playing and got a little too rough. I didn't mean to hurt Bootsie." He held out his scratched arm. "And look what he did to me."

"Oh my!" Joan's tone took a 180 degree turn. "We'd better take care of that right away. Come on inside and let me see how bad it is. Maybe we'll need to call the doctor."

Sometimes it's almost too easy, Mom, Reese thought.

For further insurance, he took some of his generous allowance and purchased a Talisman rose bush for Joan's garden. He'd heard her express a desire for one. To make the snow-job complete, he picked up one long-stemmed Talisman from a florist. When, in a seemingly sincere tone of contrition, he presented the gifts to Joan, she was won over and actually apologized for doubting him.

He never told her about the many other animals he'd hurt. Nor had she ever learned of the women he'd charmed, used, and tossed aside like a chicken bone when all the meat has been consumed. To this day, in her nursing home in Boston, Joan Sutherland believed her son to be close to perfect.

~~~

All that was years ago. This was now. Reese was a bit shaken that he'd been so rough with Lenae he'd nearly killed her. He'd never gone that far before. According to media reports, she would probably die. Reese's distress, however, mostly centered on two issues. First—before Lenae announced her pregnancy—he'd planned to string out the relationship with her a little longer. Second, and more important in his mind, was concern that the police would discover some clue that would lead to him.

Another thought came to his mind. *What if she doesn't die? What if she wakes up and talks to...*

He shook off the thought. He'd deal with it later. Right now, he needed to finish getting ready for his date with Kate Elfmon.

I'll have to go slow with her, he thought as he checked his appearance in his dresser mirror. The rust-colored blazer and beige turtleneck played up his eyes and blonde coloring and subtly revealed his muscular arms. *She's the religious sort,* his thought continued. *I saw a Bible on her desk.* He grinned at his reflection. He did love a good challenge.

As he left, he picked up the flower he'd ordered for Kate: one long-stemmed Talisman rose.

Chapter Thirty-Seven

&

Justin couldn't remember how he got to Reese Sutherland's townhouse in La Jolla. Hours ago he'd lost count of the shots of tequila he'd downed. He did recall stumbling out of the Tijuana bar and dancing to wild music coming from inside. He'd flung out his arms, swinging the tequila bottle in one hand and performing a three-beat waltz to a four-beat tune. The only reason he stopped was that another American yanked him by the elbow and took him back inside.

"Whatcha doin'?" Justin had slurred.

"You need to get a hold of yourself and get out of here, Bud. I saw a policeman down the block. You want to get put *under* the jail? A Mexican jail?"

Even in his drunken state, that got Justin's attention. He'd heard enough horror stories about Mexican jails to know that was the last place he wanted to be.

"Tell me where your car is, and I'll help you get to it. We can go out the back. I hope you're parked on the U.S. side of the border." The man maneuvered one shoulder under Justin's armpit. I'm Ned, by the way."

" 'n I'm Zshustin." Justin saluted his new friend with the tequila bottle. "You think I'm muzz, nuzz, nuts or somethin'? O'course I parked on the U.S. side." Ned took the bottle from him and led him out.

Justin wasn't sure if that had been one hour or half a day earlier. He didn't even wonder how he'd managed to get this far without being pulled over by a patrolman. He only knew that somehow he'd wound up outside Cerca de Costa townhouses and that Reese Sutherland lived on the other side of the security gate.

As a gardener on the grounds, Justin had access to the gate code. On the third fumbling attempt, he punched the numbers in correctly then angled his Honda toward the service parking lot. At the last second, in a wave of drunken defiance, he swung the car around and into the residents' private lot. Out of the car, he slammed the door and zigzagged past a thirty-something yuppie-type couple and toward Sutherland's townhouse unit. He ignored the way the young woman whispered something to her husband as Justin stormed past.

When Justin was almost to Sutherland's door, the professor himself stepped outside, his car keys in one hand and in the other, a long-stemmed Talisman rose—exactly like the one Justin had glimpsed in Lenae's loft. The amazement on Sutherland's face was replaced quickly by amusement.

"Well, well, Mr. Rhodes. How good of you to stop by today. I understand you kept your appointment with Dean Simpson yesterday."

Justin stopped and, swaying, balled his fists by his side. "You know I did! And you know you've roo— roo—"

"Ruined you? Oh come, now, Rhodes. Aren't you being a bit dramatic? I haven't ruined you. I've given you the opportunity to switch career paths into something more suited to your, um, skills and temperament." He waved his hand toward the roses lining the walk. "You really do have a talent with horticulture. Why don't you do as I suggested the other day and start your own business? I think—"

"Shut up! You *have* ruined me, and you know it. All you had to do was allow me to rewrite one lousy paper. Instead, you've deliberately trashed all I've worked for for the past ten years. You even got—" A guttural sob emitted from Justin's throat. "You got my mother on your side."

Sutherland's expression changed again, now to one of controlled anger. "I don't know anything about your mother, but I think you'd better leave, Rhodes, before you say or do something you wish you hadn't. You've already done that once with me, and I didn't appreciate your threats. Now, if you'll excuse me, I have an appointment." With a crooked grin, he held out the rose.

"You, you!" Justin lunged at Sutherland, his fist aiming for the professor's face.

Reese stepped nimbly aside and flung his arm up, blocking Justin's fist. Then he shoved Justin away, causing him to stumble on the edge of the stoop.

Through clenched teeth, Reese said, "I'm going to assume you're not yourself because of bad news and worse liquor, so I won't call the police. But if you ever come near me again, I'll have them all over you. Now, I suggest you leave quietly."

"I'm leaving—for now, Sutherland. But if I were you I'd watch my back!"

With that, Justin stumbled back to his car and tore out of the parking lot.

Justin paid no attention to the wide-eyed couple who had stopped and observed the scene.

Chapter Thirty-Eight

ॐ

Peohe's—Coronado's tropical island getaway—was nestled on the water's edge of the Coronado Ferry Landing. From the window where Kate sat opposite Reese Sutherland, the breathtaking view of San Diego Bay and the downtown skyline, sparkling with lights, spread before them. Near the restaurant, Kate knew shoppers were strolling about the Ferry Landing Marketplace, with its unique array of shops and wares.

Kate settled back in the deeply padded chair. "That mahi-mahi was to die for, but I should have stopped at the lobster bisque and all that bread I ate with it." She looked across the table at Reese, who was buttering a third (or was it fourth?) roll. "And look at you! More bread after downing a whole bass, the appetizer, and a salad. Where are you putting it all?"

Reese grinned and put on a deliberate hillbilly accent. "Gotta keep m' energy up fer golfin', ya know." He stuffed another bite of roll in his mouth.

Lulled to a benign tranquility by the food and the ambiance of quietly elegant dining, Kate leaned forward to rest one elbow on the table and cup her chin in her hand. She turned her head and stared out at the midnight blue water with its diamond-like glitters reflecting off the city lights, the ferry-side lamps, and most of all, the crescent moon. In the distance, a ferryboat that reminded Kate of a Mississippi riverboat made a smooth, watery path to the landing.

"I'd like to take the ferry over sometime," she said. "But I guess that would be silly and impractical—to drive across the bridge away from the island and then take a ferry back to it, I mean."

"I can see that you don't do enough things that are silly and impractical." Reese's tawny eyes met Kate's brown ones and held her gaze for several seconds.

Strangely flustered, Kate shrugged. "Maybe not."

Reese leaned back again, still holding her gaze. "I'll have to do something about that."

"In a way you already have."

"Really?"

"Yes. I was all set to cancel our date and spend the evening with Cami. She was pretty upset about finding Lenae Maddox on the beach."

"I heard about that, of course. Hard to believe. Let's hope she makes it."

The thought flitted through Kate's mind that Reese's statement lacked conviction. But no, his handsome face certainly seemed to reflect compassion. Unbidden, a very different face—Gunnar's—popped into her imagination. Kate had been to Peohe's a few times over the years of visiting Cami, but the most memorable until now had been the day before Gunnar returned to Boston. That was a bittersweet memory—romantic, but tangled up with the uncertainty she'd felt about their relationship.

Go away! she told the mental image. *Do you have to interrupt my pleasant evening?*

Little did she know that the day before, Gunnar had been remembering that evening as he looked out over Boston Bay.

"Kate, where are you?" Reese asked with a chuckle.

"Oh, I'm afraid my mind wandered for a minute. Where were we?"

"You were going to tell me why you decided not to cancel our date."

"Oh yes. I was going to spend the evening with Cami, but she insisted that I not do that."

"Then I'm grateful to her."

Switching gears, Kate asked, "Reese, do you know Lenae well?"

Reese seemed taken aback by the question, but before Kate could wonder why, he said, "Not really. Our paths rarely cross at the university. Why do you ask?" His last words were spoken lightly, yet made Kate feel uncomfortable.

"No reason, really. There'll be enough talk about the incident at school Monday. Let's talk about more pleasant things now."

"My sentiments exactly."

Just then a male server approached the table. "Are you ready for your hot chocolate lava cake to finish off your meal, sir?" the young man asked.

"No!" "Of course!" Kate and Reese exclaimed at the same time.

The server joined them in laughing.

"I ordered it in advance," Reese told Kate.

"You have to do that with this dessert," the server explained. "It takes about thirty minutes to prepare."

"We're ready," Reese told the server, who nodded and left.

"You already ordered it?" Kate asked.

"I did. One, to share."

"I couldn't! It would be—"

"Silly and impractical?" He waited for her answer, but she could think of none.

Reese lowered his voice to a playfully seductive tone. "Come on. You won't be sorry."

Again, something about Reese's words bothered Kate. *Of course I won't be sorry,* she told herself. *Why should I be sorry?* Her thoughts flew heavenward. *Lord, why can't I simply enjoy myself without analyzing everything?*

"Okay," she told Reese, defiance edging her tone.

While waiting for the decadent-sounding dessert, Reese launched into a list of "silly and impractical" things for Kate to do in San Diego—all with him as her escort—from taking in a downtown "improv" comedy show to riding the 1925 wooden roller coaster at Belmont Park.

As Reese talked, an inner Voice reminded Kate of her conversation with Cami this afternoon. She had said she was going to find out about Reese's spiritual beliefs tonight.

There hasn't been the right moment, Kate excused herself to the Voice. *I'll do it, though, Lord. You know that's important to me.*

Tonight?

Well, maybe not tonight. I don't want to spoil.... She crushed the thought. The Voice left her alone. She wasn't sure whether to be glad or sorry.

"By the way," she said, putting her troubling thoughts aside. "Thanks for another rose. The last one was starting to wilt. I do love Talismans."

"So did my English teacher my senior year in high school."

"Really? For you to remember that, she must have been special."

"She was. She encouraged me when my mother died and I thought I wouldn't be able to afford college. My father was already dead. Miss Baker helped me get some grants and loans and told me I could do anything I set my mind to."

"Oh, Reese, what a wonderful story."

"You remind me of her. Now, don't look at me like that. You may not think it's a compliment that you make me think of Miss Baker, but she was young, only in her thirties. And not only was she a real encourager, she was very beautiful. Small and dark-haired like you." His face took on a tender expression. "She used to keep one long-stemmed Talisman rose on her desk at all times. She told us that Talisman roses represent memories."

Kate wasn't sure how to reply.

Fortunately at that moment the server appeared and set down the small dome-shaped rich brown cake drenched with chocolate sauce and piled high with macadamia nut ice cream and crunchy Heath Bar bits. The aroma of warm chocolate floated to Kate's nostrils. She inhaled deeply and reached for her fork.

"Ready, set, go!" Reese commanded, stabbing a forkful for himself.

As Kate had scooped up a big mouthful and was salivating for that first bite, her cell phone rang. She popped the cake in and chewed slowly, ignoring the phone. "Mmm. Mmm!" she said, reaching for another bite as the phone rang again.

"I meant to turn that thing off," she told Reese. "I'll see who it is and call later."

"Of course. But don't take too long. I may finish off the cake before you're through."

"You do, and I'll hurt you." Kate looked at the phone. "It's Cami." That irritated her. Cami knew she was out with Reese tonight.

"Better answer it. Cami doesn't seem like the kind to interrupt a dinner date needlessly."

Kate nodded, annoyed that Reese was being more charitable about the interruption than she was.

"Hi, Cami," she said into the phone. "Is anything wrong?"

"Oh, Kate!" Cami wailed. "I *hate* to bother you while you're out with Reese. I *really* do! But about half an hour ago, I had a bit of a fender bender in my car and—"

"Cami! What happened? Are you hurt?"

"I had taken my friend Robin to the airport. She's going to visit family in San Francisco for the weekend. Coming back, I'd just crossed over the bridge and was heading down 4th Street when a teenage boy rammed into my passenger side. My car had to be towed."

Chapter Thirty-Eight

"Are you hurt?" Kate repeated, already reaching for her purse.

"Not much. And the boy's all shaken up, but he's okay."

"What do you mean 'not much'?" Kate heard her voice rising.

"Well, I got a bit of a cut on the left side of my head where it hit the window. The air bag kept me from getting hurt worse."

"Are you bleeding? Where are you now? I'm coming to get you."

Cami let out a shaky laugh. "I was 'bleeding like a stuck pig,' as the old folks used to say. You know how the tiniest head wounds bleed like you're dying. It's mostly stopped now. The worst part is, my new sweater is ruined. Anyway, the police are insisting I go over to the hospital and check it out—my head, that is, not the sweater."

How like Cami to try to make a joke of it. "Of course you should check it out. Where are you? Exactly where was the accident?"

"It happened at the corner of 4th and Glorietta, but I'm in a police car right now on the way to the emergency room. I really do hate to interrupt your date, but—" Cami's voice trembled. "But after all that's already happened today..."

Kate stood and looked toward Reese. "I'll get Reese to take me home so I can get my car and come back for you. I'll be there in fifteen minutes." She knew Coronado Hospital was only a few blocks away.

"Thanks *so* much, Kate. Please tell Reese I'm sorry."

"Don't give it another thought. See you in a few minutes." She pushed her chair under the table and turned to Reese, who had already flagged down the server and was taking care of their check. "You heard all that."

"Do you want me to drive you straight to the hospital and wait for you?" Though the offer seemed sincere, Kate sensed reluctance in Reese's voice.

"Oh, no. No telling how long it will take. It's not a life-and-death emergency. If you could drive me home to pick up my car, that would be great."

"Okay, if you're sure. Let's go."

~~~

Kate had been right about the reluctance she thought she heard in Reese's voice. As he led her to his car, he thought, *I don't want to be anywhere inside that hospital with Lenae Maddox there.* He looked toward

Kate. *About the time I was making some headway...*

Thinking of how he'd told her about Miss Baker and her Talisman roses, he allowed himself an inner chuckle. Miss Baker had indeed been his senior-year English teacher. But she was sixty if she was a day and had possibly never said an encouraging word in her life. As for Talisman roses, or any other kind of flowers, Miss Baker was more the dandelion, emphasis on *lion*, type. Also, Reese's mother was still very much alive, as evidenced by the huge bill he got each month from her Boston nursing home.

He looked at his watch. *Only nine o'clock. Erika Weston's party should be in full swing, and the Boat House is only about five minutes from here.*

Sunday, November 7

Chapter Thirty-Nine

&

Cami had been tempted to stay home from church this morning. Yesterday had been horrible. All day memories of Braxton's murder and Debra's beach attack had played over and over in her head. She had begun to wish she hadn't insisted on Kate's keeping her date with Reese Sutherland and that she hadn't promised Robin Byrd a ride to the airport. The little fender bender, resulting in a few easily-covered stitches at her hairline, had been the crowning offense. Kate had advised her to sleep in today.

"No, Kate. I feel like I *need* to be in God's house today," Cami had said. "What good will it do to sit around and commiserate?"

Kate had laughed. "Commiserate? If that's not a Cami-kind-of word, nothing is."

Cami had been right to come to church. Once the worship service began, she felt comforted by the familiar hymns she'd grown up singing, and Pastor Oates' simple message from Matthew 28:20 deeply touched her. "Lo, I am with you always..." Jesus had said in that verse. That promise of God's ever-presence in a Believer's life washed over her and calmed her.

Now Cami and Kate stood in the foyer of the small Baptist church on Orange Street. With her Mercedes in the shop for a few days, Cami had driven Braxton's silver Jaguar, the first time she'd been in it since he died. While Braxton was alive, Cami had attended beautiful, historic Christ Episcopal, the church the Carrington family had helped to build in 1888. As for Braxton, he had been a nominal member and often made large contributions for various projects. Occasionally he attended a service, but usually left "religion" to Cami. Even before his death, Cami had sometimes slipped into the Baptist church for their Sunday evening service. Much as she loved the minister and people at Christ Church, she felt drawn to the denomination of her childhood, even more so since she and Kate returned from their motorhome jaunt.

Cami put those thoughts aside and found herself able to smile, if somewhat soberly, and answer the other worshipers' naturally curious questions.

After listening for a few minutes, Pastor Oates placed a gentle arm around Cami's shoulders. "Thank the Lord we have such an excellent police force. I hear they got to the beach less than ten minutes after you called 9-1-1."

A teenage girl whom Cami knew only as Tracy stepped up. "I heard she was holding onto a dozen bright red roses for dear life!" She let out an exaggerated sigh, clasped her hands under her chin, and cut her eyes at her boyfriend. "Hooooow romantic."

"Roses?" Cami smiled, realizing the girl was young and not deliberately heartless. "That does sound romantic, but I only noticed a plastic florist sleeve with a bit of one flower stem in her hand. I didn't take time to examine it." She turned her attention to Pastor Oates. "Yes, thankfully the police showed up within ten minutes, and Kate was even faster. Ms. Maddox works at Grant Lauder. At least she did. I appreciate how you prayed for her during the service this morning, Pastor."

"That's what we do here, Cami," he told her with a smile that held no rebuke.

"I had met Ms. Maddox only once, but as soon as I saw her lying there on the sand, I recognized her." Cami shuddered.

Tracy gasped. "Ooooh! How horrible! Was there blood everywhere?"

"I didn't see any blood, Tracy."

"Well, the water probably washed it away."

Cami could tell that Tracy was disappointed.

"Maybe he stabbed her," the girl went on, "...over and over and—"

"That's enough, Tracy," said Pastor Oates. "That's how rumors get started."

Tracy bent her head. "Sorry, Pastor. You're right." She pulled at her boyfriend's shirt sleeve. "Come on, Brian. Let's start walking to my house before my mom makes me ride home with her and Dad."

Kate, who had been chatting with the Minister of Music, came up. Looking at the departing youngsters, she shook her head. "Teenagers!"

"Were we ever like that, Kate?" Cami asked.

Kate tilted her head and pretended to frown. "You were." She pursed her lips. "Not me, of course."

"Kate!" Cami pretended to be offended, but both knew Kate was alluding to the differences in their personalities, evident from the day they became college roommates.

As she spoke, Cami took her iPhone from her huge Prada handbag and pressed the button that took it off "Silent." At that moment, it rang. Cami looked at the tiny screen.

"It's Debra," she said. "Calling from Edinburgh. Let me get to where I can hear better." She stepped back into a small room off the foyer.

She had hardly said Hello when Debra burst out with, "Mom! What's going on there? I got some crazy text message that sounded like you found a dead woman on the beach near the house *yesterday* morning! And you're just now letting us know. Please tell me it's not true."

"That's not quite right, honey." Cami heard Debra draw in her breath. "The woman was attacked—attempted strangulation—but not killed. Just the same, finding her scared me half out of my wits, especially since I recognized her. She works at the university, and Kate had introduced us."

"Are you okay, Mom?" Cami was touched by the compassion in her daughter's voice.

"I was pretty rattled, but I'm fine now." Cami decided not to mention the car accident last night. No need to worry the twins when they were so far away. "And Detective Lopez is handling the case."

Cami heard Debra relaying the information to her brother, Durant. Cami tried to picture them in the rooming house where they shared a three-room flat.

A little after noon here, she thought. *Eight in the evening over there.* How she missed her children.

Somewhat wistfully, she asked Debra, "How are things with you, honey?"

Though Debra paused for the merest fraction of a second, Cami's maternal red flags went up.

"Things are *fab*, as they say over here. My classes are challenging, but I'm doing well. So is Durant. And Edinburgh is the *most* beautiful, fascinating city."

"Any dates?" Cami hoped her question sounded casual.

"Not that many."

"Mmmm. Anyone special?"

"Sort of. There's this guy, Reggie—Reginald Woodthorpe..." Debra's voice trailed off.

Cami could tell Debra didn't want to say more, but she pushed on with, "Sounds aristocratic. Is he Scottish?"

"English. From Yorkshire."

Cami decided not to push for more information, but the red flags were flying high now.

"Mom!" Durant had taken the phone from Debra. "You know we'll be praying for you."

In the background, Debra let out a whoosh of exasperation. Cami knew that meant Debra would leave the praying to Durant.

"I'm glad Lopez is on the case," Durant said. "He was great when Dad died and when Debra got attacked."

Cami heard Debra draw in a sharp breath. "Give me the phone, Durant. Mom! Did it happen near where I was attacked?"

"No. It was in the other direction. I found her near that big rock where I sometimes sit and relax."

"What's happening to my beach, Mom?" Debra whispered. "Will it ever be the same?"

"Nothing remains the same, Debra. But your unpleasant memories will pass and so will this. And life will go back to normal." She wanted to tell her daughter that God would help her move on, but knew the words wouldn't be welcome.

"I love you, Mom," Debra said.

"Me, too!" Durant called out.

When the twins signed off, Cami held the phone to her cheek. She had a feeling it would be a long time before life went back to normal.

Chapter Forty

&

In Stan's opinion, Erika's party last night had been a disaster. Yes, The Boat House was a perfect venue. It was catty-cornered from the Hotel Del and jutted out into the sparkling bay, with a view of luxurious pleasure boats and the majestic sweep of the Coronado Bridge in the background. Yes, the food, the ambiance, the small jazz combo were all top notch. Yes, the guests enjoyed themselves, and Erika was in her element, gushing over everything, especially the large jade, diamond-encircled pendant and matching earrings Stan gave her.

So what was wrong?

What was wrong was that Stan himself had spent the evening wondering if Reese Sutherland would dare show up. Had he? When Erika stepped outside for a few minutes about nine-thirty, did she meet him? Few people knew how many women he had enticed, then cruelly discarded.

But Stan did.

~~~

Erika could always tell when Stan was suspicious. She'd seen the signs often enough to recognize the slight withdrawal, the sidelong looks that were meant to go unnoticed, the casual questions. Besides, though he'd not mentioned it, she knew he was aware of her receiving a rose from Reese Sutherland. She was furious with him for destroying it. She was also practical minded and self-protective enough to hang onto the lifestyle Stan had provided her. Never would she go back to the near-poverty she'd known in the ultra-religious Boston home she'd grown up in.

That's why she'd been extra careful last night. About nine-fifteen, while holding out a tray of hors d'oeuvres, a waiter moved near her, looked around, and whispered, "A gentleman would like to speak with you. He said he's waiting outside near the door."

Erika had given the waiter an innocent smile and, in a voice as quiet as his, said, "Tell the, uh, gentleman that I'll be free in about ten minutes."

She went back to mingling with her guests and soon began chatting with the wife of one of Stan's elderly business acquaintances. Shortly into the conversation, she placed her fingers to her temple and frowned.

"Are you not feeling well?" the woman asked.

Erika made her answering smile weak. "Just a slight headache."

"Do you need something? I'm sure I have some Tylenol."

"No. No, thank you. I think I'll step outside for a few breaths of fresh air. Would you excuse me, please?"

"Would you like me to go with you?"

Not on your life! "How sweet of you. But, no, no. I won't take you away from the party. I'll be back in a few minutes."

Over the woman's continued offers to accompany her, Erika managed to slip away, still pressing her temple with her fingers.

Outside, a deep voice came from the shadows. "There you are. At last." The man caught her hand and pulled her into the darkened corner.

"Reese," she said in a breathy voice. "You came after all."

"Are you surprised?"

She gave him a flirty smile. "Well, no. Thank you, by the way for the gorgeous rose. I love it."

"I'm so glad you liked it, though it's a poor offering in comparison to this." He touched the large diamond-encircled jade necklace.

"It's my birthday gift from Stan. But in a way, I like the rose just as much."

He tightened his hold on her hand and led her to another shadowy spot, this one on the deck overlooking Glorietta Bay. "It's called a Talisman rose."

"Talisman? That's a good luck charm, isn't it? Kinda like a rabbit's foot."

"That's right, except a Talisman rose is no rabbit's foot. They stand for very special memories. They whisper sweet memories. I read that in a book of flower legends."

"Memories! Oh, how romantic."

Reese turned Erika to face him, hooked his finger under her chin, tipped her face upward to him, grinned, and whispered, "I shouldn't keep you too long from your party."

"I have a few minutes," she whispered back. "They think I have a headache and came out for some air."

"We don't want ol' Stan to come looking for you," Reese said, speaking in a normal tone now. "I don't think he'd be too pleased to find me here, even if you did invite me."

"Mmmm. You're right." Erika led Reese to the wooden rail at the edge of the deck. "I get the impression there's bad blood between the two of you."

Reese gave a casual shrug. "I wouldn't go so far as to call it bad blood. Simple misunderstanding based on personality differences would be more accurate."

Erika felt it was more than that, but she let the matter drop. As did he.

Standing behind her, clasping her waist in his long-fingered hands, his mouth near her ear, his low voice sounded almost magical. "Look how still the water is tonight."

"And the breeze is so soft it feels like a whisper," Erika added with a little giggle.

The two became silent, looking out at the water, dark except where a moonbeam made a bright, narrow path, and listening to the waves lapping in gentle rhythm against the deck. After a few minutes Reese tightened his hold on her waist and murmured, "What's your favorite memory, Erika?"

She thought for a few seconds, then looked over her shoulder into his eyes. She held his gaze for several silent seconds before replying, "I'm still waiting for it."

As she started to turn toward him, a raucous laugh from the party inside shattered the mood. Panicked, Erika moved out of Reese's arms. "I have to go in. Stan will be looking for me."

"You're right. You'd better go, but we'll get together again sometime soon."

Erika was annoyed with herself. Yes, she was angry at Stan for destroying the rose Reese had sent her, but there was no need to be stupid.

Besides, hadn't she promised Stan there'd be no other men in her life after that horrid affair with Braxton Carrington?

"I don't think so," she told Reese firmly. "I'm *so* glad you came, but I-I have to go now."

She glanced back as she returned to the party and wiggled her fingers at Reese. He gave her a knowing look that said he was sure they'd meet again.

~~~

Today, Erika recognized that she was already fighting a losing battle with her conscience and her good sense. With a shiver of pleasure, she wondered how soon Reese Sutherland would "drop by" again.

Chapter Forty-One

ße

Mike Jenkins' entire being burned with an all-consuming anger at whoever had nearly killed Lenae Maddox. His imagination brimmed over with ways to exact revenge. On top of the fury, he was beside himself with unanswered questions. Why had he not been able to convince the police guards who took turns outside Lenae's hospital room door to let him in—even resorting to bribery at one point? What if Lenae never came out of her coma? Why had he not realized sooner how much he cared for her?

What if he never got the chance to tell her?

Mike had even prayed, begging that Lenae would survive and be well. Considering that most of his life he'd ignored the God he now prayed to, he didn't have a lot of faith in his petitions. Still, why not cover all the bases?

Mike had rushed to Coronado Hospital the moment Detective Lopez finished questioning him and had haunted the halls of Lenae's floor ever since. He'd not changed clothing or shaved for two days, and the little food he'd eaten had been scarffed down in the hospital cafeteria so quickly he'd hardly tasted it. As for sleep, he'd been able to snatch a few minutes here and there in the waiting room; but they'd been anything but restful.

He was on the elevator now, returning to Lenae's floor after picking up a toothbrush in the gift shop. As he stepped out into the hall, he noticed a nurse coming out of Lenae's room. The nurse's face held a hint of wonder behind its mask of professionalism.

Mike caught her sleeve as she passed him. In a flash the policeman on guard stepped toward him.

"Sorry, Miss," Mike said to the nurse, while the guard continued to eye him. "It's, um ... I thought you looked ... I hoped there was some good news."

"It's all right," the nurse told the guard stiffly before saying to Mike, "I can't divulge that information, sir."

"She spoke, didn't she?" Mike demanded, struggling against the guard, who only tightened his hold. "She asked for me."

The nurse gave him a long look. "She spoke one word we could hardly make out." A hint of a sad smile played on her face. " But she didn't ask for you ... unless your name is Cami."

Chapter Forty-Two

ॐ

Cami stood by Lenae Maddox's bedside in the very room where Debra had recovered from her attack last summer. Now here she was by the side of another woman who'd also been attacked on the same beach. Oh, how she hated this hospital, despite the excellent treatment Debra had received.

Why in the world did Lenae call for me? Did she? They said she'd made a sound that may have been my name. Anyway, I only met her twice, and the second time, at the school, she was barely polite. Why didn't she ask for Kate? That would have made much more sense.

Cami moved closer. Lenae was hooked up to several tubes, many of which were in turn attached to a couple of monitors that hummed and beeped and displayed various information about the patient's condition. She touched Lenae's hand near the needle protruding from one vein. Her skin was cool. Her breathing was shallow.

"Lenae?" Cami said, keeping her voice low..

No response beyond the steady humming and beeping of the machines.

She's barely alive. How could she have said anything at all, even one word?

"Lenae," she repeated, speaking a little louder now. "They said you called for me; I'm not sure why. I came right away." Cami hardly knew how to go on. This was so difficult.

Kate said she'd pray for me to have the right words, she remembered. *Now would be a great time for her to do that, Lord.*

She sent up her own plea of *Help, Lord!* It was all she could think of. She leaned close to Lenae's face.

"They say I can only stay ten minutes." Cami said. "So I'll make it quick. First, I want you to know I'm praying for you to absolutely, completely recover. Also, don't forget you promised I could come over sometime and see your paintings. I'd love that, though I'd probably be jealous of your talent." Cami thought of something. "If you can hear me, try to squeeze my hand. Doesn't have to be hard. Only enough for me to feel it."

Lenae's hand lay still.

"Lenae, I want you to know that God loves you and He is here with you." Cami bowed her head. "Dear God, I know you love Lenae. Please help her." Cami couldn't think of anything else to say.

She reached for the white hand on the white sheet and squeezed it gently. The slender fingers remained still, and Lenae's breathing became even shallower.

Just then the door opened and a nurse spoke to Cami. "Time's up, Mrs. Carrington."

Disappointment flooding her, Cami leaned over to kiss Lenae's cool cheek. Outside the room, the nurse gave Cami a questioning look. Cami shook her head no.

The nurse patted Cami's shoulder. "Well, you tried."

With a weak smile, Cami walked away.

~~~

The nurse closed Lenae's door, not noticing the wet lashes on the still, pale face.

Chapter Forty-Three

ᘒ

Mike sat outside Coronado Hospital in his black Escalade. He watched the entrance, hoping to see the woman Lenae had called for, though he had no idea how he'd recognize her. About fifteen minutes later, a pretty blonde woman wheeled into the last parking slot in front of the hospital and hurried inside. Instinct told him this was the one. As she hurried by him, he thought she looked familiar.

All at once, Mike's photographic memory took charge. Of course! The woman's face had been plastered all over the San Diego Union Tribune—and papers across the country—back in August after her husband was murdered at the Hotel del Coronado. Her name was *Cami* Carrington!

Mike couldn't sit still. He got out of the SUV and paced the sidewalk in front of the hospital. In about twenty minutes, his vigil paid off. He caught a glimpse of Mrs. Carrington as she approached the large glass front doors, but couldn't tell her mood until she came out. His heart plummeted when he saw the droop to her slender shoulders. He stepped near and touched her arm.

When she looked up at him, he saw only sadness in her smoky blue eyes.

"I'm sorry to bother you, Mrs. Carrington, but I'm a good friend of Lenae Maddox, and I know she called for you."

"How—"

"The nurse told me." Mike didn't see any need to explain the circumstances. "Could you... would you... Did she speak anymore? How is she?"

"She didn't speak to me at all, Mr.—"

"Jenkins. Mike Jenkins."

"Well, Mr. Jenkins," she said, her tone somewhere between discouragement and hope, "if you're a praying man, now would be a good time to pray hard." Then, as though reminding herself, she smiled slightly and added, "She's in the Lord's hands."

As she walked away, Mike allowed himself a tiny glimmer of hope.

Chapter Forty-Four

ॐ

Two nurses entered Lenae Maddox's room. Lenae felt one of them wrap a blood pressure cuff around her forearm. She sensed the other one moving to what Lenae assumed was the heart monitor and oxygen machine.

"Poor thing," a young-voiced female said. The voice came from the one pumping up the BP cuff. "Nearly choked to death by her lover."

"How do you know it was a lover?" A male, also young-sounding, spoke now.

"Well, maybe not a lover, but at least a date. Why else would a young woman go out on the beach alone at night? I mean, Coronado is pretty safe—"

"If you ignore that woman who was hanged from the balcony of the Spreckels mansion."

"The police called that a suicide."

"And Braxton Carrington's murder at the Del back in August?"

"Um, yes."

"And the murder-suicide involving some Navy pilots on New Year's Day?"

"Okay. Okay. But those were the first incidents in nearly two years. What I was going to say is, even though Coronado is a pretty safe area, it's dumb for a woman to go out on the beach alone at night. I don't think Ms. Maddox did."

"Who knows?"

Lenae felt the male move nearer and sensed he was looking down at her. He let out a growly sound. "I'd like to get hold of the lowlife who did this."

"If only she could tell the police who it was."

"*If* she knows."

I can hear you! Lenae screamed from within herself. *And I do know! It was Reese Sutherland!* She tried to force out words to tell the two nurses that "lowlife" was the right word for Reese, despite his good looks and charm. Despite all her mental effort to speak, her throat remained shut and her voice silent.

"How's the blood pressure?" the male asked.

"Not good." Lenae felt the BP cuff release and knew the nurse was rolling it back up. "Eight-three over forty-five. Could be worse. It was forty-two over eighteen when they brought her in yesterday."

The male nurse whistled. "Heart beat's weak, too. You through here?"

"Yes. Let's go." A gentle hand touched Lenae's face, and she felt as much as heard the gentle voice. "Hang in there, girl."

Chapter Forty-Five

※

Kate knew that sometimes it was more important to let her students talk through some current event rather than force them to stay on track with the lesson. This was one of those days. Even as they entered the classroom, the young men and women were chattering about Lenae Maddox's attack, right here on the sands of Coronado's own beach.

"It's horrible," a tight-jeaned, auburn-haired co-ed named Aubrey said. "I can't imagine!"

"It is not safe anywhere anymore," her friend Juana said.

"Well, at least, according to the news, she wasn't, well, you know..." a shy, prim girl put in.

"It's okay if you say raped, Susan," said Aubrey, taking her seat. "All the same, I'm not going out on the beach alone at night."

"Did you ever?" Paul, the skinny boy who took the seat next to her, shot her a sly look and snickered.

"Hmmpf." Aubrey lifted her chin and slanted her head away from him.

Kate walked around to the front of her desk. When the buzz died down, she held up her notes. "Looks like I won't be using these today." She put down the notes and looked around the room. Carefully avoiding mentioning that Cami Carrington, who had found Lenae, was her own best friend, she said, "I know you all want to discuss Friday night's horrible incident, especially since Ms. Maddox works here at the university." A chorus of agreement met her ears. She held up one hand. "That's fine, as long as we keep the discussion orderly."

As soon as the words left her lips, several voices clamored for attention.

"I said orderly," Kate reminded the students in mock sternness. "Aubrey and Juana have brought up important points about safety. Let's begin with that."

"Well, I think Aubrey mentioned the most important one," Paul said. "Girls ought not to go to lonesome places alone."

"What about guys?" Susan put in. "They're vulnerable, too, you know."

"And what about daytime?" That was Aubrey.

That prompted a spirited discussion that Kate let run its course. About fifteen minutes before time for class to dismiss, she decided to direct the conversation to a different subject.

Just then Dexter Driscoll burst into the room.

All eyes turned toward the lanky, awkward sophomore with his thick, rimless glasses hooked around protruding ears. From the beginning, despite the way he often challenged her in class, Kate had felt sorry for Dexter. Poor brilliant guy was definitely a *nerd* in the eyes of the other students. A friendless nerd, at that.

"Sorry," he muttered. "I spent the weekend with my family in Tucson. Took a red-eye back, and it was late getting in." Obviously embarrassed, he stopped.

"Please take a seat, Dexter," said Kate. "We're having an *orderly* discussion about Ms. Maddox's unfortunate attack. Since you were away, you may not have—"

"*What?*"

"You didn't know, Dex?"

Dexter's head jerked toward Paul.

Aubrey spoke up. "Friday night, Ms. Maddox was attacked on Coronado beach, a couple of blocks down from the Del."

"Choked," said Paul.

"Is she—" Dexter began, trembling.

"She is alive." Melancholy filled Juana's brown eyes. "Barely."

"Where—" Dexter seemed unable to go on.

"She's in Intensive Care at Coronado Hospital," Susan explained, sympathy touching her soft voice. "She, she may not make it."

Dexter spun around and ran out of the room, his lanky limbs flailing in all directions.

~~~

Despite his fatigue, Dexter ran the full mile and a half from Grant Lauder to Coronado Hospital. He paid no heed to the quaint cottages or the luxurious mansions he passed. He simply ran.

As he ran, his mind reeled. How could this be happening now? He'd entered Dr. Elfmon's classroom in the best spirits he'd been in for years. The short trip to visit his family in Tucson had been uncharacteristically pleasant. His father claimed to have experienced a kind of spiritual renewal—"born again," he called it. Dexter could hardly believe the difference in the normally gruff man's demeanor and attitudes. He had trouble reconciling the image of this man with the excuse-for-a-father Dexter had known since birth.

Though the long years of crushing criticism were impossible to dismiss out of hand, a pathetically eager Dexter was more than willing to forgive his father. During the next two days the two talked more than in the previous twenty years. Dexter left Tucson in a state of near euphoria.

And now this. Lenae attacked. Probably dying. Maybe already dead.

Dexter ran faster, and as he ran, the memory of Mike Jenkins' twisted countenance when he rushed out of Lenae's loft grew sharper and sharper in his mind.

Chapter Forty-Six

ප

The sound was like some kind of babbling. To its uneven rhythms, Lenae drifted into a light consciousness.

"Lenae! Lenae!" the voice seemed to say. She felt long, skinny fingers squeezing her hand. "I'll get him. He'll never get away with it."

Dexter. Dexter Driscoll. That's who it was. Sweet, caring Dexter. He babbled on some more. At one point he seemed to be saying something about his father. Something to do with God, but Lenae drifted in and out and understood little of Dexter's words. Until—

"First he gets you pregnant, then he tries to kill you." Anger. Indignation. "I know you must hate it that the baby didn't make it, Lenae."

A deep sadness fell over Lenae. She'd not wanted to get pregnant, but as soon as she'd suspected she was, she'd begun to develop a bond with the little person growing inside her. She'd even wanted the child to have a home with its father present. Now that "little person" was gone. It was all her fault. Everything was her fault, beginning with the immoral lifestyle she stepped into as a teenager and up until the moment she felt Reese Sutherland's fingers around her throat. Her stomach knotted at the thought of the person she'd become.

Dexter was still babbling on. He stopped for a moment, then nearly shouted, "The world's better off without that monster's kid."

Don't say that Dex! Not about that innocent child. It wasn't his fault that Reese Sutherland was his father.

Lenae vaguely remembered that though she'd told Dexter about the two men in her life, she'd been sure not to mention the name of either.

"Don't you worry, Lenae, I'll see that he pays for what he did. Mike Jenkins will not—

No! Not Mike! Overwhelmed with frustration that she couldn't make her vocal cords comply with her thoughts, she managed a low groan.

"Lenae!" Lenae felt Dexter's breath an inch from her face. "Are you awake? Oh man! What are you trying to say?"

Lenae exerted every possible bit of effort, but "Riiiiizuh" was the only part of "Reese Sutherland" she could force out.

"What's the reason I'm so mad?"

Oh no! Dexter had misunderstood. He thought she was trying to say "reason."

"You know the reason!" Dexter cried. "I'm not going to let Jenkins get away with what he did to you!"

Chapter Forty-Seven

&

"Cami, this is Kent Jacobs."

Kent cleared his throat. "I'm sure you're surprised to hear from me."

"Yes, I guess I am."

"Maybe you don't know I'm Chairman of Deacons at Coronado Baptist." Cami didn't know, but Kent went on before she could say so. "I've been to the hospital. They let Pastor Oates and me in to see Lenae Maddox. The nurse on duty told us you visited her yesterday, so Pastor Oates thought you might like to know we visited her, too. I offered to make the call."

"The news isn't good, is it? I hear it in your voice."

Kent let out a long sigh. "Ms. Maddox improved for a while, but her blood pressure has dropped again, and her breathing is shallower than ever."

"I'm so glad the two of you visited her."

"Me, too, though I'm not sure how much good it did."

"I felt the same way when I left. I appreciate your calling me and letting me know what's going on."

Cami laid the phone in its cradle next to the leather recliner she was stretched out in. She picked up the mystery novel she'd been engrossed in when Kent called, but had trouble getting back into the story.

She closed the book and thought of what she knew about Kent Jacobs. Unlike the Carringtons, whose Coronado roots went back to the late 1800s, Kent had moved to the island from somewhere in the Midwest "only" about twenty years ago.

Kent was as unassuming as he was rich and was often seen at the local

158

Von's grocery store in worn jeans and an old sweatshirt, his grey-tinged sandy hair a bit unkempt. He did "clean up good," as Cami's grandmother would have said. He looked sharp, even kind of handsome, in his Sunday suit or the tuxedo Cami had seen him in a few times. His tuxedo didn't get much use, though. He participated little in island social life, especially after his wife died of a lingering cancer two years ago.

Cami's thoughts shifted to the supposed reason for Kent's call. Why did Pastor Oates feel that she should know about his and Kent's visit to Lenae? And, if so, why would Kent offer to do it for him?

Oh well, she *was* glad to know about their visit. Cami went back to her mystery novel.

Chapter Forty-Eight

❧

"**I**s this the eminent, delightful Dr. Kate Elfmon's classroom?"

Kate looked up from her desk to see Reese Sutherland. Leaning one wide shoulder against the door frame, he had crossed one ankle over the other and slipped a hand into his pants pocket. In tan slacks, burgundy crew-neck pullover, and brown suede bomber jacket, he looked like an ad for Neiman Marcus.

Imagining what he'd look like modeling for a golf magazine, Kate smiled widely. "Neither eminent nor delightful, but Dr. Elfmon here, present and accounted for."

Reese ambled in and stood looking down at Kate, a confident, one-sided grin on his face. "You know you're beautiful," he said. His words were low, seductive.

Kate was dumbstruck. She was often called attractive or cute or sometimes even pretty, but not beautiful. That was Cami's territory. Oh, sometimes someone told Kate her brown eyes were beautiful or that her thick, dark brown hair was great, but "You're beautiful"? Almost never.

Almost. The thought came unbidden. Joel had said she was beautiful *to him*. And more recently... She didn't want to remember right now that Gunnar called her beautiful—inside and out. She recalled how she could feel herself blushing as she gave Gunnar a simple "Thanks." Now, to Reese, she said that same simple word, then rushed on. "And thanks for being so understanding about our dinner being interrupted Saturday night." Only briefly did she wonder why he hadn't called on Sunday, to check up on Cami if nothing else.

"What are friends for?" Reese sat on the edge of the desk and folded his arms across his broad chest. "But that's why I'm here—to see if we can make up for lost time. Are you free tonight?"

"Tonight? Monday?"

"Too silly and impractical?"

"Well, if you put it that way..." Tilting her head to one side, Kate pushed aside thoughts of the papers she needed to grade. "What do you have in mind?"

"There's a little bistro in downtown La Jolla that features local musicians every night, even Mondays. Tonight there's a young clarinetist named Amy Jones, calls herself AJ. I haven't heard her myself yet, but I hear she's great."

"I love the clarinet," Kate said. "And I'd love to hear AJ."

"Pick you up at seven." Reese gave her a thumbs up and started to leave. Then he stopped. "By the way, a few minutes ago I saw one of your students tearing out of the building like something was after him."

"Oh, that was Dexter Driscoll. He came in late while the class was discussing Lenae Maddox's attack."

Reese became still. "Oh, really?"

"Yes. He was out of town over the weekend and hadn't heard about it. You should have seen how he reacted. Turned as white as that wall over there. Then as soon as he heard she was at Coronado hospital, that's when he ran out. Do you know if he had a crush on her or something?"

Reese shrugged. "Who knows about college students? Well, I need to run. See you tonight."

Watching him leave, Kate had a sudden disturbing thought. Reese had not once expressed concern for his fellow staff member, Lenae Maddox.

Chapter Forty-Nine

&

"The end!" Cami snapped her mystery novel to with a sense of satisfaction. Just before the moment the author revealed the name of the killer, Cami had known who it was. She'd have to tell Kate about this one. With its elements of intrigue mingled and tangled with intensely romantic but not graphic scenes, it was perfect. With all their differences in personality and tastes, Cami and Kate shared a love of a good mystery.

Laying the book aside, Cami kicked in the footrest of her recliner and wandered to the kitchen. Edith had cleared away the remains of the delicious clam chowder she'd made for Cami's supper and had taken some upstairs to the servants' apartment to enjoy with her husband Edwin. So Cami had the rest of the big, lonely house to herself.

Determined not to lose her upbeat mood, Cami decided to do something positive to fill her evening. She fixed herself a glass of diet cola and got a dark chocolate candy bar from her chocolate stash. Nothing like chocolate to foster a good mood, and having diet soda took away the guilt of consuming so many sugary calories—at least in Cami's mind.

Back in the den, her eye fell on her powder blue Bible. She plopped herself back down in the recliner, placed the soda on the table, tore open the candy bar wrapper, and flipped the footrest back up. Then she opened the little Bible and, putting aside the doubts that assailed her about the effectiveness of her visit, soon began to pray for the young woman who lay at the point of death in a hospital not two miles away.

Chapter Fifty

ॐ

Le Petit Bistro was snuggled between one of dozens of trendy boutiques and a fine-arts gallery on Girard Avenue in the area of downtown La Jolla known to locals as "the Village." Inside, at a small round table, complete with a wine bottle dripping with candle wax, Kate Elfmon and Reese Sutherland closed the colorful menu. Both had settled on the house salad, grilled baguette sandwiches with camembert cheese, and the restaurant's signature French onion soup.

The walls of the little bistro featured whimsical Renoir-style murals—tourists gazing up at the Eiffel Tower on one wall, left-bank artists on another. Kate and Reese's table, with its dark red cloth under the wine-bottle centerpiece, echoed the outdoor café mural on the wall opposite them. Kate closed her eyes and breathed in the delightful aroma of fresh-baked baguettes and rich French sauces.

Reese gave their orders to a buxom dark-haired waitress dressed in a short, low-cut black dress and a white ruffled apron tied tight around her tiny waist. A frilly white lace cap sat jauntily behind her jet black fringe of bangs. Kate couldn't help noticing the appreciative stare Reese gave her as she walked away. Like the one he'd given Erika Weston at the gym.

Well, she chided herself, *what red-blooded man wouldn't?* She pushed the thought aside.

In the background, the clear, pure tones of AJ's clarinet, accompanied by a young man on the piano, filtered across the room in a haunting melody.

"The adagio from Mozart's 'Clarinet Concerto,'" Kate told Reese when the waitress was finally out of sight.

"You know your music," said Reese, leaning back and giving Kate an amused smile.

"My parents wanted me to play an instrument. Said it would round out my education. I hate to think how much they spent on piano lessons."

"Not money well spent?"

"Well, I play a really cool 'Chop Sticks.' That was the closest to Chopin I could get."

Reese laughed; then they gave themselves up to the music for a while. At length, Reese said, "Mozart is a fitting background for 'The Legend of the Talisman Rose.'"

"Legend? Did Miss Baker tell it to your English class?"

"Miss Baker?" For a moment Reese looked confused. Then he chuckled. "Yes, she did. The girls loved it and the boys pretended to hate it. It was supposed to be tragic, but was really kind of inane—the usual story of a beautiful girl named Rose who was in love with a poor gardener who tended the roses."

Kate broke in. "But her father tries to force her to marry a wealthy land-owner. Poor Rose refuses and in her distress, throws herself over the cliff."

"Hey, you've heard it."

"No, but those legends seem to have similar themes."

"Didn't I say it was inane?"

"I prefer your version of Miss Baker always keeping one rose on her desk." Kate smiled. "And encouraging her most promising student."

Reese reached across the table and squeezed Kate's hand. "Me, too." He lowered his voice. "Especially the part about the Talisman rose whispering wonderful memories."

~~~

That was close, Reese thought as the server brought their food. *I almost forgot I'd told Kate the Miss Baker version of the whispering Talisman. That's the same one I told Lenae Maddox. She ate it up.*

Thinking of Lenae reminded Reese of Saturday night. He looked at the fingers that were squeezing Kate's and remembered how they had felt around Lenae's throat. His hand stilled as a tremor of fear fluttered in his stomach.

I wasn't trying to kill her. But who will believe that if she comes out of her coma and points a finger at me?

Reese consoled himself with the reminder of how unlikely it was that

Lenae Maddox would ever open her eyes—or her mouth—again.

~~~

In an ICU room at Coronado Hospital, an oxygen machine worked at full capacity. The heart monitor graph was almost flat, and the blips much too far apart. The movement of Lenae Maddox's chest was barely visible to nurse Nancy Foster at her bedside.

~~~

AJ and the pianist had switched gears. From Mozart, the music flowed into a medley from "Fiddler on the Roof."

"If I were a rich man..." Reese Sutherland sang along in a low, melodic voice, moving his shoulders back and forth in a sensual imitation of Reb Tevye, the irrepressible father in the Broadway play and movie. "...Ya ha deedle deedle, bubba bubba—"

"Reese!" Kate slapped at Reese's arm. She was relieved that the romantic moment had passed. She hardly knew what to do with it. "Stop!" She scolded. "People are looking at us!"

A young woman at a nearby table giggled, proving Kate's point.

"Oookay." He put on a playful pout and stabbed a cherry tomato with his fork and pointed it at her. "If you insist."

"I insist."

AJ's notes moved to the haunting tones of "Anatevka," the tearful closing number of "Fiddler." Kate felt the smile die on her lips. Two disparate images implanted themselves in her mind. Her Jewish husband Joel lying dead in a Columbian jungle. And Lenae Maddox possibly dying in a Coronado hospital.

"What's wrong?" Reese asked.

"Huh?"

"You went off into la-la land there for a minute."

"Oh, sorry. I guess I did."

"Do you have another date after I take you home?" he teased.

Kate rolled her eyes and shook her head. "It's nothing important."

"If it's spoiling your enjoyment of my singing talents, it's important. Tell me."

Kate hesitated. Then, since she wasn't accustomed to being indirect, she looked straight at Reese and said, "The music made me think of ..." She couldn't mention her thoughts of Joel. No need to be *that* direct. "... of Lenae Maddox."

Reese became still, so still that Kate thought he was angry. He recovered so quickly she thought her imagination must be on overdrive.

"Don't be so sad, Kate," he said. "With all the modern medical advances, she has a good chance of recovery."

Kate wondered why his words seemed insincere.

~~~

Nurse Foster had stood by Ms. Maddox's bed in Room Three for several minutes before going back to her station to finish some paperwork before her shift ended. In the middle of filling in some information for another patient, she heard a beep on the heart monitor that duplicated the one in Room Three.

Oh, no, she thought. Then she saw that the graph was drawing mountains, not tiny hillocks, and that Lenae Maddox's heartbeat had become almost steady.

Springing from her chair, Nurse Foster buzzed for the doctor on duty, then ran to Room Three.

~~~

AJ coaxed out the last swinging notes of "String of Pearls" from her clarinet. As Kate and Reese were pushing aside their now-empty dishes, Kate's cell phone sounded the text message tone. She started to ignore it, but something told her to at least see who it was from. Besides, Reese was engrossed in studying the dessert menu. She got the phone out of her purse.

After a few seconds, she caught her breath.

Reese looked up from the menu. "What is it?"

"I got a text from Cami."

"Again? That's the second time she—"

"Reese! It's great news. Lenae Maddox's vital signs are much better."

Reese didn't reply for a moment. Then he cleared his throat and said,

"That's wonderful. Is she awake?"

Kate looked down at the rather lengthy text message from Cami. "No, she's still on oxygen, and she hasn't gained consciousness, but they hope that will happen soon."

"Really? Soon, you say?"

"Yes. And when she wakes up, she can tell the police who tried to strangle her!"

"You're right. That will be ... great, won't it?" Reese wrapped his fingers around Kate's.

Just then, the shapely waitress arrived with a tray of coffee. As Reese turned toward her, his arm hit the tray. Hot, dark liquid spilled onto Kate's white blouse.

Kate shrieked, shoved her chair back, and jumped up.

"Oh, no!" the waitress wailed. "I didn't mean—"

Reese interrupted her. "My fault. I bumped your arm." To Kate he said, "What an ox I am. I'm so sorry. Looks like we're going to have to leave without dessert."

Deflated, Kate gave her blouse a useless wipe with her napkin, then gathered her things to leave.

AJ had switched musical styles again. Now she was playing the melancholy theme melody from "Phantom of the Opera."

Chapter Fifty-One

ॐ

She's been in a coma since Friday night, Mike Jenkins thought, getting a soda from the refrigerator in his kitchen. *Three days.*

Mike knew people often remained in comas for long periods, then recovered; but he had trouble taking comfort in that fact. Gone was the glimmer of hope he'd sensed from Cami Carrington's assurance that Lenae was in God's hands. He kept wishing Lenae had called for him rather than Mrs. Carrington, though there was no real reason she should.

One thing Mike refused to do was let himself fall into the funk he'd experienced after Melanie's death. He had a business to run, people depending on him. So, although Lenae was on his mind during every waking and sleeping thought, he had forced himself to go to his office this morning and bury himself in his work. Now it was a little past ten-thirty p.m., and he felt he had to be near Lenae.

Knowing it was a stupid thing to do—and not normally inclined to stupid acts–Mike made a snap decision. He was going to the hospital.

Chapter Fifty-Two

 ∂

Coronado police officer Lenny Black, clad in his dark blue uniform, stood guard outside Lenae Maddox's room. Earlier the room and hallway had been abuzz with nurses and doctors exclaiming over the way Ms. Maddox was beginning to rally. Though she'd muttered two words—the name Cami and something unintelligible to a young male visitor—she had not fully regained consciousness. Also, she still required the help of the oxygen machine, but the general atmosphere was hopeful.

Now, eleven-oh-four by Lenny's watch, the hall was quiet. No one was in sight. At this hour Lenny guessed that not even that Mike Jenkins guy would try to get in to see Ms. Maddox. Lenny fidgeted. Not only was he sleepy, but he needed desperately to go to the restroom. He opened Ms. Maddox's door far enough to see that everything seemed to be okay. Closing the door, he looked down the quiet hall to the Men's Room sign.

I'll be quick, he thought.

~~~

In her half world, Lenae had learned to recognize certain sounds, one of them being the slight squeak her door made. Now she was marginally aware of the sound and anticipated someone entering. A second squeak told her the door had been shut again, but she could tell no one had come in.

~~~

Mike had managed to sneak into the hospital and make his way to the stairs. All the way over, one fact had kept repeating itself through his mind.

She doesn't know I love her. I never told her. What if I never get the chance?

She doesn't know I love her. I never told...

Taking the stairs two at a time in the dim stairwell, he thought, *I have to see her. Somehow I've got to get past that guard. I've got to tell her I love her. Maybe she'll hear me and maybe she won't. But I've got to try.*

Chapter Fifty-Three

&

I'll have to be quick, Reese Sutherland told himself as the guard neared the Men's Room. He left the shadowed area where he'd been waiting for the right moment and quietly entered Lenae Maddox's room.

~~~

Lenae sensed a presence. An evil presence. Terror pressed on her chest and throat. For the first time since the attack, she managed to force her eyes open. Trembling inside, she looked toward the intruder.

Reese!

Reese looked her full in the face and grinned.

No! No! Lenae tried to scream as Reese bent toward the wall beside her bed.

~~~

Less than a minute after he'd entered, Reese left the room and headed for the door leading to the back stairs.

Inside Room Three, the oxygen machine sighed to a stop.

Chapter Fifty-Four

ॐ

Mike knew his chances of carrying out his plan to get past the guard were slim to none. Well, he'd faced impossible odds before. He had to try. At Lenae's floor, he reached out to the door to the hall.

It flew open, hitting him on the head. Stunned, he fell hard against the wall, then to the floor, hitting his head again.

Someone rushed past him and clattered down the stairs.

~~~

There. That didn't take long. Lenny Black congratulated himself as he left the Men's Room. The self-congratulation stopped when he saw Lenae Maddox's door wide open. Lenny's heart plummeted to his feet.

He ran in. The heart monitor. Barely blipping. Almost a flat line. Frantically, he jerked the emergency cord several times and turned to run out and yell for a nurse.

Wait. What's that? An unplugged cord! The oxygen machine!

Lenny dove for the floor.

~~~

Hand pressed against the side of his head, Mike struggled to his feet. His hand felt sticky.

Blood! his dazed brain told him.

He hardly knew what had happened; he just knew he had to get to Lenae. Somehow that seemed a desperate need now.

Whoever had knocked him down with the door had also left it

ajar. Mike steadied himself against the frame and stumbled out into the hallway.

"There he is!"

Someone was shouting. The noise hurt Mike's head. He leaned against the wall, trying to will himself to stand straight.

"Get him before he gets away!"

The same voice. Shouting again. What was going on?

Mike looked up to see two burly orderlies and a policeman bearing down on him. He felt like he should try to run, but when he turned, he faltered. The orderlies grabbed him and pushed him back against the wall.

"You stay right here, buddy," one of them growled. "Don't even think of trying to get away. More police are on their way right now and they're going to be on you like Elmer's on glue."

Mike opened his mouth to speak and hardly recognized the sound that came out. "Lenae," he croaked. "Lenae."

"What's he talkin' about?" the second orderly asked.

"Ms. Maddox," Mike slurred. "How is Ms. Maddox?"

"He's talking about that woman he tried to kill." Mike recognized that voice as the first orderly. "Two times," the orderly added. "Be a miracle if she makes it."

Mike's vision blurred. Blood streaming down his neck and soaking his shirt, he slumped to his knees.

Chapter Fifty-Five

&

"So we meet again, Detective," Mike's words to Detective Lopez held no pleasure.

"So we do," Lopez's tone matched Mike's.

The detective slapped a file folder shut. Keeping his face devoid of expression, he looked at the man across the desk from him in his CPD office.

Lopez had been dead asleep when the phone rang about 11:15 last night, the first time in days he'd made it to bed before one a.m. He'd heard Ella, his wife, groan before turning over. She was used to his late-night calls.

Lenny Black, who had supposedly been guarding Lenae Maddox's room, apologized for waking Mike, then haltingly explained the situation, including his own part.

Before Lopez could blast him, Black went on to say that Mike Jenkins was being kept overnight because of his head wounds.

"Should I go ahead and arrest him, Sir? Disturbing the peace, maybe?"

If the situation had not been so serious, Lopez might have felt sorry for Lenny Black. Instead, he railed at the young officer with a few choice words before calming down enough to say, "Don't arrest him. Sounds like he's a victim not the perp, at least in this case. And, Officer Black..."

"Yes, Detective?" The man was clearly forcing himself to use a steady tone.

"In an hour or so, your replacement will show up. Do you think you can suppress your ... urges until then?"

"Y-yes sir."

"Make sure you do, and report to me tomorrow afternoon. I'll have the hospital tell Jenkins to come to my office as soon as he's released."

Muttering angry words to himself, Lopez had made the call to the hospital, then snuggled back under the covers and was asleep in seconds.

Now, though only eight-thirty this Tuesday morning, Mike Jenkins had already been answering Lopez's questions for half an hour. An hour ago, he'd declared himself able to leave the hospital, checked himself out, and headed straight to the police station. The top of his head was wrapped in a wide white bandage, his shirt was dark with blood stains, and he looked a little pale; but Lopez guessed he was a tough cookie and would be fine.

Lopez leaned back in his chair and gave Jenkins a long, steady stare. "So tell me again what you were doing at the hospital at eleven o'clock last night."

Jenkins let out a ragged sigh of resignation. "For the tenth time, I wanted to try to talk to Lenae Maddox. I've been seeing her."

"Seeing her?" What does that mean?"

"I already told you—"

"Tell me again."

Another sigh. "We've been dating for about six months. And, again for the tenth time, yes, our relationship was intimate. And yes, I knew she was also seeing someone else. She never kept that from me."

"And this 'someone else'? You mean to tell me you didn't try to find out who?"

"No. Up until recently I was okay with our arrangement."

"Gave you space to pursue ... other interests as well, huh?"

Mike shrugged and looked unhappy. "Yeah."

Lopez let that go. He opened the folder again and took his time looking at the papers inside. He had already made himself well familiar with each one, but he wanted Jenkins to squirm a little. Instead, the man's rugged face kept its unmoving granite-like expression.

After a couple of minutes, Lopez held up one sheet of paper. "I thought your name sounded familiar when I talked with you at Ms. Maddox's loft yesterday. I see you're the owner of MelJen Industries."

"That's right."

"Widowed, I see. No children."

"Right. My wife died eleven years ago, in childbirth. Baby boy died, too."

"So now, along with who knows how many other women, you're

dating Lenae Maddox, whom you've gotten pregnant, by the way."

"I told you, the baby isn't—in fact couldn't be—mine. I was out of the country at the time she would have conceived. And, no, I don't know who the father is. I never asked the name of the other man she was seeing. She only told me about the baby a few nights ago."

"And you reacted by—"

"I was upset."

"Only upset?"

"Okay, I was furious, not to mention confused, hurt—"

"Jealous."

"Jealous. Sure. I'd gone to Lenae's loft to tell her that in those weeks I was away I realized I was in love with her. Wanted to marry her."

"Then she tells you she's pregnant with another man's child. Didn't set too well, did it?"

"Of course not." For the first time in the interview, Mike raised his voice. "Of course not! I left mad, okay?" He lowered his voice to a whisper, and his eyes became moist. "She was crying her heart out. I left anyway." He pressed his fist against his moist eyes. "As I've told you before, I took a moment on the way out to look at the card attached to the rose on the table."

"And?" Lopez knew the answer, but he wanted to hear Jenkins say it again.

"All it said was 'R.'"

A ring from Lopez's phone interrupted the interview. The detective picked up the receiver.

"Lopez here."

"It's Pitt, at the hospital."

George Pitt, who often accompanied Lopez when he needed a back-up, was on morning guard duty at Lenae Maddox's room. Lopez wasn't sure who would replace Lenny Black, for tonight's late shift. Seemed like a nice enough young man, but he was certain to receive disciplinary action.

"What is it, Pitt? I'm in the middle of an interview."

"I think you better get down here. Some annoying guy calling himself Dexter is wanting to get into Ms. Maddox's room."

"Don't see why you needed to call me about that. You should be able to handle it."

"I thought so, too, but he's raising such a stink that I thought you might want me to bring him in."

"Okay. Arrest him for disturbing the peace and bring him to me." Lopez cut the call.

Jenkins stared at Lopez for a moment. When he spoke again, his tone strengthened. Now he sounded like a man used to giving orders. "Look, Detective, I've told you everything. I know it looks bad, that you're considering me a 'person of interest'—even when you should be trying to find out who slammed me with the door in his rush to get away. That's your man."

"Believe me, Jenkins, we are not ignoring that angle."

"And what about the guy I saw leaving Lenae's place? He was mad as a hornet that she wouldn't let him in."

"Oh, we thought we'd ignore that little detail." Lopez hoped his deadpan expression didn't reveal that he hadn't yet learned who that person was.

"Very funny," Mike said, his expression matching Lopez's. "So, for the second time in three days, am I under arrest? If not, my head is killing me. I'd like to go home and rest."

"You can go, Jenkins. One of the officers will drive you to your car. For now—for the second time in three days—don't leave town." He paused, giving greater impact to his next instruction. "And don't even put your little toe anywhere near that hospital."

A stony-faced Mike left without bidding Lopez good-bye.

Chapter Fifty-Six

❧

"Mrs. Carrington, this is Detective Lopez."
Cami had been singing little praise songs almost non-stop all morning and thanking the Lord for the improvement in Lenae Maddox's condition. Now this. A call from Detective Lopez could not mean good news.

"Oh, um, good morning, Detective."

"Mrs. Carrington, I have something to tell you."

"Please, please say it isn't bad."

"It's not good." Detective Lopez paused as if reluctant to continue. "I, I thought you'd want someone to tell you. Late last night, someone managed to sneak into Ms. Maddox's room and unplug her oxygen machine."

"Oh no!" Cami felt as if the detective had slammed her in the chest with a hammer. "Is she, is she—"

"No, she's not dead, but she's at least as bad off as she was before."

Cami sat down hard in a kitchen chair. "Oh, Detective!" she wailed. "Who, oh who, could have done such a thing?"

"I wish I knew. You can be sure, though—we'll catch him."

"Or her."

"Or her."

Cami took a deep, shuddering breath. "Well, Detective, God is still in control. I'm trusting Him to help you find that, that— whoever did it."

Cami replaced the phone in its cradle on the wall of her blue and yellow kitchen that combined state-of-the art equipment with a cheery atmosphere. Though she employed Edith Stern as live-in housekeeper/cook, she still enjoyed preparing many meals herself. Now, however, her mind was far from food.

Another murder attempt on Lenae! I can't believe it.

Agitated, Cami flung open the french doors that led to the sunroom and stepped through. She moved to one of the large windows that looked out onto a magnolia tree in the backyard. Early in her marriage to Braxton, he had humored her by letting her plant the tree that reminded her of the ones in her yard back in North Carolina. Usually she loved admiring the large glossy leaves on the spreading limbs, but now her mind was not on magnolias. Instead she wondered why Lenae Maddox's situation had touched her so deeply. She'd only met the woman twice before the attack on the beach; and the only common ground she knew of was their mutual interest in art.

Pushing a strand of hair behind one ear, she turned from the window and caught sight of her Bible. She had brought it from the den this morning, and it lay on a table next to one of the comfortable wicker chairs in the pleasant sunroom. She walked to it and ran her fingers over the name engraved in gold on the right-hand corner: *Camilla Leigh Stewart*, her maiden name.

The Bible had been a high school graduation gift from her parents. For years it lay on a bedside table, not completely neglected, but certainly not read often. Even at her Christian college in North Carolina, she'd taken only the required Bible classes, much preferring to focus on drama and art. And a full social life.

Well, at least I kept attending church regularly after Braxton and I got married, she excused herself. *And I always made sure the twins went, too. I even changed denominations and went to the Carrington family's church. Not that Braxton went himself any more often than was necessary to keep up a good front.* She picked up the Bible. *Well, he did go more often after he decided to run for mayor of Coronado.*

Cami shook off that thought and remembered how after Braxton's death she had found herself turning to the little Bible every morning, sometimes highlighting verses that touched her heart. During the month-long motorhome trip, she and Kate often read together Sometimes Kate explained certain passages from her more intense studies over the years. At other times, Cami recalled points gleaned from college Bible classes and from the church she'd grown up in and where, as a twelve-year-old, she'd made a decision to follow Christ.

Now she opened the Bible. Before she'd read more than a few verses, Lenae's face seemed to superimpose itself over the words.

Chapter Fifty-Seven

❧

"Someone got into Lenae's room? How in the world did that happen?" Kate asked Cami, who had called on Kate's lunch break with the bad news.

"The guard left her door long enough to go the Men's Room."

"I wouldn't want to be him today."

"Me either. I almost feel sorry for him. Enough of that for now. You haven't told me much about your date with Reese last night."

"Up until you texted, it was, well, memorable."

"Oh, Kate. I'm sorry. I shouldn't have bothered you. Sometimes I don't think."

"I'm the one who's sorry. I'm glad you told me about Lenae. I didn't mean that to sound like a rebuke."

"No offense taken."

"You know how Reese has sent me Talisman roses several times?"

"Uh-huh."

"The night we ate at Peohe's he told me his high school English teacher used to keep one Talisman rose on her desk at all times. And last night, we joked about a legend about them. He says that Talisman roses represent memories."

"Memories. I like that. What about you and Reese, Kate? Are you hoping to establish memories with him?"

Kate thought for a moment. "I wouldn't go that far. I like him a lot. He's wonderful company, fun to be with, intelligent."

"Not to mention good looking," Cami put in.

"That, too. But..."

"But?"

"Well, at times I get an uneasy feeling about him."

"In what way?"

"It's hard to put my finger on, but once in a while I wonder if he's really saying what he means."

"Makes me think of when I was dating Braxton and had a teeny weeny bit of doubt. You told me it was a 'check in my spirit,' that it came from God and I shouldn't ignore it."

"Hmmm."

"As we both know, I did ignore it. Completely. And things weren't all bad for Braxton and me. I loved him desperately, and he gave me the two most beautiful children in the world."

Kate couldn't help laughing. "Spoken like a true mother."

"Have you talked with Gunnar lately?"

"Not since I called to tell him about Lenae. The time before that, our conversation didn't go well. This time I made the call short and sweet."

Cami grinned. "Just the facts, ma'am, huh?"

"You watch too many old re-runs. You sound like Jack Webb on 'Dragnet.' That was already old when you and I were kids. I bet your parents watched it. Not mine of course. Too frivolous for them."

"A little bit of frivolity is okay now and then," Cami said. "It doesn't hurt to be silly and impractical once in a while."

Reese's exact words, Kate thought. She set aside that "teeny weeny bit of doubt" that Cami had mentioned and thought of how Reese had told her he wanted to make up for how badly last night's date had ended. He was taking her somewhere really special tonight. Kate rarely went out on a school night, preferring to make sure she was completely caught up with grading papers and going over her plans for the next day's classes.

How silly and impractical of me, she thought with a little smile.

Wednesday, November 10

Chapter Fifty-Eight

❧

Lopez was back at his desk in what he thought may be the country's most stunning police department, with its low Spanish-style building fronted by three arches and set among palms and one or two other trees. Ordinarily, he enjoyed looking out the window at the meticulously cared-for grounds. Today, after a full morning of interviews concerning Lenae Maddox's attack, frustration tempered his enjoyment this afternoon. His eyes glazed over the roses edging the property, while his mind drifted to the interviews he'd conducted today.

First, soon after Mike Jenkins left his office, twenty-year-old Dexter Driscoll was brought in. The young man was so strung up with anxiety that half Lopez's time was spent trying to calm him down. In the end, he gleaned two pieces of information: one, that Dexter actually considered Ms. Maddox his best friend, and two, that the young man was fully convinced that Mike Jenkins was the father of her child and was the one who'd attacked her both times. Nothing Lopez could say would convince him that the second statement was unlikely seeing that Mike himself had been hurt as the supposed perpetrator ran off.

Next Lopez had driven to Grant Lauder University. There he spoke with several faculty members, as well as a few students. Nothing concrete had come through. Ms. Maddox had always been friendly enough, everyone said, but kept mostly to herself. No one knew of anyone with a grudge against her.

The same couldn't be said of Dr. Reese Sutherland. If it were an attack on him rather than Lenae Maddox that Lopez was investigating, he'd put Dr. Alfred Bainbridge at the top of the list. Lopez had learned that Sutherland had been appointed head of the Law Department over Bainbridge. Interesting, but the dapper little professor seemed to have no connection with Lenae Maddox beyond normal interaction at the university.

As for Sutherland, with his athletic good looks and charm, he'd certainly be the kind of man a young woman might be attracted to. And he had the right initial: "R". He had expressed genuine-sounding indignation over Lenae's attack. That meant next to nothing to Lopez, but Sutherland's alibi did. He had spent the early part of the evening at a gym right here in Coronado, with Kate Elfmon, no less. Later he'd gone to the university and worked in his office until midnight, facts confirmed by Kate Elfmon and the security guard, respectively. Lopez instinctively disliked Sutherland. The man was several shades too sure of himself and his charm, but that didn't make him a suspect. Too bad.

Unfortunately, neither Ms. Maddox's computer and cell phone had been of help. Her few emails were all either school related or junk mail.

Smart girl. Maybe she took heed of all the trouble some well-known and very stupid politicians have gotten into recently because of emails.

Lopez kept coming back to Mike Jenkins as a suspect, but some mismatched facts and gut instinct always stopped him.

His stomach growled. No wonder. It was two o'clock, and this was getting him nowhere. Might as well get a bite to eat. He rolled back his chair and was about to rise, when his gaze went to a manila folder on the desk. It held a copy of the watercolor painting he'd retrieved from Lenae Maddox's loft. Without knowing why, but trusting those gut instincts, he picked it up and took it with him.

~~~

The Coronado Ferry Landing's Market Place shops were frequented mostly by out-of-town visitors, but Cami Carrington liked the quaint, colorful atmosphere. Besides, her favorite island boutique, Robin's Byrd Cage, owned and operated by her friend Robin Byrd, was there. Cami had steered a number of island residents to Robin.

This afternoon, in an attempt to put aside deep concern for Lenae Maddox for a little while, Cami had driven to "The Cage." She knew Robin was back from her weekend trip to San Francisco. Finding a wonderful periwinkle blue cashmere twin set, matching "bling" jewelry, and two trendy belts had helped a little.

"I always know I'll find something I like here," Cami told Robin as she paid for her purchases.

"May that never cease," said Robin, dressed in a black broomstick skirt and a silk blouse in the signature red that she wore to remind her customers of the name of the red-breasted bird whose name she shared.

"But now I'm starved," Cami told her. "Want to join me for a late lunch?"

"Love to, but my assistant is about to leave to run a personal errand, so I'd better take a rain check."

"Okay, but you'll be sorry you missed out on Taco Bell."

"Not going to Il Fornaio's or Peohe's?"

"Not today. I'm in the mood for plain ol' rolled tacos."

"You and your rolled tacos. Don't know how you keep so skinny." Robin patted her own slightly round tummy.

A few minutes later, having stowed her purchases in Braxton's Jag, Cami crossed the street to the restaurant that housed KFC and Taco Bell. She ordered five rolled tacos piled high with guacamole and sour cream, then looked around for a seat.

"Detective Lopez!" she said, spotting the detective at a window seat. Though other places were available, she walked to Lopez's table. "May I join you?"

"Please do." The detective gave her a genuine smile and rose while she placed her food on the table. Eying her pile of tacos, he said, "Do you plan to eat all that?"

"Every bite. I'm a taco-holic. Hope you weren't thinking I'd share with you."

Lopez laughed. "Taco-holic. That's a new one. And I have plenty to eat, thank you." He indicated his nearly empty plate of chicken and biscuits.

"Mind if I thank the Lord for my food?" Cami asked when she was seated.

"Please do," Lopez said again. "I like to do the same thing."

Cami bowed her head and silently thanked God for the food, the beautiful sunny day, and her successful shopping. Then she prayed aloud a few words for Lenae Maddox's recovery and for Lopez to discover her attacker.

"Thanks," Lopez said when Cami raised her head.

At first Cami avoided the subject of Lenae Maddox and chatted with Lopez about everyday subjects, including his artsy wife and their three teenage children. She liked the way this hard-nosed detective's eyes grew soft but proud when he spoke of "my Ella" or one of their children.

After a while, she couldn't avoid the subject uppermost in her mind another second. Wiping a bit of sour cream from her lips, she became serious and told Lopez, "I'm so glad you're investigating Lenae Maddox's attacks."

Lopez eyed Cami with speculation. "All this has to be hard on you. Especially coming so close after..."

Cami gave a remorseful shrug and answered simply, "It was. I don't know if I ever told you how grateful I'll always be for how you handled all that...mess...first with Braxton, then with Debra. Firm and thorough, but caring." She paused. "I know you can't talk about your investigation much, but have you had any success?"

His grin disappeared and he shook his head. "Not as much as I'd like." Then he brightened. "Hey, you may be able to help me with something." He picked up a manila envelope lying near his plate and started to extract a sheet of paper.

"Hey, Cami!" Robin Byrd's cheerful voice rang out. "My assistant is already back. Did you leave a few rolled tacos for me?"

"Ha! Go get your own."

Lopez slid the paper back into the envelope.

Thursday, November 11

Chapter Fifty-Nine

&

"Hello, Erika."

Erika recognized the strong masculine voice at once. With a mixture of nervousness and guilty pleasure, she pressed the phone closer to her ear. "Reese!"

"Look, I'll get right to the point. I have an unexpected afternoon free and thought you might like to join me for a bite to eat."

"I-I don't know, Reese. Stan wouldn't like it, I'm sure."

"Now why would Stan mind your having lunch with a friend?"

"You know better than that. Not only would he be furious at me for going out with another man, but as I said the other night, I get the feeling there's bad blood between the two of you. Something to do with when you were both in Boston."

"We aren't the best of friends, I admit, but it's nothing for you to worry about. Besides, who's going to tell him?"

"Um..." Erika thought of how Stan had once hired a detective to follow her.

"Nobody, that's who," Reese said. "Especially if we choose an out-of-the way place."

In the few seconds that she hesitated, several conflicting thoughts whirled through Erika's head.

After all that horror with Braxton, I promised Stan I'd be a good, faithful wife...

Well, I have been. Not once have I gone out with someone else since I made that promise...

Meeting Reese at the boatyard was accidental, and seeing him on the night of my birthday party was unplanned...

Reese is so charming and good looking...

Stan is so bald and fat and old...

I'm only twenty-five. I deserve a little fun with someone near my age...

It would only be lunch.

"So, how about it, Erika?"

"I'd love to have lunch with you."

"Great. I know the perfect spot. In Del Mar, there's a quaint little inn that has a small dining room."

"Sounds wonderful." Erika put aside the fleeting suspicion that at some time Reese had taken someone else to the "quaint little inn."

"And Del Mar's about forty-five minutes from the Cays," Reese continued. "It's 11:30. How soon can you leave?"

Without further hesitation, Erika gave Reese a cheerful "Give me the address. I'll be there in an hour."

After hanging up with Reese, Erika called Stan. "There's a great a sale at that little boutique I like up at North County Fair mall in Escondido. I'm heading up there right now and may not be back by dinner time."

"I know you and your shopping sprees." Stan chuckled. "I won't look for you before the mall closes."

Perfect, Erika thought, pleased that Stan had agreed so quickly and even had unwittingly given her plenty of time with Reese. *I'm sure he wouldn't hire a detective to follow me again.*

Erika shouldn't have been so sure.

~~~

The Del Mar inn was as charming as Reese had said it was. Their table, covered in blue linen and nestled next to a huge clear-glass window, offered a breathtaking view of the white-sanded beach, the blue-green waves rolling in from the ocean, and the brilliant winter sky above. Even the food was perfect, the shrimp heavenly.

So, what's wrong? she asked herself. *Why does everything feel so... so flat?*

Reese seemed to sense her unease and put on a heavy dose of charm. He complimented the emerald green silk blouse she'd worn.

"Matches those matchless eyes," he said.

She attempted a seductive look with those eyes, but only managed a quick, weak smile.

"Okay, so that was corny," he joked. "But here's something that isn't." He reached out and slipped one finger into a thick red curl that had fallen across her cheek. "There are women who'd give up their last chocolate bar for your hair."

"Thanks," she said with another weak smile. "Thanks, too, for the rose." She had laid the rose across the middle of the table. Now she caressed one silky golden-coral petal. "It's fabulous."

"I hope it makes up for the one Stan destroyed."

Why had she told Reese that? She wished she hadn't, but what could she say now except, "Oh, sure. It does." She cleared her throat and repeated, "It's fabulous."

He gave her that lopsided grin that had nearly stopped her heart the first time she saw him. It still did. In a way. So, what was wrong?

"You already said that," he told her.

"Huh?"

"You already said the rose was fabulous."

"Well, some things bear repeating, don't they?" She went back to concentrating on her shrimp salad.

At last, the meal finished and the server paid, Reese slid the rose nearer to Erika. Then, with a sensual lift of his brows, he cocked his head toward the steps leading upstairs. "I've reserved a room overlooking the beach."

"No." Erika's words came out with such force that Reese shrunk back. She had figured why she was in such a funk.

Reese's brows dropped and drew together. "No?"

"No."

"Why not?" The disbelief on his face was almost funny. "You seemed willing enough when we spoke on the phone."

"Well, I've changed my mind." Erika lifted her chin.

"What's wrong, honey?" he sneered. "Got a sudden case of jitters?"

"I prefer to call it a sudden case of loyalty. I don't want to do this to Stan. I don't want to hurt him. I know he wouldn't do anything to hurt me."

Reese caught her wrist and squeezed it in his strong fingers. "I wouldn't be so sure if I were you," he said.

Reese's face had such a knowing look, it frightened Erika. She jerked her wrist free and rubbed it back and forth with her other hand. "What do you mean?"

"What do you know about the death of the eminent Dr. Stan Weston's first wife?"

"Margo Cramer? She had a heart attack. Stan didn't do anything to her."

"You don't think so? Why don't you ask him?"

For a moment Erika couldn't speak. She felt as if all the breath had been sucked from her body. *Get a hold of yourself,* she thought, forcing herself to breathe again. "I don't know what you're talking about, Reese." She pushed her chair back. "I'm leaving."

She was glad that she'd driven herself to the inn and didn't have to depend on Reese to get her home. She picked up the Talisman rose, tossed it on the floor, and left.

Friday, November 12

Chapter Sixty

✌

"**L**ucas Richards here, Dr. Weston."

The tone of the African American detective's voice on the phone didn't sound encouraging to Stan. He'd been careful not to question Erika last night when she came in around ten o'clock. That was about the right hour to have stayed at North County Fair mall till it closed, then drive back to Coronado Cays. His gorgeous flame-haired wife was loaded down with several shopping bags, but didn't act as excited as usual to show off her purchases.

In fact, she'd acted off-key all evening. Several times he caught her staring at him with an odd expression he couldn't read, though he feared it somehow involved Reese Sutherland. The thought that Erika may have been with Reese earlier in the day made him crazy with jealousy. Also, what if Reese told Erika about how Margo died? No, he wouldn't do that. It would implicate him, too.

Though he needed to get up early for surgeries, he waited until he was sure Erika was asleep, then looked through the receipts she had thrown down amongst the perfume bottles and scattering of cosmetics and jewelry on her dressing table. Yes, each of the stores had a branch at North County Fair, which was several miles inland, off Interstate 15, but none of Erika's purchases had come from there. They were all from Horton Plaza, a funky mall off Interstate 5, which ran by the coast. Also, the earliest time recorded on the receipts was five-twelve p.m. Erika had left the house before noon.

She had lied to him—again. But he wanted concrete proof from Detective Richards before confronting her. He was glad he'd had Richards start following Erika the day after her birthday party.

Now, at ten-thirty a.m., Stan had already performed two cosmetic surgeries: an eyelid lift on an aging movie star, who'd come down from Beverly Hills, and a thigh liposuction on a local woman. He felt good about the outcome of both procedures. He wished he felt good about the conversation he was about to have with Lucas Richards.

"So what did you find?" he asked the detective. "Where did she go before Horton Plaza?" He explained how he knew about the location of Erika's shopping expedition.

"She went to a little inn at Del Mar."

"Not alone, I'm sure."

"No, Doctor. She met a man there."

Despite his certainty that Richards' report would be like this, Stan felt like he'd been kicked in the stomach. Controlling his voice as much as possible, he asked, "Good looking? GQ-type blonde?"

"That's right. The two had lunch together at the inn's dining room."

"And then?"

"I'm embarrassed to tell you this, Dr. Weston, but I got an urgent call from my wife and stepped away for about three minutes. When I came back, Mrs. Weston and her gentleman friend were gone."

"Gone? Where?"

"I don't know for sure. I'm still kicking myself. But I was able to see the man's name on the room register when I asked the desk clerk for some info about the inn."

"Sutherland. Reese Sutherland."

"Right."

"Well, how long did they stay upstairs?"

"Again, I can't say. My wife's call was about our son. He fell at school and hit his head on a cement block. He was unconscious and had been rushed to the hospital. As soon as I saw Sutherland's name on the guest register, I left."

"And your son?"

"He got a bad concussion, but thankfully will be okay."

"Well, you had to do what you had to do."

"I got a few photos before I left. They're pretty innocent."

"I'll be the judge of that. Can you bring them by the clinic today?"

"Will do," said Richards. "By the way, there's one other thing."

Feeling as though he couldn't take "one other thing," Stan said, "Well?"

"Sutherland brought her a rose. Long-stemmed. Kind of gold colored."

"Only one?"

"Only one."

Chapter Sixty-One

ℰ

Clad in dark blue sweat pants, hoodie, and running shoes, Kate breathed in the cold, salty air as she took a run down Ocean Boulevard, which ran in front of the beach and past Cami's mansion. At 6:30 on this November morning, the air was chilly, the iron-grey water rough and angry looking. Kate hummed along and ran in rhythm with the upbeat tune coming from her iPhone. She often listened to praise music as she ran, but Reese had downloaded a recent Coldplay album for her, and that was her choice today. She hummed and smiled. Smiled and hummed. And thought of tonight's date with Reese. They planned to attend a comedy at the island's Lamb's Theater. She tried not to spoil her cheerful mood by examining the excitement she felt in Reese Sutherland's company while still deeply caring for Gunnar Volstad.

But...*Face it*, she thought. *How can I help comparing the two men?*

Gunnar had eased into her life over a period of a few months after they met at church. Reese had swept in like...like a tsunami. Gunnar had steadily wooed her with telephone calls, Red Sox games, church outings, walking tours of historic Boston. She had enjoyed it all. Still... in the two weeks since she had known Reese, he had already taken her to two pricey restaurants—Peohe's and La Jolla's Georges at the Cove—and, last night, a romantic cruise of San Diego Harbor. Every time they went out, he brought her one perfect long-stemmed Talisman rose. She hated to admit that in comparison to vibrant, exciting Reese Sutherland, good, steady Gunnar Volstad was slightly...ordinary.

She veered away from the beach and approached the back side of the Hotel del Coronado. The white Victorian style, red-roofed hotel rambled over about an acre of land and had been Coronado's best-known landmark and tourist attraction since it opened in 1888. To Kate it would always be the place where Cami's husband Braxton was murdered in the Oceanfront Ballroom.

Not dwelling on that, she concentrated on the song. She passed only a few people, mostly other joggers or people walking their dogs, before stopping at last in front of Café 1134—so named for its address on Orange Street. Only one brave soul, an elderly man, sat at one of the outside tables, gripping a Styrofoam cup with steam rising from it.

Inside the narrow café, a number of islanders occupied tables near the large window, their muted conversations matching the grey sky outside. At the long, curved bar she ordered a large coffee, toasted bagel with cream cheese, and a side of fruit. She took them to the second-level loft, where she was presently the only customer.

As was her custom, before beginning to eat she bowed her head and offered thanks to God for her food and for her health and for this morning, glorious despite overcast skies. She pushed aside the thought that not once had she bowed her head for a blessing when dining with Reese. When she was about half finished with her bagel and fruit, her phone rang. She fished it out of her sweatshirt pocket and looked at the caller ID.

Gunnar. For a moment her feelings skipped from pleasure to guilt to a touch of annoyance. Pleasure won out as she answered cheerfully.

"Good morning, Gunnar."

"Finally." His voice was anything but cheerful, instantly putting a damper on Kate's good mood.

"Finally?"

"Finally. I've lost count of the messages I've left for you in the past few days. And that's not counting the times I ended the call before your voice mail came on."

Kate bristled at his tone. She had planned to call Gunnar today and apologize for not getting back to him sooner, but that intention disappeared like the mist dissipating outside the café window. "Well, you've reached me now," she said. "What was so important?"

"What was so..." Gunnar paused, and Kate imagined him trying to collect himself and recover from surprise at her cool reply.

She waited, not helping him out.

After a few seconds he said, "Kate, what's going on?"

It was Kate's turn to pause. What *was* going on? She wasn't sure she knew.

"It's that *fellow professor*, isn't it?"

"What do you mean?" Kate knew how ridiculous that question sounded.

"You've been going out with him a lot, haven't you?"

Kate hated how that sounded like an accusation, and she hated even more the way she felt she deserved it. Abandoning her usual, level-headed style, she snapped at him. "Yes. I have. Is there a reason I shouldn't?"

She heard him draw in his breath as though he couldn't believe the way she was talking. She was about to relent and apologize, but he cut her off.

"Well, I see you're well occupied out there, so I'm sure you won't be at all upset with what I was calling to tell you."

A premonition of dread hit Kate. She tried to hide it by saying, "And your news?"

"Not news exactly. But I have a business conference in Vancouver next week." He let her digest his words. It didn't take long.

"Vancouver! Isn't there where Natalie transferred to?"

"It is."

"And you plan to call her?"

"I wasn't planning to, even though, as I've told you, she's called and emailed a few times."

Yes, he had told her. He'd been completely open about Natalie's attempts to contact him and his consistent disregarding them—because of Kate.

"I had wanted you to know I was going there, so it wouldn't be a surprise to you. I had planned to let you know I wouldn't be seeing Natalie."

Kate's dread increased. So did her pride. "And now?"

"Now I see I was wrong to think you cared."

She could feel Gunnar waiting for her say she did care, that she didn't want him to see Natalie. And she didn't.

It's just that... Just that what? Just that I'm in love with another man? No. I'm not in love with Reese. Am I? Of course not. I barely know him. Oh, dear Lord, I'm not falling in love with him, am I?

Her confusing thoughts kept her from answering right away, and now Gunnar was saying, "Give me a call sometime, Kate."

She heard the click from his end.

She was still processing her feelings about Gunnar's call when her phone rang again.

Reese! Kate's good mood returned. She greeted Reese with the same cheerful "Good morning" she had given Gunnar. "You're up early," she added.

"No earlier than you. Out jogging already, I bet."

"You got it. And you? Golfing this morning?"

"I was planning to, but I had to cancel. I got a distressing call a few minutes ago."

"Oh! What's wrong?"

"It's my favorite aunt, up in Sacramento. She's scheduled for surgery this afternoon."

"I didn't realize you had relatives there."

"Aunt Bertha is my mother's sister. I've always been close to her. In fact, she's like a second mother to me."

Kate was touched. She wished she could reach out and squeeze Reese's hand. "I'm so sorry," she said.

"Aunt, uh, Bertha fell and broke her hip in several places. Bad breaks. She's in her eighties and really frail. She's begun to have a lot of falls. Also, she's in early stages of Alzheimer's. Anyway, she's in the hospital and has been asking for me. Wants to see me before the surgery."

"You have to go. There's no question about it. Besides the injury, you never know how much longer people with Alzheimer's will recognize you."

"What a woman you are, Kate. That's exactly what I was thinking. If I get up there and she doesn't know who I am...." He let the implication hang.

"Well, I'll pray that doesn't happen." The words came out naturally.

Reese didn't respond immediately, and in the few moments before he did, Kate recalled how the one time she approached the subject of God with him he'd teasingly said, "How can I not believe in God when I look into your beautiful brown eyes?" That had sent up red flags in Kate's mind. At the same time she was flattered.

"Prayer never hurts," Reese continued now. "Especially yours."

Kate smiled, glad to hear him make a statement that seemed to indicate some interest in God.

"When do you leave?" she asked.

"In a couple of hours. I've already booked a ten o'clock flight."

"Do you need a ride to the airport?"

"No! I mean, I'll leave my car in the long-term parking area. I'll be getting back late tomorrow night, and it'll be convenient to have the car handy."

Disappointed, Kate said, "I guess that's more practical."

"Definitely. But you know what this does to our evening plans. I was looking forward to the play at Lamb's."

"Well, we can catch it when you get back. It's playing all this month. I'll call and change the reservation to next weekend."

"Maybe you should cancel the reservation until I see how things are with Aunt Bertha, or maybe go with someone else. What about Cami?"

"She saw it last night with her friend Robin. Anyway, I agree that you should keep your options open in case your aunt needs you again."

"I repeat—what a woman you are." He cleared his throat.

"Take care, Reese. I hope you'll find things aren't as bad as they seem with your aunt."

"Me, too, I'll see you at The Glue on Monday. Good-bye, Kate."

Kate stared at her phone. Two calls in the space of a few minutes from the two men in her life. Being honest with herself, she wasn't sure which had upset her most—Gunnar's implication that he would look up Natalie—Kate didn't even know her last name—in Vancouver or the missed date with Reese. Well, at least Reese was going on a kind of mercy mission.

Suddenly feeling depressed, Kate tossed the half-eaten breakfast into a trash container and left to walk home. She no longer felt like jogging.

Chapter Sixty-Two

‱

For several seconds Gunnar stared at the receiver he'd just slammed into its base on his home desk. In one swift motion, he sent a stack of papers flying across the floor, then kicked at the waste basket beside his rolling chair. Leaning on his elbows, he pressed his fingertips hard against his temples, with the ridiculous image of pressing away his heart-searing hurt.

What's going on here, Lord? A week ago, I was almost crazy with excitement thinking of Kate coming back to Boston when the Grant Lauder semester ends in December. That engagement ring I looked at yesterday—it had Kate's name written all over it. Gunnar pictured the square-cut diamond rising between two smaller diamonds. The simple style suited no-nonsense, straight forward Kate, yet hinted of her romantic streak. The sparkling gems symbolized to him the faith that shone from her life—bright and solid.

Can it be only a little over a year since I met her? He allowed himself a sad smile. *It took me half that time to convince her she could treasure her memories of Joel and still find love again. Like I had had to do after Brita died.*

During that year, Gunnar had fallen deeply in love with a woman with ordinary physical beauty made dazzling by an inner glow that came from her firm dedication to Jesus Christ. He knew instinctively from the loyalty she had shown to Joel that she would be a passionate and devoted wife to any man who could win her heart again.

Gunnar rolled the desk chair back and stood up. Hands in his pockets and shoulders hunched, he stood still and studied the brown-on-brown pattern in the carpet.

O Lord, was I wrong about Kate? Did I completely misjudge her?

He kicked at the waste basket again. *Kate Elfmon! Who are you? You're the last person I'd have suspected of having your head turned by an overdose of charm and a few roses.*

He looked up, feeling the bleakness in his face. *Lord....* He couldn't think how to go on. He kicked the waste basket yet again, harder, till it fell over, scattering balled-up papers across the floor. *I'm better off without her!* he told himself.

He didn't believe it.

His thoughts turned to Natalie. Those short-lived romantic thoughts of her were long gone. Still, what would it hurt to look her up when he got to Vancouver?

Chapter Sixty-Three

ॐ

Reese Sutherland had, as he'd told Kate, received a call that morning, but that and the fact that he was headed to the airport were the only accurate information he'd given her. He thought of their telephone conversation as he parked his black Mercedes in the *regular* parking lot rather than the long-term one.

I hope she didn't notice how I stumbled over "Aunt Bertha's" name that second time I mentioned it, he thought, then excused himself with, *How was I supposed to remember a name I made up two minutes earlier? Should have written it down. Kate's pretty sharp, but ...* he reminded himself *... trusting. That's one of the things that's appealing about her.*

As he had done at the gym Monday night, he wondered at himself for being even slightly interested in a woman so different from the ones who usually appealed to him. Of course, her "religiosity," though not aggressive, did put him off a little. At the same time, the idea of helping her overcome her inhibitions challenged him. He'd played the gentleman to the hilt, only giving her chaste good-night kisses at the end of the past two dates. He had even toyed with the idea of seeing Kate exclusively, at least for a while.

Then he got the call this morning from Raquel Wells. Reese happened to know Raquel's birth name was Ruth Williams, but she'd changed the prosaic moniker to one that reflected her obsession with some of the provocative classic film stars. She probably thought that would further her own goal to break into the movie industry. However, her three years haunting the major, minor, and never-heard-of studios in Hollywood had yielded only a few commercials and minuscule roles in forgettable films.

"Reesie," she'd said in that breathy voice that was an obvious attempt to imitate Marilyn Monroe, "I got called for a TV commercial at Fiesta Island. It's only about a twenty-minute taxi drive from your place. It's not until Monday, but I could snag a commuter flight this morning and get there by ten. That is if..." She left the rest to Reese's imagination.

Memories of their three days in Martinique last summer had made an evening at Lamb's Players with a highly principled date seem tame. Now, Raquel's flight was due in any time. His blood raced as he retrieved one long-stemmed Talisman rose, its gold and coral beauty enclosed in a funnel of plastic, from the back seat and got out of his car. With long, eager steps, he strode to the terminal and the long, wide steps where incoming passengers descended.

~~~

A secret smile played about Raquel Wells' full red lips as the small commuter plane flew over the cliffs of La Jolla before swooping southward toward San Diego's Lindbergh Field airport. From her window seat, she leaned forward and placed her hand against the glass.

I can hardly wait to live in La Jolla! She pushed her white-blond hair behind one ear. *That's the most ritzy part of San Diego County. And Reese's townhouse is one of the fanciest homes I've ever been in. He says he can afford it because of some kind of inheritance he got. Anyway, I'll make sure we'll plant several Talisman rose bushes, like we'll be planting memories.*

Looking away from the scene below, Raquel thought of the romantic story Reese had told her—how back in 1929, when the movie industry was in its infancy, a wealthy producer had fallen in love with a beautiful blonde starlet named Rose. Nearly every day he sent her one beautiful gold and coral rose that he himself had developed in the garden of his Beverly Hills mansion. He said each rose represented a memory of their time together.

"Maybe one day someone will make a movie of that story," Reese had told Raquel, "with you playing the role of the starlet, of course."

Raquel held out her left hand. *I wonder if he's already bought my engagement ring. He knows what I want—I showed him the exact one online.*

She remembered Reese's reaction when he saw the ring on the jeweler's website. "Isn't that a bit, um, gaudy?"

"Oh, no! It's big, but I don't think its gaudy."

He had kissed her and said, "Whatever you want, Baby. Whatever you want."

Raquel gently caressed her ring finger with the other hand, imagining that she could feel the largest diamond in the seven-stone set.

What I want is you, Reese Sutherland. And it won't be long now.

~~~

Reese saw Raquel before she saw him. Tall, her Monroe-styled hair bleached nearly white, buxom, wearing a very short, form-fitting skirt. She swayed her way down the corridor that was visible from his vantage point below. As she put one foot in its five-inch heels on the top step, their eyes met. She gave him a knowing smile. No wave. Just that alluring smile.

Seconds later, she had grasped the Talisman rose and was in his arms.

Reese thought of the two contradictory natures of Raquel Wells: the seductive, street-wise, ambitious starlet and the simple-hearted Kansas girl who wanted a home and husband. He was growing a bit weary of both—but not weary enough to break off with her. Not yet.

~~~

Grant Lauder student Mindy Lewis had come to the airport to meet a friend who was visiting from Los Angeles for the weekend. Mindy had been assigned to do clerical work in the Human Resources office while Lenae Maddox was hospitalized. She'd gone into the office this morning, even though it was Saturday, and had let the time get away from her. Arriving at the airport later than she'd planned, she ran to the bottom of the steps, hoping her friend had not already come down. She glanced at the nearby baggage area and saw only a few people at the carrousel for her friend Kaylie's flight. She breathed a sigh of relief and blew out a whoosh of air that puffed up her cheeks, then searched the faces of the descending passengers. Not seeing Kaylie, she glanced around at the others waiting at the stairs.

That tall, blonde man nearest the steps looked familiar from behind. Mindy admired the long-stem gold-and-coral rose he clasped in one hand. He turned his head to one side and upward, an eager expression on his face.

Professor Sutherland! Mindy, always open and friendly, made a step toward Dr. Sutherland. He was one of the nicer professors at The Glue, not all stuffy like Dr. Bainbridge. She was about to touch his arm when a provocative blonde stepped off the stairs, took the rose from the good-looking professor, and fell into his arms.

Chapter Sixty-Four

֍

The waves were angry today. A bitter chill nipped the air. Cami felt the water and the wind reflected her mood. A few minutes ago, she'd picked up her Bible, thinking to go out to her favorite boulder on the beach and read for a while.

My rock is spoiled now, she thought, as she stood staring at the huge rock. *The whole beach is spoiled. Just when I get past thinking of Debra's attack here in August, I find Lenae lying by 'my rock', looking like she's dead.*

I've visited her and talked with her about Jesus every day since Tuesday, but she doesn't seem to be responding. Now and then I think I feel a muscle twitch in her finger, but I can't be sure. How much longer can she last in this coma?

And what's going on with Kate? From the day she accepted Christ, she's been the much stronger of the two of us, even though I was a Christian first. Now here she is going out with a man she hasn't bothered to learn about spiritually. She even slept late Sunday morning and didn't make it to church. Oh, I know that's not a sin. But it's not Kate.

And what's going on with my children? Especially Debra. I don't like the feeling I get when I think of her dating that English lord or earl or whatever this Reggie person is. And Durant? Last time he called, he was coming down with a cold. I hate being so far away when he may be sick. He did say he's found a good church to attend, but I know Debra's not going with him. Even with phone calls and emails, I feel so disconnected from my children.

Oh, how I wish Braxton were here. That thought brought sudden tears to Cami's eyes. She let them flow unchecked. *Despite his faults, he was able to see things more clearly than I did sometimes. I need him. Why did God take him away and leave me alone?*

After a few moments, she swept the back of her hand across her eyes. *And...*

Cami, you're commiserating with the wrong person. Yourself.

The thought interrupted Cami's melancholy musings. She strode to the boulder, pulled her jacket close about her, and opened the little blue Bible. She thought she knew where to look. Kate would be able to turn right to it. She scanned a few pages near the back. Ah, there it was. First Peter five, verses six and seven.

"Therefore humble yourself under the mighty hand of God, that He may exalt you in due time, casting all your care upon Him, for He cares for you."

Cami bowed her head and cast her anger and complaints and frustrations on the One who cared for her.

Sunday, November 14

Chapter Sixty-Five

❦

Sitting across from him at the glass-topped breakfast table in Reese Sutherland's luxurious townhouse, Raquel Wells leaned her elbows on the table and feasted on the handsome man's square-jawed face, strong but finely shaped nose, incredible long-lashed eyes the color of a lion's mane streaked with brown, and the blond wave dipping over his forehead. No man had ever fascinated her like Reese Sutherland did.

He gave her that crooked smile that always caused a little flutter inside. "Enjoy your lunch?" He indicated the sparse remains of the salad he had made for the two of them when they finally got up about noon.

"Mmmm. Delicious. I didn't realize you were a cook."

Reese grinned. "One of my many talents. Can't quite match Mr. A's," he said, speaking of Bertrand at Mr. A's, the elegant top-of-a-skyscraper restaurant he'd taken her to last night.

Raquel stretched her arms over her head in a languid way she knew revealed her curves and said in that whispery voice she'd worked so hard to develop, "Know what I want to do, Reesie?'

He pulled her forward and kissed the tip of her nose. "Let me guess."

"No, silly boy." She fluttered her lashes at him. "I want to go for a walk on the beach. I know it's chilly, but that will make it fun."

Reese let out a mock sigh of disappointment. "Oh, well, a walk on the beach it is. One of the best in San Diego is practically at my doorstep."

"We've done that lots of times, Reesie. Today I want to go to Coronado Beach."

That was the exact moment the weekend began spiraling downhill.

206

Reese hadn't been able to hide something that seemed like panic from his face. The look was gone so quickly Raquel thought she must have imagined it.

"Why Coronado?" he asked, displeasure oozing from his words.

Though his tone made her feel hesitant, she answered, "I've heard a lot about that fabulous hotel on the island, right on the ocean. It's where Marilyn Monroe made 'Some Like It Hot' with Jack Lemmon and Tony Curtis. I've seen the movie a dozen times, but I've never been to the hotel." It must have been nervousness that made her want to show him she wasn't the complete bimbo he seemed to think she was. "Did you know Coronado isn't really an island, Reesie? It's really—"

"A peninsula." Reese let out a huff of exasperation. "Of course, I know that, Raquel."

"Oh," she said, deflated. Determined not to show it, she took in a deep, dramatic breath and went on, "Who cares about a silly old hotel when we can stroll hand in hand on the shore?"

Reese snorted. "Sounds like a line in one of those bit parts of yours."

That really stung. What was wrong with Reese all of a sudden? Sure, her few movie roles had been miniscule, but hey, she was trying hard to make it in this business. Look at all the money she'd spent on acting lessons, hair salons, and wardrobe, not to mention regular Botox treatments and various surgeries.

It took great effort not to respond to Reese's dig. Well, she was an actress, wasn't she? She could act as if the barb didn't bother her. Stepping into the role, Raquel let out a careless laugh.

"Caught me. That was from *Miami Magic*. Didn't exactly catch on with the public. Too artsy, I guess. Anyway, Reesie, come on. Let's get out of here and go to Coronado."

"No!"

At his sharp bark, Raquel clapped one hand to her chest and moved away from him.

He softened his tone. "Sorry. Didn't mean to bite your head off. We'll go beach-walking if you'd like, but not at Coronado."

"But why not? I've heard it's really beautiful. And..."

"Not Coronado. Um, I don't like Coronado."

"But, Reesie—"

"Look, Raquel, I'm all for 'walking hand in hand on the shore,' right here in La Jolla, not—I repeat not—Coronado."

Raquel forced out her bottom lip. "Well, okay, if that's what you want."

"It is. Look, while you get changed, I need to make a phone call."

Chapter Sixty-Six

❧

Gunnar hadn't slept well Saturday night and had nearly fallen asleep in church this morning. Now, mid-afternoon on Sunday, he was restless. The situation with Kate kept playing over and over in his mind. He had thought and prayed over and over during the night and throughout the day today. Now he knew what he needed to do.

He was going to fight for the woman he loved.

And he couldn't do that from Boston.

~~~

Perusing the political editorials of the *San Diego Union Tribune,* Kate pushed aside an annoying feeling of guilt for missing the morning church service. When her phone rang, she recognized the number on the incoming call and answered on the first ring.

"Hi, Reese." She heard the lift in her voice.

"Hi, yourself. Just checking in to see how things are in Coronado."

"They're fine here. What about there? Is everything okay with your aunt?"

"She's holding her own. Poor old thing. There's not much I can do for her except sit here and hold her hand."

Kate's heart went out to Reese. "I'm sure it means more than you can imagine that you dropped everything and flew up there."

"I think so. Aunt Beulah means the world to me."

"When will you get back?"

"Probably not before late Monday night."

Kate heard a voice in the background that seemed to be calling out "Reesie."

209

"Excuse me, Kate. A friend of Aunt Beulah's is here. I need to go. See you Tuesday." He ended the call.

A recurrence of the uneasy feelings Kate occasionally felt about Reese stilled her as she clicked off her own phone. At first, she didn't know the reason. Then it came to her. Hadn't Reese said his aunt's name was "Bertha"? A minute ago he had called her Aunt "Beulah."

I must be mistaken. After all, the names are similar.

Another thought came to Kate. The aunt's friend had called out "Reesie." And she didn't sound like an elderly woman.

I must have misunderstood. She mused for a few seconds. *Yes, that's it. I misunderstood.*

Chapter Sixty-Seven

ॐ

Raquel and Reese dressed warmly and made their way down the one-hundred-plus wooden steps from the cliff top in front of Reese's house to the beach below. At the bottom they removed their shoes. Holding hands, they strolled barefoot in the cold, wet sand. Reese was almost like his old charming self, but it felt like an effort to Raquel. She felt so miserable that she barely listened as he explained the name of city.

"*La Jolla* is Spanish for 'The Jewel.' And that's what La Jolla is, as a town and an ocean view. He dropped her hand and held his arms out toward the water. "Look. See how the water sparkles like a million diamonds."

To Raquel, the view was indeed breathtaking, but more importantly, Reese's little travelogue gave her the opportunity she'd been looking for to bring up a subject foremost in her mind. She took his arm and snuggled close.

"Speaking of jewels and diamonds, Reesie, I'm sure a ritzy town like La Jolla has dozens of jewelry stores."

"Jewelry stores?"

Reese looked genuinely puzzled. That frightened Raquel. Something was wrong here. What she may lack in talent, Raquel made up for in determination. She hid her dismay and gave him a meaningful smile. "You know," she said playfully, "those places where you buy rings."

"Rings?" He spoke as if he were clueless as to her meaning.

She held on to the smile with great effort. "We need to shop for my engagement ring."

"Oh, yes. Of course. Sorry. I let my mind wander there for a minute. You're right. We need to shop for your engagement ring."

Raquel brightened. She'd have preferred he be the one to bring up the subject, but.... Well, whatever. The first time Reese mentioned marriage had been three months ago. Now she felt a bubble of excitement to think they may be closer to an official engagement.

His next words burst that bubble. "But not today."

She pulled away from him. "But why not? What are we waiting for?"

He paused and looked down at the sand. "If you must know...."

He was going to break the engagement. She knew it.

"Yes, I must know."

"Well, I hate to admit it to you, but I've had some reverses in my stock market investments and am a little short of cash right now. We need to wait till I get my finances straightened out before making a big purchase like the kind of ring you want." He put his arm around her waist and pulled her close. "And deserve."

"I see," she said, returning his hug, but thinking with sudden, shocking clarity, *What I see is that Reese doesn't intend to marry me. Ever.*

After that the day went flat. Raquel couldn't tell what Reese was thinking. As for herself, her excitement at the beginning of the weekend had changed to grief at the loss of a dream. A dream that was turning into a nightmare.

~~~

During the rest of the day, Raquel's feelings of grief grew into an anger that slowly built to a near breaking point. However, she was a better actress than Reese credited her to be, and she continued to smile and flirt. Despite the anger, though, Raquel was a natural optimist. Also, despite her immoral lifestyle, at heart she was old-fashioned enough to want marriage and a home. That night, back at Reese's house, she convinced herself to give it another shot.

Things didn't quite shake out the way she'd hoped. It didn't help that after a rather awkward dinner—if you could call take-out fish and chips dinner—Reese suggested they watch a late-night movie on TV. An old World War II movie called *The Longest Day.*

"A war movie?" She was astounded. "You've got to be kidding."

Reese shrugged and pointed the remote at the TV.

Halfway through the movie, which Raquel thought was appropriately named, she slipped into a slinky nightgown and paraded in front of him. After a few provocative twirls, during which he tried to look around her at the TV screen, she asked, "Aren't you ready for some...shut-eye?"

He actually moved her from in front of the screen. "Not yet. I want to see the end of this. You go on."

He hadn't even said he'd join her, but still Raquel lay awake waiting for him—waiting and trying to rationalize away her moment of clarity on the beach. Finally, she knew her natural optimism wasn't going to fix this.

She fell asleep with hot tears of rejection and anger spilling onto her pillow.

Chapter Sixty-Eight

ॐ

Kate curled up on one of two comfortable matching leather recliners in Cami's den. She and Cami had returned from the evening service at Coronado Baptist and were enjoying bowls of aromatic kettle corn. Picking up a handful, Kate said, "Pastor Oates has a way of hitting home, doesn't he?"

Cami, seated in the other recliner, took a sip of diet cola and grinned. "You mean how he talked—for about forty-five seconds out of a forty-minute sermon—about faithfulness to church services, on a day when you slept in and didn't attend this morning?"

Kate let out a rueful chuckle. "You hit the nail on the head." She popped a few of the sweet kernels in her mouth.

"And you didn't even stay out late last night since you and Reese didn't go to the Lamb's play."

"But I was so tired from being out several nights in a row before that that I didn't hear my alarm this morning. I didn't even stir under the covers until ten o'clock!"

"Kate Elfmon sleeping 'til ten? What is the world coming to?" Cami paused and became serious. "You were really disappointed that he had to cancel, weren't you?"

"I really was. Especially after that unpleasant confrontation with Gunnar." Kate made a face. "Reese is so incredibly charming, Cami. And I love the roses he sends me. Always just one—so much more romantic than a bouquet."

"Sounds wonderful. Has he kissed you?"

"Only at the door when he brings me home. He's been a total gentleman." Kate fell silent. Looking down, she began stirring her popcorn with her index finger.

"Then why suddenly so glum? I mean, are you, um, sorry he's being so gentlemanly?" Cami put on a coquettish look.

Kate matched her look. "Maybe a little. No, not really."

"But you're ... having some ... concerns? Is it because of..."

Kate could tell that Cami was nearly biting her tongue off to keep from pressing her to say more about Gunnar. The woman was *so* transparent. Kate lifted one shoulder in what felt like a too-casual gesture. "Oh, it's little things. Silly, unimportant things."

"Such as?"

"This will sound petty, but it really bothered me how Reese practically devoured Erika Weston with his eyes at the gym. I told you about that."

Cami's face darkened at the mention of Erika, but Kate knew she couldn't stop now. "I've even wondered if he actually showed up at her birthday party. There was plenty of time after we left Peohe's and he took me to pick you up at the hospital."

Cami groaned. "After my little fender bender. You don't know how I hated interrupting your date."

"No problem. Anyway, Erika might as well have posted a personal invitation to him in the *Coronado Eagle*, she was so obvious."

"Hmmm. Well, you may have a prejudice concerning Erika because of her affair with your best friend's husband." Cami pointed to herself. "What else?"

"Little inconsistencies here and there, the most obvious being that he called his 'sick aunt' by two different names. And when he called me on Sunday, I got a weird feeling. I'm not sure he was even in Sacramento. But maybe I'm being overly suspicious."

"Maybe. Maybe not. You should listen to your instincts." Cami tilted her pretty head at Kate. "I'm sure you've prayed about it."

"Not much, Cami," Kate admitted. "Not much."

Chapter Sixty-Nine

&

Raquel's sleep was so fitful that she awoke before six a.m. The first thing she noticed was that Reese's side of the bed was untouched. Fighting angry tears, she flung back the covers on her side.

She needed to be up anyway. She had to be at the film site by eight and ready for shooting the TV commercial at ten. She wished she were more excited, but how excited could a girl get about wearing a bikini on a beach in chilly November? This one, sponsored by a local surfboard establishment, would feature San Diego's "Over the Line" contest on Mission Bay's Fiesta Island, and wouldn't be shown until next July. Raquel had heard the boisterous three-on-three softball game described as more "beers, babes, and bats on the beach" than athletic prowess. The weather forecast had promised skies sunny enough to make the action seem to occur in mid-summer. Fortunately, the film site was only a twenty-minute taxi ride from Reese's townhouse.

Hearing the TV still blaring, she made her way to the living room, where Reese was sound asleep on the couch. His sun-streaked hair was slightly tousled, and his firm lips were slightly parted as a gentle snore puffed through. He looked so innocent and endearing that Raquel had to force herself to remember how he'd treated her yesterday.

Inexpressibly depressed, she turned off the TV and went back to the bedroom. When she was dressed, she went back to wake Reese up. As she reached out to touch him, she noticed a florist receipt on the table by the couch. The way it was folded, she could see the words "Talisman rose, long stem" and the number "one."

Raquel picked up the receipt. *Must be for the rose Reese brought to the airport.*

Her eyes widened in horror. The date on the receipt was four days before Raquel arrived in San Diego! Realization and fury hit her so hard she clutched her stomach. Reese had bought *her* rose for another woman.

~~~

Reese knew the exact moment Raquel found the rose receipt. He had left it out on purpose so she'd see it. He'd pretended to be asleep and heard her run out and slam the door two minutes later.

For some time Reese had realized it had been a mistake to imply he would marry Raquel, but she was such a paradoxical combination of world-liness mixed with an old-fashioned desire for a home and husband that he'd played along with it. Yesterday her insistence on getting an engagement ring had shown him it was time to break it off. Besides, her bimbo personality had really grated on his nerves all day.

Could that be because of the time he'd spent with Kate Elfmon recently? What a contrast! Raquel with her fake Marilyn Monroe voice and her inane comments about Coronado not being a real island. Kate with her bright, easy intellectualism. Maybe it was time to ease up on his gentlemanly pose with her and move in in earnest. He began to imagine how he'd begin that process. Maybe he would even give up his pursuit of Erika Weston.

Well, maybe not.

A sudden roiling in his stomach cut Reese's pleasant musings short. He leapt to his feet and ran to the bathroom. He made it barely in time to keep from throwing up onto his pale blue carpet. When he'd emptied his stomach of last night's greasy fish, he stumbled to his bed, vaguely noting that only one side was disturbed.

I'll lie here for a little while, then get up and get dressed for work, he told himself.

An hour later, having made three more dashes to the bathroom, he called his office and told Cecelia he wasn't feeling well and wouldn't try to go in today.

The ever-faithful admin assistant gave him sympathetic, motherly advice to take it easy and said she'd hold down the fort.

Reese thought about texting Kate, but the thought of the effort seemed like too much. He fell back onto the couch and squeezed his eyes shut against the spinning of the room.

Chapter Seventy

ॐ

Kate couldn't believe she'd slept late again—not 'til ten o'clock like yesterday morning—but still arriving only minutes before her eight o'clock class. When she didn't see Reese's car in the staff parking lot, she wondered if he'd even got back in town yet. Maybe he was still with Aunt Bertha—Beulah—whatever. Kate really wanted to give him the benefit of the doubt.

After her class, Kate headed to the staff cafeteria for a cup of much-needed coffee. On her way, she peeked outside and still didn't see Reese's car. He must have some kind of meeting this morning, and he wasn't obliged to inform her of his plans. She was disappointed but not worried.

Soon after she sat down with coffee and a blueberry muffin, Dr. Albert Bainbridge appeared at her table. His cane hooked over his arm, he said, "May I?" Without waiting for a reply, he set his tray down across from Kate.

She watched in fascination while he removed his own coffee and muffin and a cup of fruit from the tray and placed them as carefully as if he were setting a formal table, even folding his napkin and placing a knife and fork on top of it. When he was settled, he unfolded the napkin he had just folded, picked up his knife and fork, and cut the muffin into quarters. Before taking a bite, he leaned forward and spoke in a conspiratorial tone, almost whispering. "I'm sure *you're* aware Dr. Sutherland didn't show up for work today."

Not liking that emphasis on the word *you're,* Kate made an effort to hide her surprise. "No, Dr. Bainbridge. I didn't know." Well, that wasn't entirely true. She knew his car wasn't in the lot when she arrived, but he could be on campus now without her knowledge. "Why should I?"

Dr. Bainbridge raised one perfectly groomed eyebrow. "Well, I hear the two of you are a bit of an item these days."

"An item?" Kate frowned.

"Come now, Dr. Elfmon, news gets around on a college campus—especially when the *acting* head of the law department bestows his favors on an attractive new faculty member."

Kate felt herself color. She disliked being the object of campus gossip.

Before she could reply, Bainbridge went on, "Of course, Dr. Sutherland has rather eclectic tastes in the women upon whom he bestows those favors." He turned down his mouth in an expression of distaste.

He's thinking of someone Reese has gone out with. A sick feeling hit Kate's stomach as she wondered, *How recently? This past weekend maybe?* This was her first conversation with Albert Bainbridge, and already she disliked him—so much that she heard herself reverting to a sarcasm she had worked at squashing since the day she became a Christian.

Matching his formal phrasing, Kate said, "And you, Dr. Bainbridge, upon whom do you bestow your favors?"

The little man's face turned a dark purple, and Kate thought he would choke on his muffin. "You—you— That was quite uncalled for, Dr. Elfmon."

"As was your snide remark, Dr. Bainbridge."

Bainbridge patted his lips with his napkin and pushed away from the table. He began to place his lunch items carefully back on the tray. "I can see my presence is distressing you, Dr. Elfmon. I shall take my leave."

Is this man for real? Kate wondered as Bainbridge rose and left.

Chapter Seventy-One

ಬಿ

As he maneuvered his Escalade over a rough road off Interstate 8 several miles beyond the East County mountain town of Alpine, Mike Jenkins felt like one of his construction workers was using his head for a sledge hammer. Between worry over Lenae—Would she ever wake up? Would he have a chance to tell her he loved her and ask her to marry him?—and a slew of problems at MelJen's, he had begun to think he couldn't take any more. Even as his body left the seat when the SUV flew over a pothole in the road, he welcomed this morning's excuse to check on a possible house site for a new client.

About nine-fifteen he had been agonizing over Lenae while trying to concentrate on a knotty architectural design. A minute later, he swept the paperwork aside, shoved his chair back, snatched a denim jacket from a hook on the wall, and marched out of his private entrance at the back of the building. His assistant was away from her desk, and he didn't stop to leave her a note.

So what? he thought. *I'm the boss. I can leave unannounced if I want to.*

Soon Mike turned off onto another bumpy road that lead up a steep incline and to the location the client had suggested. He got out of the vehicle and sucked in the cold, clean air so unlike the overcast skies so common in the mornings at San Diego's beaches. For several minutes he stood motionless before the panorama of mountains and valleys stretching into the distance. What a view! His client's choice was right on the money. And a lot of money it would take to prepare this mountaintop for a house, but the client could afford it and it would be worth it.

After half an hour of pacing the area and making some mental notes, Mike got into the Escalade and began driving back down the mountain.

He'd been able to set aside thoughts of Lenae for these past few minutes, but now they came back and hit him so hard he swerved the SUV.

He clenched his fists on the steering wheel as he thought of the deliberate disinterest he'd kept in the other man in her life...until recently. Now he wanted to thrash himself. Because of his cavalier attitude, the only clue to the man's identity he could think of was the "R" on the card attached to the rose he'd seen in Lenae's flat.

He clenched his fists tighter and swerved again, almost landing in a big pothole.

There must be something! Something she let slip.

As he left the rough off-road and pulled onto the smooth highway, he searched his memory. Suddenly a scene flashed in his mind as though it were in living color on the sixty-inch TV in his den. He and Lenae were standing on the deck of the Lord Hornblower harbor-cruise yacht, enjoying an early evening tour of San Diego Bay.

As the boat moved slowly under the Coronado Bridge, Lenae pointed to the land opposite the mainland. "Over there is Coronado," she said. "You can't see the Hotel Del from here, but soon we'll be approaching the Ferry Landing."

"Oh, you've done this before," Mike said, a bit disappointed. "This is my first time, even after all these years in San Diego." He started to say he'd never gotten around to taking Melanie on a harbor cruise, but decided that would be inappropriate. Instead he asked, "Have you done this often?"

"No, only the once with someone from the g—" She stopped, then quickly went on to say, "with a friend."

At the time, Mike had thought little of it. Now he wondered what Lenae had stopped her herself from saying. Something that started with a "G." Someone—probably some man—from, from where? The "government"? The "group"? The "galaxy"? Ridiculous.

Great. Now I really have a lot to go on. Two letters of the alphabet: an R and a G.

Mike was almost to the exit to his own home when it hit him. *The G. They call Grant Lauder University "the Glue"! She went on a cruise with someone from the university!*

Mike's mind raced, his anger merging with excitement. *I've got to find out who works there with a name beginning with R. Somebody she'd be likely to go out with.*

Mike sped up. At his house, he sprinted inside to his computer and pulled up the Grant Lauder website.

~~~

About the same time Mike Jenkins was remembering Lenae's chance remark during the harbor cruise, Dexter Driscoll was doing his own recalling. At first, he'd been convinced that Mike Jenkins had attacked Lenae on the beach and a few days later unplugged her oxygen machine. Little by little, though, he'd faced the fact that Mike was a victim, along with Lenae, in the oxygen machine incident. It must be the other man, the one who sent the roses, the one who always signed his name "R".

Well, not always.

Once, when Dexter was visiting Lenae, he had noticed what he thought was a piece of trash on the floor. He picked it up and saw it was the florist card from the most recent rose offering. As he laid it on the table and was about to turn it over, he caught sight of two letters: the usual "R" and another one that had been marked out, as though to obliterate it. Dexter had always respected Lenae's privacy, even secrecy, about her private life; but this time his curiosity got the best of him, and she was busy at the sink. While her back was turned, he peered closely at the card and deciphered the marked-out letter: "S." About that time, Lenae started to turn around, and Dexter moved away from the table. He gave no more thought to the card.

Until now.

Chapter Seventy-Two

&

This commercial was a real bust so far, Raquel thought. About 7:25, dressed in red sweats and a black calf-length sweater coat and carrying her large purse and overnight bag, she had cast one last look at Reese, still asleep on the couch. She slammed the door and stepped outside into a grey sky that was predicted to clear up by 10 o'clock.

At the Cerca de Costa gate, she got into the taxi she'd called for. Minutes later, she arrived at the large beige dressing tent set up on the edge of Fiesta Island beach. There, along with eight or nine other shapely actresses, she submitted herself to the wardrobe stylist, who'd made her try on eight bikinis before proclaiming a tiny gold and black number suitable. Next came the make-up artist, whose own face was innocent of even a touch of lipstick. Then a hairstylist with ultra-bright blonde hair streaked with purple took fifteen minutes to brush out Raquel's usual Marilyn Monroe style and pull it up into two high, untidy pony tails, one on each side of her head.

"The casual, windblown look," the stylist said.

Several of the other actresses knew each other from other San Diego shoots and chatted together during and after their preparations. Raquel was the only one who'd come down from L.A. and, though usually friendly, she had no desire for idle chatter today. She wrapped her sweater-coat over the itsy-bitsy bikini and retreated to a director's-type canvas chair in one corner of the tent.

She felt like crying, but knew the make-up artist would start screaming if she saw tears making black mascara streaks in Raquel's foundation. Instead, she curled her feet under her and relived the past couple of days. Remembering how cocky and hopeful she'd been as she flew into San Diego to meet Reese, she felt embarrassed and ashamed. Rejected. That evening and night and even the next morning had been wonderful, but from the moment she'd mentioned going to Coronado right to when she walked out of Reese's house this morning had been one humiliation after another.

How could I have loved that louse? And how could I have thought the creep cared about me? He's the one who should be in acting. He could get an Oscar.

For several minutes, Raquel inwardly blasted Reese with names far more colorful than louse and creep, then thought, *All those compliments and promises. Well, I thought they were promises, but now that I think about it, he was careful about how he worded them. Like he wanted to be able to say they weren't really promises, that I'd misunderstood his intentions.*

And the roses. What a classy touch! One beautiful rose at nearly every date. He said they represented the memories we were making together. All the time, he was sending the same rose to some other woman. Or women. How I'd love to get my hands around his neck and—

A voice interrupted her musings. The director had stuck his head back into the tent. "Hey, Raquel. We're waiting for you. Are you in dreamland, or something? Come on. Now."

"Oh, sorry. On my way." Raquel shed her sweater coat and went out to the chilly beach to join the other actresses.

Shivering and stumbling over her own feet on the way, Raquel took her place on the sand with a baseball bat in hand. A brunette with hair to her waist tossed the ball. Raquel swung, missed, and dropped the bat. On the next attempt, her swing went wild and almost hit another actress in the head.

Thirty minutes and several more miscues and mishaps later, a disgusted director stopped the shoot. "Raquel!" he growled. "I don't know what's eating at you today. Let's try this one more time from the top."

Another fifteen minutes later, the director shouted out, "Cut!" He threw a towel onto the sand. "I think we need to take a break. It's eleven o'clock. Be back here by one." He glared at Raquel. "And see if you can get your act together."

Raquel suppressed a groan. This gig paid Screen Actors Guild minimum wage, a good portion of which she'd used on airfare; and she could see that her visibility on the screen would be minimal. One bikini-clad actress among nine others.

I only accepted it because it's in San Diego, and it gave me a chance to be with Reese. Ha. What a laugh. She opened up her large purse to get out her brush. *Oh no! I left it at Reese's. And it's my favorite one—pure boar bristle. Cost me over two hundred dollars. I have time to go back and get it. Wait. Reese is at work by now. How am I going to—*

Then she grinned to herself. *I know the gate code and where he keeps a spare key—right behind that golf bag–shaped plaque next to the front door.*

Saying nothing to anyone on site, she hightailed it out of there.

Chapter Seventy-Three

⪘

It felt like *déjà vu*. As he had back in August, when Erika had been involved with Braxton Carrington, Stan spread out photos of her and another man—this time Reese Sutherland—on his desk. As PI Richards had said, the pictures were pretty innocent looking, with the two simply having a meal at the restaurant of a Del Mar inn. In some of them, Erika didn't even appear to be having a good time. She definitely wasn't giving Sutherland the bold, suggestive looks Stan knew so well. Still, if it was all so innocent, why had they chosen to meet way up in Del Mar? And why did they choose a restaurant in a romantic inn with private rooms?

And why haven't I confronted Erika by now? I've had these photos for three days. When Richards gave me the photos of her and Braxton Carrington last summer, I blasted her that very day.

I must be avoiding the inevitable this time.

Maybe it's because she's been so loving for the past few days. But maybe that's an act. Still, after Carrington was murdered—and we each learned the other hadn't done it—she promised me there would be no other men in her life. I really don't think there have been. Until now.

Richards hasn't reported seeing Erika and Sutherland together any more since Thursday. Maybe there really wasn't anything to it.

But I'm twice her age. And Sutherland's a real ladies' man. He's the kind who'd find it amusing to move in on Erika just to annoy me.

For the next hour, instead of looking over his follow-up notes from several recent surgeries, Stan scourged his mind with excruciating torture. One minute he could convince himself that there really wasn't anything romantic between Sutherland and the woman who'd been an obsession to him since the first time he saw her. The next, he was sure the two were having a torrid affair, and burning rage would nearly take his breath away.

Finally he couldn't take it any longer. *I have* to *know the truth.* Acting on anti-typical impulse, Stan looked up the number for Grant Lauder University. He had no plan about what he'd say, but he knew he had to talk with Reese Sutherland.

Moments later, he heard an efficient-sounding voice say, "Dr. Reese Sutherland's office. Cecelia Hanson speaking." When Stan asked to speak to Dr. Sutherland, the woman said, "Who may I say is calling?"

Stan thought fast. "This is Dr. St— Stephen, um, W— East. Stephen East. I'm with the law department of New York City College. I'd like to talk with Reese about a paper he published in the *New York Law Journal* last month." Using Reese's given name was a spur-of-the-moment decision. Hopefully, Ms. Hanson would think that meant Stephen East and Reese were friends.

Well acquainted, yes. Friends? Hardly.

"I'm sure Dr. Sutherland would like to discuss that with you, Dr. East," said Ms. Hanson, "but he's not in. He's not fee— He's not in. Could I take a message?"

"No, no. I'll call back later. Thank you very much, Ms. Hanson."

When Stan hung up, he said aloud, "She was about to say Reese isn't feeling well. That means he's at home." Stan sprung from his chair and headed for the back door of his office.

~~~

Cecelia Hanson began jotting down the info about the call: "Dr. Stephen East, 10:15 a.m., November 15. Wants to discuss—" She stopped. Something wasn't right. For one thing, the man had stumbled over his own name. Also, Cecelia knew that though Reese had had several articles published during his sixteen months with Grant Lauder, none had been with the *New York Law Journal.*

Who was this "Dr. East"?

Chapter Seventy-Four

ॐ

Usually a trip to Neiman Marcus at Fashion Valley, San Diego's largest and most upscale shopping mall, brought a major thrill to Erika Weston. Having grown up in near poverty in a Boston tenement area, she still sometimes literally pinched herself as a reminder that she really could afford NM's outrageously high prices. The only expensive clothing she'd ever worn before marrying Stan were the outfits she'd modeled. Today, she'd already purchased a pair of Yves Saint Laurent two-tone metallic sandals costing $995. Plus tax! Now she was headed to a cash register to pay for a formfitting one-shoulder top by Ralph Lauren with a $455 price tag.. She loved the asymmetric neckline and the shiny gold fabric.

So, why wasn't she feeling the usual thrill? Had she become so used to extravagant spending sprees that it wasn't fun anymore?

No way.

She paid for the top and walked outside to the walkway between Neiman Marcus and Nordstrom's. She was about to enter Nordstrom's, but felt an inexplicable aversion to shopping one more minute. Well, maybe it wasn't inexplicable. Ever since Thursday the back of her mind had swirled with thoughts of her lunch with Reese Sutherland.

I'm glad Stan doesn't know, she thought.

Still, she'd been trying to make it up to him by being extra attentive. She had learned to care about him and had felt both disloyal and cheap when she was out with Reese.

In the parking garage, Erika stowed her purchases in the backseat of her little red Corvette and got behind the wheel. Instead of starting up the motor right away, she concentrated on the part of her lunch with

Reese that was worrying her most: his words about Stan's first wife, Margo Cramer. When he'd implied Stan might have had something to do with Margo's death, she'd been too frightened to ask more. "What you don't know won't hurt you" was her motto.

"What she didn't know" was occupying more and more of her thoughts. Had Stan caused Margo's death in order to marry her, Erika? If so, how? The doctor who'd pronounced Margo dead said it was a heart attack. No surprise for a woman her size. Still...

Reese had implied he knew the truth. What if his hints were true? Would he go to the police? Would Stan be put in prison, not only hurting the dear man but possibly ending Erika's luxurious lifestyle? She had to find out what Reese knew. She *had* to convince him to keep silent.

~~~

Leaving a student intern in charge of the office, Cecelia Hanson left for a coffee break soon after "Dr. East" called. She returned fifteen minutes later.

"I'm back," Cecelia told the young co-ed, who was writing something on the missed-calls pad. "You can go now. Thanks for filling in,"

"No problem. There was only one call for Dr. Sutherland."

"Oh?"

"Some woman."

Cecelia suppressed an inner grin. Reese and his "women." She knew she should disapprove, but felt a guilty excitement at being in on some of the details of the handsome man's love life.

"Did she leave her name?"

"No. When I told her Dr. Sutherland was out sick, she said she'd call back."

"You told her he was out sick?"

The co-ed looked embarrassed. "Um, yes. Guess I shouldn't have, huh?"

Chapter Seventy-Five

&

"Hi, Mindy." Kate smiled at the pretty blond co-ed who was taking care of Lenae Maddox's clerical work.

"Hi, Dr. Elfmon," the girl replied, obviously wondering why the political science professor had asked her come by the office.

Kate looped her hair back over one ear as she rolled her chair away from the desk. It was five o'clock, and she had been reading and grading essays since her unpleasant mid-morning encounter with Albert Bainbridge. She foresaw several more hours of work ahead. She could gather up the essays and take them home to work on, but that would interrupt the flow, and she wanted to put this batch behind her.

"Thanks for coming in," she told Mindy. "You look lovely today, by the way. I love that rust color top on you, and you've done something different with your hair."

Mindy pretended to fluff up her blonde curls. "It's my hair that does something with *me*, Dr. Elfmon," she said. "It has a mind of its own."

"Well, it made a wise decision today." Kate smiled at the bouncy girl, who reminded her in some ways of a young Cami. "Did I hear that you live in Coronado?"

"That's right. An elderly friend of my mother's—Mrs. Townsend—is renting me a room dirt cheap. In return, I drive her places now and then. Only way I can afford to live here. And I love it!"

"Who wouldn't? Are you heading home soon?"

"In about ten minutes. As soon as I clean off my desk."

Kate waved at the pile of essays. "Looks like it's going to take me a while to do that. I'll probably be here another couple of hours."

"Can I help you? I don't have a lot of homework tonight, and I'm pretty good at catching spelling and grammatical errors. Maybe getting that part out of the way would save you some time."

"Thanks. That's tempting. But I need a different favor." Kate swiveled her chair and lifted a large gift bag from the floor. "I picked this up for a friend this afternoon and told her I'd get it to her in time for a birthday party tonight. But I really need to stay here."

"Oh, I'd be glad to take it to her for you. What's her address?"

Kate began to scribble on a sticky note. "Here it is," she said, handing it to Mindy. "You're probably already familiar with the house. On an island of gorgeous homes, Cami's is one of the *most* gorgeous."

"Cami Carrington? The woman whose husband was murdered last summer?"

Kate nodded.

"Mrs. Townsend showed her house to me the second day I was here. Claimed she knew a couple of the murder suspects from her volunteer work at the hospital."

"I have a feeling Mrs. Townsend is a fountain of information."

Mindy laughed. "You bet! And I have to admit..." She put one hand near her mouth and put on a falsetto whisper. "...I enjoy it."

Kate gave Mindy a noncommittal "Mmmm" and handed her the package.

As Mindy left, Kate silenced her cell phone. The campus switchboard had shut down at four, and though Kate hoped Reese would try to call, she really needed to get these essays done. If she saw his name on the caller ID, it would distract her even if she let the call go to voice mail.

Forcing aside the uneasy, even suspicious, feelings about Reese that had plagued her all day, she picked up the next essay in her pile.

Chapter Seventy-Six

&

Mindy felt nervous as she rang the front door bell of the beach-front Tudor-style Carrington mansion. Having grown up in a modest home in a small town in Ohio, she was not accustomed to being around wealthy people. This fabulous house, with its steep pitched roof, wood beams, and tall diamond-paned windows was enough to intimidate any normal person, she thought.

Her nervousness didn't lessen when a stern-faced maid in a light-blue uniform the door answered the door.

"May I help you?" the maid asked in a tone that made Mindy excruciatingly aware of her inexpensive pants and jacket, wrinkled from a day of classes and work in the HR office. Trying to smooth her pants with one hand while hanging onto the large gift bag in the other, Mindy wondered if she should have gone to the back door.

She bit her lip to keep from stuttering and was pleased to hear her words come out steady. "I'm from Grant Lauder University. I have a package for Mrs. Carrington."

"Thank you. I'll be sure she gets it." The maid firmly took the bag from Mindy and started to close the door.

"Wait, Edith," Cami called out from somewhere in the house. "Is that Mindy with my gift for Robin?"

"Yes, ma'am."

"Have her come in. Bring her here to the den."

"Yes, ma'am."

Mindy couldn't believe how the maid managed to fill those two words with such disapproval as she opened the door wider and stepped aside. Mindy followed the stiff-backed woman across a marble entrance. From it a wide staircase curved upward and a large, multi-faceted chandelier cast a glittering sheen onto a four-foot high cloisonné vase at the bottom of the stairs. An elegant formal living room opened to the right, with an equally elegant and formal dining room to the left.

Then, Mindy entered the den and into a different world, as warm and cozy as the entry was formal. She had only seen Cami Carrington once, with Dr. Elfmon and Lenae Maddox, having lunch at the Burger Lounge, the very day before Ms. Maddox was attacked. Now, wearing dark blue pants topped by a smoky blue cashmere pullover, Cami strolled toward the arched entry to the room, both hands extended toward her.

"Mindy! We meet again," said Cami, clasping Mindy's fingers in her own. "Thanks so much for dropping this by." Without giving Mindy a chance to respond, she took the gift bag, led the girl to a comfortable leather chair, and chatted on while she perched on the edge of a matching chair. "I'm the world's worst for waiting 'til the last minute to get a gift. And this is for one of my dearest friends. The party's in an hour, so your timing is perfect. Good thing it's here on the island. Thank you *so* much."

"I was happy to do it, Mrs. Carrington. I..."

"Oh, call me Cami, please. Mrs. Carrington was my mother-in-law." Cami wrinkled her nose. "So, tell me about yourself. What year are you at the...what do you kids call it?...The Glue?"

Mindy laughed. "That's right. I'm a freshman, undeclared major, and as you know I've helped out in the H.R. office since Miss Maddox... um, until she..." She stopped herself and rushed on, "I'm from Ohio, and I love living in Coronado."

"With Mrs. Townsend, I hear." Cami looked like she was trying to suppress the giggle that slipped out. "Sorry. She's quite a woman. Volunteers at the hospital even though she's nearly eighty."

"She's wonderful. And a lot of fun."

"I can imagine. What about your office work? Do you have a lot of communication with the professors?"

Mindy thought that was an unusual question, but then, Cami Carrington seemed to be a most unusual woman. "Some," she answered. "Now and then one of them drops off some work for me."

"What about Dr. Sutherland?"

That question seemed strange, not simply unusual, but with an inner shrug, Mindy replied, "Yes, he comes in sometimes. He's one of the nicer professors. Always friendly, never stuffy. I like him. Actually, I saw him Saturday morning at the airport, but he didn't see me."

"Oh?"

"Yes. I was there to meet a friend who spent the weekend with me." Mindy couldn't help wondering about Cami's interest in the professor.

"I heard he was flying up to Sacramento to be with an ailing aunt," Cami said.

Before she could stop herself, Mindy giggled. "When I saw him, he was meeting someone, not flying out, and that was no 'aunty' hug he gave her. If that was an ailing aunt, I'm your uncle."

"What do you mean?" All trace of levity had escaped Cami's voice. Suddenly, Mindy felt uncomfortable.

"Well, the woman he was meeting looked like a model or movie star or something. And he gave her a flower."

"A flower? What kind?"

"A long stemmed rose. Don't know what kind, but it was gorgeous, all coral and goldy colored."

Mindy was shocked at how pale Cami's face turned.

"A Talisman rose." Cami's mouth tightened, and her eyes narrowed. *She's angry!* Mindy thought. *What did I say wrong?*

Chapter Seventy-Seven

ॐ

Kate pushed the essays aside and pressed her forehead with the heels of her hands. She had worked steadily since Mindy left and had finally graded the last paper. Moving her hands from her face, she looked at the wall clock and saw that it was nine-thirty. Wow, that had taken even longer than she'd feared it would. Kate straightened her desk, then got out her phone. She wondered if there would be a message from Reese, who had never showed up for work today. As she restored the sound, she saw she'd missed a call, a voice mail message, and two text messages, all from Cami.

How odd, she thought, checking the text messages first.

"Call me," was all the first text said. The second one, sent an hour later, read, "No matter what time." The voice mail only added, "Something important to tell you."

Cami and her dramatics. Kate shook her head. *Probably wants to tell me about Robin's birthday party. This is as bad as when we were in college and she couldn't wait a single second to give me all the details of her latest date.* Kate started to return the call, but all at once the long hours at her desk hit her. She was exhausted and hungry. She'd call when she got home.

Kate locked her office and walked down the dimly lit hall, realizing she was the last person to leave the building. Though not given to jitters, she couldn't help feeling a little spooked. Thank goodness the campus and parking lots were brightly lit, and several security guards wandered the grounds every night. Still, she'd be glad to get to her car.

She had just stepped out into the cold night air, when a hand touched her shoulder. She sensed a large body looming behind her. She spun around, ready to scream if she had to.

235

~~~

"Where *are* you, Kate?"

Frustrated beyond words, Cami paced the floor of her bedroom. Tonight no images of the years she had shared the room with Braxton invaded her mind. Every thought focused on Kate. And Reese Sutherland. And his roses! What a— Cami forced herself away from a number of names that came to mind — what a jerk!

"Where *are* you?" she repeated, still speaking aloud as though Kate could actually hear her. "Why don't you return my calls? I have something important to tell you!"

A disturbing thought occurred to Cami. Was Kate with Reese right now? Was he plying his oh-so-alluring charms on Kate at this very moment? Was Kate even safe with a man like that? A man who clearly used the women in his life?

Finally she thought to pray that God would keep Kate safe in every way.

~~~

Two strong hands gripped Kate's shoulders as she turned. She tried to jerk free, but the grip only tightened. Heart thudding against her chest, she looked up at her attacker.

Very tall. Pale blonde hair made nearly white by the nearby pathway light. Blue eyes filled with ... concern. And love.

"Gunnar!"

Without a second thought, she fell into his arms.

Chapter Seventy-Eight

Sitting with Kate in front of a blazing fire in the den of this delightful craftsman cottage, Gunnar felt like he was on both ends of a seesaw in a kiddie park.

How wonderful to hold Kate in his arms here on the comfortable sofa. She'd never looked more beautiful to him than the moment she fell in his arms an hour ago at the university. *Up.*

Across the room he could see several gold-colored roses in a vase, a few of which were in various stages of drooping. From Reese Sutherland, of course. *Down.*

Kate had seemed so glad to see him. *Up.*

He had a hard time keeping his gaze away from those roses. *Down.*

He was here. He loved Kate Kelly Elfmon. He was going to fight for her with every ounce of his energies. *Up.*

Kate broke into his musings."You haven't told me how you were able to get away to come here. I thought you were going to Vancouver."

Was that a note of jealousy in Kate's tone?

"For the second time in three months, I turned a responsibility over to my young, very ambitious assistant, Keith Johnson, in order to come to Coronado."

"Like you did the night Braxton Carrington died."

"Yeah. If I do this again, they may replace me with Keith."

"Not likely." Kate snuggled closer. "What are you thinking about, Gunnar?"

Gunnar chuckled. "A playground."

"What!" She pulled away and sat up straight.

"Never mind." He pulled her close again. "The question is, what are *you* thinking?"

She buried her cheek deeper into his shoulder and didn't answer right away. "I wish I knew."

"Me, too," he growled.

"The only thing I know for sure is that everything else flew from my mind the moment I saw you."

"And now? Has this *fellow professor*..." Gunnar made no attempt to keep disdain from his voice. "Has he suddenly flown into your mind?"

"Flown in? No. Snuck in? Yes." *Down.*

Kate moved out of his arms again. "I have to be completely truthful with you, Gunnar. The thing is, I care about you more than I can say. But I have had a really good time going out with Reese. We've done some fun things. He's been a perfect gentleman, by the way."

"Bully for him."

"Gunnar..."

"Sorry. Go on. You've done fun things. You enjoy being with him."

Kate bent her head and nodded.

Gunnar tucked one finger under her chin tilted her face up. "Look at me Kate."

She did. And what he saw put him back on the seesaw.

"Kate," he said, "do you enjoy being with him more than with me?"

"It—It's different."

"He's more exciting. Is that what you mean?"

"Well, yes."

Down, down, down. Sometimes Gunnar wished Kate were not quite so forthright.

Lord, help me! Where do I go from here? Do You want me to give up? Do You want me to let Kate go?"

The *NO!* Gunnar felt in his spirit made him start.

"I'm sorry, Gunnar," Kate went on, "but you asked."

"I did. And you gave me an honest answer. I appreciate that—sort of. Now, let me be completely honest with you. I don't 'care about' you, I love you. And unless you can tell me straight out that you're in love with another man, I won't give up fighting for you."

A look of disbelief and trust swept over Kate's countenance. She took his face in both hands and kissed him, long and deep.

"Please don't give up, Gunnar," she whispered.

She kissed him again.

Up. Up. Up!

Chapter Seventy-Nine

ɮ

"Wow, you were hungry!" Cami told Gunnar.

Late last night, Kate finally had returned Cami's calls. She'd intended to tell Kate about Mindy's seeing Reese Sutherland give a rose to a woman at the airport. Kate's news about Gunnar being in town made Cami decide to hold off for now. She hated the thought of spoiling Kate's news.

Now, mid-morning, after giving Gunnar time to sleep in at the island hotel he'd booked, she was treating him to breakfast while Kate was at work. The Day & Night Cafe was a tiny Coronado landmark with a 1950's arrow-shaped sign over the door out front. It was squeezed between a carpet company and a pizza parlor on Orange Street. Gunnar had just finished off every bite of one of the restaurant's specialties, a huge California omelet stuffed with bacon, cheese, avocados, and tomatoes, as well as a healthy serving of hash browns.

Gunnar leaned back with a deep sigh of satisfaction and patted his stomach. "I was starving. No food on the plane from Boston, unless you count peanuts and pretzels. And last night, with Kate..."

Cami laughed. "You weren't thinking of food." She loved the sheepish grin Gunnar gave her for a reply. "How did that go? Kate sounded upbeat but a little guarded when I talked with her after you left her place last night."

"It went well, considering the fact that Kate's been seeing another man."

Cami didn't know how to answer that, so she kept silent, debating about how to tell Gunnar about Reese. She'd deliberately waited until he had a good breakfast before saying anything. Now she was bursting to spill out her indignation and anger at Reese's deceitful treatment of her friend.

They both need to know. I'll go ahead and tell him. She opened her mouth, then shut it. *Maybe I should wait and tell Kate first.*

Gunnar folded his large arms across his chest and gave Cami a level stare. "So, what do you think, Cami? What's going on? What's this guy like? First I heard of him was when he sent her the first rose. She told me the kind. An unusual name."

"Talisman. Same word as for a good luck charm, but Reese told Kate it represented memories. He also told her a legend supposedly connected to it. But last night, I Googled 'Talisman Rose' and didn't find one single thing about memories or a legend. He always sends Kate one. Only one." *Even to other women,* Cami thought, wishing she could kick Reese Sutherland right now.

Gunnar let out a snort. "Interesting, but you didn't answer my question. "What's Reese Sutherland like?"

"What's he like?" She shrugged. "Movie star good looks. Sophisticated law professor. Sharp-dressing golfer. Attentive, easy to talk to. Could charm the fur coat off an Eskimo."

"Hmmpf." Gunnar's mouth turned down. "Hard act to follow."

Cami gave him a long look, dying to go ahead and tell him what she knew. Instead, she said, "I wouldn't be sure about that."

Gunnar blew out a whoosh of air and unfolded his arms. "And spiritually?"

Spiritually? It may be judgmental, but on a scale of one to ten, I give him minus nine. Again, Cami held back and simply said, "Kate has been reluctant to dig deep on that subject with Reese."

"That's completely out of character for her."

"Completely."

Gunnar searched Cami's face as if hoping to find encouragement. "So, what do you think? Is Kate falling in love with him?"

Cami paused, wanting to encourage Gunnar, yet knowing he needed her honesty. For a moment, she asked herself the question: *Was* Kate falling for Reese? After all, she didn't know what Cami did about him. Finally, she answered what she felt in her heart about her friend.

"Charmed, yes. Flattered? What woman wouldn't be? Falling in love? I doubt it, Gunnar. I really do."

"Ever the gentle diplomat, aren't you, Cami?"

"Oh no, I—"

"It's okay. I get your drift. Besides, as much as I love Kate and as hard as I plan to fight for her, in the end I want God's will for us. And I want her happiness, even if that means giving her up."

"Now that's real love," Cami whispered. Speaking normally again, she became somber. She couldn't wait any longer. "I tried to call Kate several times yesterday, but her cell phone was off."

"She told me about that. What was so serious?"

"I learned something about Reese that she needs to know. But she sounded so happy last night when she finally called—after you left—that I didn't have the heart to mention it then."

"What was it?"

"One of the girls from the university came over last night. And she told me—"

"Mrs. Carrington!" The male voice came from behind Cami, whose back was to the door.

Cami turned her head. "Detective Lopez! We keep running into each other at eating, um, establishments." She waved her hand at the long, narrow ultra-casual room.

"No tacos, today?"

"No. I went for the veggie omelet." She gestured toward Gunnar. "Do you remember meeting Gunnar Volstad when you were investigating Braxton's death?"

"Sure do." Lopez and Gunnar exchanged a hearty handshake.

"I'd ask you to join us," Cami said, "but these teeny tables are definitely meant for only two."

"No problem." Shifting a black leather attaché case from one hand to the other, Lopez settled himself on a counter barstool, no more than three feet away.

"Are there any further developments about who tried to kill Lenae, Detective?"

Lopez shook his head. "'Fraid not. But hey, I have something I started to show you at Taco Bell, but right then your friend came in." He snapped open the attaché case and drew out a manila envelope, which he handed to Cami.

"What's this?" Cami asked, undoing the envelope clasp.

"Probably nothing. A copy of a small watercolor painting I found in Lenae Maddox's loft."

"Oh," Cami said sadly. "We talked about my seeing her art work sometime." She opened the envelope and pulled out the single sheet of computer paper and turned it over.

Cami stared at the picture, exquisite even on cheap printer paper. In the background, out of focus, was the Hotel del Coronado. In brilliant contrast, one stunning long-stemmed gold and coral rose curved over the page. She drew her brows together.

"What is it, Mrs. Carrington?" Lopez insisted.

Cami raised her eyes.

"Detective Lopez. I think I know who attacked Lenae!"

Chapter Eighty

❧

On a break after her ten o'clock class, Kate got a latte from the cafeteria and took the steaming brew outside. She strolled through the eucalyptus-dotted lawn where Cami had fallen and was rescued by Reese. Reese's car was missing from staff parking lot again this morning, and Kate didn't know for sure if he'd come to work or not. She hoped he was feeling better today, then wondered why she wasn't more concerned about him.

It's probably a cold. Maybe I'll text him later. Don't want to bother him if he's resting.

From Reese, her thoughts flew to Gunnar and the moments they'd spent together last night. She took a sip of the latte and remembered how warm his lips had felt against hers. Despite the hot drink, a delicious shiver rippled through her body.

Mmmm, mmmmm! She ran the tip of her tongue over her lips. *Good thing Gunnar insisted on leaving when he did.*

Hugging herself, she entered the path to the beach. It was the same one she'd seen Lenae Maddox returning from the day Kate met her. The woman was still in a coma from the two attempts on her life. Kate began sending up a prayer for Lenae's recovery, but in the midst of her plea, her thoughts skipped back to Gunnar, and a smile tugged at her lips.

Near the end of the path, a wind-scarred wooden bench beckoned to Kate. She settled on it, slipped off her shoes, and flexed her feet out in front of her. Unlike most San Diego mornings, there had been little fog. The sun shone bright on the water, and the breeze that ruffled the choppy blue-green waves was enough to make Kate tighten her sweater.

For several minutes, Kate allowed the continuous motion of the waves rolling into shore and back out again to hypnotize her.

Like I let Reese Sutherland practically hypnotize me. What happened to me, Lord? Where has my mind been?

A better question might be, where has your heart been, Kate?

My heart, Lord? My heart has never left You.

You could have fooled anyone but Me. Look how you kept putting off trying to learn about Reese's spiritual life.

The inner Voice stung Kate. Yes, she had held off questioning Reese about spiritual issues. She didn't ask herself why. In her heart, she had known she wouldn't like what she learned and would feel she had to stop seeing him. Not only that, but ever since her first date with Reese she'd been out late so many nights and slept as long as possible the next morning that she'd either rushed through or skipped her morning devotions.

All of that is so unlike me. A few weeks ago, if anyone had told me I'd skimp on my time with God this way, I'd have said I'd never do that.

You were pretty sure of yourself, weren't you? There's a word for that, you know, Kate.

That stung even more.

Yes, Lord, I know the word: pride. Worse yet, spiritual pride. Chest tight with regret, Kate bowed her head and begged forgiveness for her cocky self-assurance and for neglecting her Lord.

You know I forgive you, Kate. So, what now?

What now? Suddenly she knew.

She pulled out her phone and speed-dialed Gunnar's number.

No answer. Maybe he was still sleeping. Kate started to leave a message, but noticing the time on the cell screen, she saw that her next class would begin in five minutes. She put the phone back in her pocket. As usual, it was on silent mode during most of the school day.

It's better if I wait 'til I see him anyway. Tonight I'll tell Gunnar I love him and we can get married as soon as the semester at Grant Lauder is over. Maybe we can have a Christmas wedding in Boston!

Chapter Eighty-One

ॐ

Gunnar's phone vibrated in his pocket, but he was so startled by the statement Cami had just made that he ignored it.

"I think I know who attacked Lenae!" she'd said.

"Wait a minute," Lopez said. "Mrs. Carrington, are you telling me you know who attacked Ms. Maddox from looking at this painting?"

Cami turned the sheet of paper so that both Lopez and Gunnar could see it. Gunnar felt the blood drain from his face.

"It was Reese Sutherland!" Cami went on, looking like she was about to rise from her chair and go after Sutherland. Gunnar placed a restraining hand on her elbow.

"Hear her out, Detective," he said.

Lopez gave Cami a tight-lipped skeptical look. "Okay, I'm listening."

Cami looked toward Gunnar, then back at Lopez. "When you came in I was about to tell Gunnar something I only found out about Reese last night."

"Which was?"

"It looks like sending a Talisman rose—that's the kind in this painting—is Reese's signature date offering. He has been sending one to Kate before every date."

"Could be a coincidence," Lopez said, sitting stock still, but alert.

"Even if I know he has sent one to at least one other woman?"

Now Lopez leaned forward. "Go on."

"Last night a young woman from Grant Lauder brought something by my house. While she was there, she mentioned seeing Reese Friday morning at the airport. He had told Kate he was going to Sacramento to visit a sick aunt."

"Which would explain his presence at the airport," Lopez said.

Cami tightened her lips, and her eyes flashed. "He wasn't there to catch a plane, Detective. He was there to meet someone—a woman."

Anger washed over Gunnar. Not only was this Sutherland guy trying to make time with the woman he, Gunnar, loved, but the man was playing her for a fool at the same time.

"Not a nice thing to do," Lopez said, "but not an indication that he attacked Lenae."

"According to Mindy, this woman was a seductive looking blonde, Marilyn Monroe wannabe, and—"

"Mrs. Carrington, you're making guesses."

"Well, Detective, my *guess* is based on the fact that Mindy said Reese gave this woman one long-stemmed gold and coral rose, the same kind he gives all his women, including Lenae. My *guess* is that it was a Talisman."

~~~

"Sutherland isn't answering his phone," said Lopez, still reeling with the information Cami had shared with him. Followed by her and Gunnar Volstad, he had stepped outside the tiny restaurant and called the university to get Sutherland's phone number and address, including the gate code. "And he hasn't shown up at work today."

"I've been trying to return Kate's call, but she isn't answering either," said Gunnar.

"I have a really bad feeling about this, Detective," said Cami.

"Yeah. Me, too. I'm going over there," Lopez said.

"I'm going with you," Cami told him.

"You can't do that, Mrs. Carrington. This is police work."

"No, Cami," Gunnar put in, "we have to let the police do their job."

Cami ignored him. "Kate Elfmon is my best friend. What if she's in danger?"

"Mrs. Carrington..." Lopez tried to speak patiently. "Mrs. Elfmon probably silences her phone during class time."

"Well, yes. But what if that's not why she's not answering? What if she's with Reese for some reason?"

Lopez saw Cami glance back at Gunnar with a look of apology. *This woman is too much,* he thought. "I understand your concern, but—"

"I don't think you do."

"I do. Really." Lopez was tired of being patient. "But the answer is no."

Chapter Eighty-Two

Ᏸↄ

K ate had assigned her students a project to do in class, and she was pleased to see them engrossed in it. She was also pleased that, after missing class yesterday, Dexter was back today. He looked rattled, but that was par for the course for Dexter, especially since the attempts on Lenae Maddox's life.

As the students worked silently, Kate's thoughts swung back and forth like a pendulum. One moment she was feeling delicious anticipation of seeing Gunnar's face light up later today when she told him of her decision. The next she was feeling bad about how Reese might react to that news.

We did have some great times together. And I have to admit I was starting to have feelings for him. It seems heartless to simply announce, "Hey, I realize I'm in love with someone else. Thanks for the roses and the 'memories.'"

Kate had heard Cecelia Hanson, Reese's admin assistant, tell a female staff member that he wasn't in again today and hadn't even called. He must be really sick.

Well, Kate was sorry if he was sick and she hoped he'd soon be better, but that didn't change the fact her heart now belonged to Gunnar Volstad. She'd have to pray—*Never again let me forget to pray, Lord!*—for the best way to tell Reese about him.

A horrible thought came to Kate. *Gunnar. He didn't answer my call. What if he wasn't sleeping? What if he's having second thoughts about us?*

She was tempted to call him right now. No. Not during class time. That would be unprofessional. Again, she decided she'd wait and talk with him when her work day was over. Thank goodness today she'd be finished at noon.

Chapter Eighty-Three

It hadn't been hard for Cami to talk Gunnar into heading over to Reese Sutherland's home, despite Detective Lopez's stern words. After all, he too wanted to be there. It had been a little harder for Cami to convince Gunnar to let her accompany him.

"Look," she'd said, using the most reasonable tones possible, "neither of us needs to go inside. We can stay in the car and wait for Detective Lopez to come out. We know where Reese lives. We both heard Lopez repeat the address and gate code out loud when he called the school. The code is easy. Remember? One seven, one eight. Seventeen, eighteen."

Gunnar's phone vibrated. He got it out and looked at the caller ID.

"It's Kate again." He started to return the call, then put the phone back in his pocket. "I can't talk to her now. Not until we know more about Sutherland."

"I think you're right."

"Come on. We can take my car."

"And show up in that Honda rental? I don't think so. We'll take the Jag."

~~~

Lopez got no response when he rang Reese Sutherland's bell. The CPD officer he'd phoned to meet him at the townhouse had a lock kit ready, but when Lopez tried the door, it wasn't locked.

The two stepped inside the room. Though the sun shone brightly outside, heavy drapes obliterated most of its light, so that at first Lopez only saw outlines of furniture. He flipped a switch on the wall, blinking at the sudden brightness.

He and his companion didn't need to search the home. There on the couch lay Reese Sutherland, dried brown blood coating his forehead. Beside him lay a bronze statuette in the shape of a golfer swinging a club. Across his chest rested one long-stemmed Talisman rose.

~~~

Cami clenched her fists to her face and screamed.

Detective Lopez swirled around and shouted at her. "What are you doing here? Get out! Get out right now!"

Gunnar ran up behind her and grabbed her sleeve. Jerking her out the door, he said, "Sorry, Detective. I tried to stop her from coming in."

Seconds later, they were back in the Jag. It was too late. Cami knew that every detail of what she had seen would haunt her forever.

Chapter Eighty-Four

ॐ

Not waiting for the elevator, Mike bounded up the stairs leading to Lenae's floor. His head rang with the words he'd just heard on his office phone.

"Mr. Jenkins, this is Jan Foster. I'm a nurse at Coronado hospital."

The hospital calling me? Mike had steeled himself for bad news. "Go ahead," he'd said as calmly as possible.

"Dr. Feldman told me to call and let you know that Lenae Maddox is awake and—"

"Awake? She's awake? What—"

"Please let me finish, Mr. Jenkins. She has been having moments of wakefulness all day, and during one of them, a few minutes ago, she called for you."

"I'll be right there!" Mike didn't bother to say good-bye.

Now, as he approached the door to Lenae's floor, he opened it cautiously, remembering how it had slammed into him last time he was here. After checking in with Nurse Foster and showing her his ID, Mike followed her to Lenae's room. He was glad to see there was no longer a police guard. That was the last thing he wanted to deal with today.

"Ten minutes, Mr. Jenkins," the nurse told Mike.

Lenae's eyes were closed, but her color was good, her breathing even; and the heart monitor graph only a little erratic. Almost reverently, Mike tiptoed to her bedside and pulled up a chair. He desperately wanted to wake her up, but maybe it was best not to.

I only have ten minutes, he reminded himself.

He touched her hand. To his utter delight, her eyes fluttered open and she gave his fingers a nearly imperceptible squeeze.

251

"Mike," she whispered. Her voice was hoarse in the manner of someone who hasn't spoken for a long time. Saying that one word seemed to take tremendous effort.

"Shhh, Lenae. You don't need to talk. I'm here and you're awake. That's all that matters."

Mike didn't hear the door open behind him

"Want ... to ...," she forced out. "Want ... to ... tell ... you ... who ..."

"Shhh. You want to tell me who hurt you?"

She nodded and closed her eyes again, though Mike could tell she was still awake.

"You don't need to tell me." He gently stroked her cheek, but clenched his teeth. "I know who it was. It was Reese Sutherland. Right?"

Mike had to lean close to hear Lenae's answer. "Right."

"Mike Jenkins!"

Mike jerked his head toward the stern voice. A CPD officer!

"I need you to come with me to police headquarters," the solemn-faced officer told Mike. "Now."

Chapter Eighty-Five

❧

A s her students left chattering from the room, Kate looked at the clock on the wall. Noon. She felt almost giddy that she was finished for today and could see Gunnar soon. She rushed to her office and got her things together in record time, then headed for the exit. Heading down the outside steps, she pulled out her cell phone. She saw that he'd tried to return her calls.

"Kate!"

Startled and pleased at hearing Gunnar's voice, she looked up. She was less pleased when she saw that Cami was with him. She'd hoped for time alone with him. Then...

Their faces. Gunnar's was stone-like, and Cami's nearly matched the white blazer she wore.

Oh, Lord, she thought, *something is terribly wrong.*

With Cami not far behind, Gunnar was at Kate's side by the time she touched the bottom step. He pulled her to him and held her tight for a moment.

"What—"

"Not now. Let's go to my car."

"I-I'll wait here," Cami said, her voice weak and shaky.

~~~

Cami could see Gunnar's car from where she'd perched herself on the steps. She was inexpressibly relieved that he'd offered to tell Kate about Reese's murder. She had no idea what words he used, but she knew the exact moment he told Kate what he and Cami had seen an hour ago.

Kate—strong, stoic, indomitable Kate—covered her face, and her body began to shake all over. Then Gunnar pulled her to him, as he'd done at the steps, and let her sob into his shoulder. What was Kate feeling, besides natural horror over the violent act? Was she simply grieving the loss of a man she'd grown close to, or was it for the fact that now they'd never have an even closer relationship? And what about Gunnar? What was *he* feeling, and how was this going to affect him and Kate?

As for Cami herself, she felt cold all over, and it wasn't only from the breeze that had blown in from the ocean beyond the school grounds.

Chapter Eighty-Six

જી

Carlos Lopez stood on the cliff of Point Loma, a narrow peninsula jutting out between San Diego Bay and the Pacific, a few miles from downtown San Diego. A brisk breeze flicked at his short, dark hair, while bright afternoon sun warmed his back. Behind him a few tourists wandered in and out of the historic 1855 Point Loma lighthouse. From there many would make their way to the point of the peninsula in order to peer down at the "new" lighthouse, built in 1891 to replace the original one, which was not often visible through dense fogs and low clouds. Across the bay, lay Coronado.

But it was the Hotel Del that dominated the scene. Lopez's eyes strayed up the beach from the hotel to the area where Lenae Maddox had been attacked—by Reese Sutherland, he now knew. Yesterday Lenae had regained consciousness long enough to call for Mike Jenkins and to verify that it was also Reese who had pulled the plug on her oxygen machine.

The man tried to kill her twice, Lopez thought, disgust and loathing threatening to overcome him. *And now he's dead, too.*

Lopez scrunched his shoulders against the breeze and shuffled to the head of a trail that led down to a spot a few feet above the water's edge. Because he had been the one to discover Sutherland's murdered body, the La Jolla Police Department had allowed Lopez to take charge of this new development. On the way down the trail, he ticked off possible suspects, name by name, and put them into separate mental file folders.

First, there was Mike Jenkins. After seeing Reese dead, Lopez had called CPD headquarters and ordered Jenkins to be picked up. He'd been furious to learn the station's newest rookie had given the hospital permission to let Jenkins into Ms. Maddox's room. Of course, if Jenkins was Sutherland's murderer, the woman he'd killed for would be safe with him. Still…

The coroner had tentatively guessed the time of death to be between eleven a.m. and two p.m. on Monday. When Lopez questioned Jenkins, the man claimed he'd left his office about nine-fifteen and driven to Alpine to inspect a building site, alone of course. His secretary couldn't confirm either the time or the location, and no one had seen him at the off-road site. He'd had plenty of time to go to Sutherland's La Jolla Shores townhouse during all those hours. Naturally, Jenkins denied ever setting foot near Reese Sutherland's home and said he'd never even met the man. Well, with sufficient motive, you didn't have to meet with a man very long before you killed him.

Mike Jenkins: Revenge "file folder."

Lopez stumbled over a rock in the path, straightened himself, and went to the second name on his mental list. Raquel Wells, a bit-part actress who had spent Sunday night with Sutherland. Upstairs, in the master bedroom's waste basket, Lopez had found a boarding pass from L.A. to San Diego, with Ms. Wells' name on it. A little before eight a.m. she'd arrived at a commercial shoot at Fiesta Island, a twenty-minute drive from La Jolla. However, the director had called for a break from eleven to one. Plenty of time to get to Reese's home, do the dirty deed, and get back. When questioned, Ms. Wells had erupted into sobs that seemed genuine—until she admitted that Sutherland had led her to believe he planned to marry her, but all the time was sending roses to another woman.

Hell hath no fury like that of a woman scorned. Lopez had learned that phrase in 11th-grade Lit class and had had cause to recall it many times in his years as a police detective.

Raquel Wells: Rejection file.

Interviews at Grant Lauder University had yielded three more people—a professor and two students—who hated Sutherland.

Dr. Albert Bainbridge, Professor of Corporate Law, had been vocal about his resentment toward Sutherland, an outsider, being chosen interim head of the Law Department over him. However, the fussy little man's secretary had confirmed that Bainbridge was in his office from about ten o'clock until three grading essays on the day of Sutherland's murder. If he had left, she would have seen him walk through her office and out the front door. Unfortunately, that eliminated Bainbridge.

Third suspect: Law student Justin Rhodes. Make that former law student. He'd been expelled from school after punching Sutherland for refusing to allow him to redo an important essay. Now, his chances of going into law looked dim indeed. Not only that, but Lopez had learned that Rhodes had tried to get Lenae Maddox to go out with him. He'd sent her flowers and practically stalked her. Maybe he had learned about her relationship with Sutherland. His shaky alibi hinged strictly on his mother's statement that her son was dead drunk in his room almost all day. Mrs. Rhodes seemed like a very nice lady, but she wouldn't be the first to cover up for a son. Rhodes had not been at home when Lopez went there earlier today. His mother said he was out job hunting. Lopez had already made a mental note to go back and interview the man in person.

Justin Rhodes: Another Resentment file candidate. Possibly Jealousy file, as well.

Fourth: What about that other Grant Lauder student, Dexter Driscoll? The young man had been distraught about both attempts on Ms. Maddox's life. Claimed she was his only true friend, despite their age and station differences. Driscoll was pretty unstable. Lopez could imagine him attempting to get even with the person he thought had ended that friendship. He hadn't gone to school on Monday. Said he was too upset and had stayed in his room all day. No witnesses, of course.

Dexter Driscoll: Another candidate for the Revenge folder.

Better head back to the station, Lopez told himself. *Probably shouldn't have taken time to come out here, but I had to get away and try to get some perspective.*

Refreshed, but no nearer to a solution to Reese Sutherland's murder, Lopez cast one longing look at the sparkling blue bay and turned to head back up the trail. About halfway up, his phone vibrated.

"Lopez here. What is it, Pitt?"

"You might want to get back over to Sutherland's place and talk to a woman who just called the station. She says she saw two people, a woman and a man, arguing at Sutherland's door about noon the day of the murder. Name's Stephanie Winslow."

"Call her back. Tell her I'm on my way."

Chapter Eighty-Seven

❧

Gunnar sat on the bed in his hotel room thinking these past two days had been among the worst in his life, even worse than last summer when Kate had told him she was going to step away from their relationship for awhile. This time, she hadn't said anything about their relationship. She'd just cried. And cried. And cried. It was so unlike her that he hadn't known what to do.

About fifteen minutes after he'd told her about Reese's murder, he'd given her car key to Cami and told her to meet them at Kate's house. There Cami, though pale and shaken herself, had taken charge and insisted that Kate come to her home for a day or two.

"I'll call the school and tell them you won't be in tomorrow," she'd told Kate.

Still crying, Kate had submitted to Cami and began getting an overnight bag together while Gunnar and Cami drove to the Day & Night Cafe. She picked up the silver Jag, and Gunnar followed her back to Kate's house. Before getting into the Jag to drive away, Kate turned to Gunnar and held on to him with a strength that was amazing in such a small woman.

"I'm so sorry, Gunnar. I'm so sorry," she'd kept repeating.

That was yesterday. Gunnar hadn't heard a word from Kate since, and it was already one o'clock. Plenty of time for her to get in touch with him.

What's going on with Kate, Lord? Was she really in love with Sutherland? So much in love that there's no hope for me and her?

Gunnar stood and began prowling the spacious room. He paid no attention to the sea-foam-green chairs and comforter or the sand-colored carpet or the Polynesian posters against sky-blue walls. He went back and lay down on the comfortable bed, but it may as well have been a paddle board. Too restless to lie still, he sprang up again and went to the white sugar-cane desk where he'd laid his airplane ticket. Now, he wondered if he should call the airline and move up the date.

I want to be here for Kate, but not if she doesn't want me. And if she was in love with Sutherland, I'm the last person she'll want around. I competed for her against a dead manonce. I can't do it again.

He noted the airline's reservation number and picked up his phone. An indecisive finger hovered over it. It rang.

Kate.

"Gunnar, we need to talk," she said as soon as he answered. "May I come over?"

~~~

Kate felt like she'd been dragged across the sharp tentacles of a coral reef and knew she looked like it, too. She was glad Gunnar had suggested they meet in a screened-off sitting area off the lobby. His room would have been too intimate, too... She stepped around the bamboo screen and stood for a moment watching Gunnar, who sat with his head back and eyes closed.

"Gunnar," she said softly.

He opened his eyes. She hated the wary look in them.

"Kate."

His chair was love-seat style, large enough for two people. He frowned when Kate chose the easy chair across from him. She had come here ready to reveal her innermost feelings to Gunnar, but when she opened her mouth to speak, the words froze in her throat. So she folded her hands in her lap and stared down at them.

After several long, silent moments, she looked up. "Gunnar, I don't know where to begin."

"Kate," he commanded, "tell me what you came to say. I'm a big boy. I may not like it, but I can take it."

She took a deep breath and made herself look at him. "These past few months have been so confusing for me. You were so far away. And... and things were not completely settled with us, with me. I have to admit that Reese's attention was very flattering, I'm embarrassed to say he turned my head with a few roses and some fun dates."

She waited for him to respond. Instead, he crossed one leg over the other and glared.

Stumbling over her words, she continued, "The moment I saw you Monday night I realized that no one—no one—could ever mean what you do to me. Nobody could ever take your place."

As Kate spoke, Gunnar's expression had become less wary. Less, but not completely.

"Gunnar, I'm afraid of something."

"Afraid?" His expression became wary again. "Afraid of what?"

"Afraid that all this has changed your feelings about me."

Gunnar got up slowly and walked a few steps away. His back to her, he said, "I need some time to process this, Kate. Let's talk again tomorrow."

~

A few minutes later, back at Cami's, Kate told her friend every detail of the few minutes she'd spent with Gunnar.

"Cami, what have I done? What if I've blown it with Gunnar? I don't think I could stand that."

Cami had no reply.

Chapter Eighty-Eight

&

"Thank you for stepping forward, Mrs. Winslow." In his usual speedy manner, Lopez assessed the woman before him—about thirty, medium height, somewhat attractive in her flawless make-up and straight brown hair cut in a short, practical style. He'd learned that she was a window designer for one of the local Macy's stores. Her own home—two doors down from Reese Sutherland's—with its pure, clean lines in teal and browns, reflected not only her talent, but her attention to detail.

"It was my duty, Detective," Mrs. Winslow said in a matter-of-fact tone. "As soon as I heard what had happened to that gor— uh, nice Reese Sutherland, I knew I had to get in touch with the police."

Nice? Reese Sutherland nice? And she almost called him gorgeous. Even in death that worm is charming women. Lopez wanted to refute Mrs. Winslow's opinion. Instead, he said, "You did the right thing. I came as soon as I was notified."

Mrs. Winslow nodded. "Well, why don't we sit down?" She waved a neat, short-nailed hand at a couch lined with decorative pillows. "Please excuse the mess." She brushed her fingertips across a glass table-top and blew off imaginary dust. "And do call me, Stephanie."

Not seeing one thing out of place, Lopez was tempted to make a sarcastic comment. Instead, guessing that "Stephanie" was fishing for a compliment and needing her full cooperation, he smiled and said, "Everything looks perfect, Stephanie."

Looking pleased, Stephanie took the easy chair. "I'll tell you every-thing I know, Detective."

"Please do. Start at the beginning."

"Well, there's not much to tell really. I wish there were."

I bet you do, Lopez thought.

"Whatever you can tell me will be helpful, I'm sure. I believe that when you called Coronado Police Headquarters, you said you saw someone at Sutherland's townhouse the day of his murder."

"Make that *two* someones. A man and a woman. I'd come home to get a design book I needed for the window I'm working on. When I drove in, I noticed two unfamiliar cars. One was in a visitor's spot, but the other was in one of my spots. It didn't really matter, though, because my husband was at work. He's a financial consultant. Anyway, I couldn't help noticing that the one in our spot was a red Corvette with a vanity license plate."

She stopped and looked at Lopez expectantly. He obliged her by asking, "What did it say?"

"Two—the number two, that is—ERIKA. That's Erika with a 'k' not a 'c'. You can see why I noticed it."

"Of course. What about the other car? Did you notice anything about it?"

"Cadillac. Grey. Very conservative. I didn't pay attention to the license plate."

"That's all right. Go ahead and tell me about the people you saw at Sutherland's door."

"The man was short and plump and almost bald. He was dressed in a business suit. Probably about fifty."

"And the woman?"

"She was the complete opposite. Tall, early twenties, dressed in a russet-colored pants outfit. She was quite stunning. Looked like a model."

Lopez felt his detective instincts honing in. "What else do you remember about her?"

"Her hair. She had the most wonderful, long, thick red hair."

Erika Weston and her husband, Dr. Stan Weston! Has to be. Can't be another beautiful red-head married to a short, bald man driving a car a '2 ERIKA' license plate. Lopez tamped down his excitement. "What was this couple doing?"

"Arguing. I could tell from the way he was shaking a fist at her and she was jabbing her hands into her hips."

"Could you hear them?"

"They were loud, but not plain enough to make out what they were saying."

"I see."

"Except for one thing."

Lopez raised his brows.

"I heard him yell out something like, 'He wouldn't dare!'"

"Could you tell if they went into Sutherland's house?"

"No. They could have been going in or coming out. Anyway, I decided it was none of my business, so I went inside."

"And that's all you know?"

"Except that when I came back to the window a few minutes later, they had left."

"And the time all this occurred?"

"Noon. I had come home during my lunch break."

Lopez got up and extended a hand to Stephanie Winslow. "You've been a big help, Stephanie. If you think of anything else, please call me." He handed her a card.

"You can be sure I will." She rose and followed Lopez toward the door. "Poor man. So many people causing trouble for him."

Lopez stopped. He turned toward her. "What do you mean?"

"A few nights ago, my husband and I were out for a walk when a young man stumbled up to Reese's door as he came out. The guy started yelling at Reese. He was drunk and really mad. Reese told him off, but still kept his cool."

"I think we'd better sit down again, Stephanie."

Chapter Eighty-Nine

ॐ

"I'm sorry, Detective. Justin isn't at home right now."

Chrissy Rhodes had invited Lopez into her small duplex home in a run-down area of Imperial Beach and offered him a seat and sat down opposite him. As when he'd come by earlier, he was again impressed by the expert landscaping that made the yard stand out in the midst of other yards that were a mixture of reasonably tidy and trashy looking.

"Can you tell me where he is, Mrs. Rhodes?"

"I-I'm not sure."

Lopez felt a twinge of compassion for the sweet-faced woman who looked as though she hadn't slept well for days. "What do you mean, you're not sure?"

"I mean I haven't seen him since last Saturday."

That surprised Lopez. "That's more than a week ago. When I spoke with you earlier, you told me your son was home drunk on Monday, day before yesterday. You also said he was out looking for a job and would be home later this afternoon."

Chrissy hung her head and tightened her lips, then looked up and searched his face with a haunted look in her own. "I lied."

Lopez bit back an angry response and forced himself to speak calmly. "Why did you do that?"

Chrissy clutched her arms and began to rock back and forth. When she spoke, tears had begun to stream down her cheeks. "I had heard about Reese Sutherland's murder, and I was afraid you'd suspect Justin." She let out a soft sob. "You do, don't you?"

"Mrs. Rhodes, your lie hasn't helped him."

Chrissy reached out and clasped Lopez's hand. "Justin didn't kill

Reese Sutherland, Detective. I know he didn't. He's a good son. You can't imagine how many sacrifices he's made to provide for me and his sisters since his father died. He was angry with Dr. Sutherland, yes, but he'd never kill him. He'd never kill anyone." She released Lopez's hand and pressed her fingers to her forehead. "I'm so worried about him. What if he's been in some kind of accident? What if he's lying dead somewhere? I'm going crazy with worrying over him and trying to keep the girls from suspecting anything."

Lopez was about to question Chrissy further when his phone vibrated. He got it out. "You again, Pitt? ... You sure about that? ... When? ... Where?.. He said what? ... SDPD won't let him go anywhere. I have a couple of other stops to make; then I'll head over there."

Lopez ended the call. "You can quit wondering if your son is lying dead somewhere, Mrs. Rhodes."

Her expression brightened, then clouded at Lopez's tight face. "Wh-what do you mean? Where is he?"

"Main San Diego police headquarters. He's drunk and keeps muttering something about getting into a fight and hitting someone on the head."

Chrissy jumped up. "I'm going to him."

"Not yet, Mrs. Rhodes. I need to speak with him first."

Seeing the woman's stricken expression, Lopez added, "I'll have someone call you."

Chapter Ninety

ᏏᎤ

Erika Weston answered the door of the Tuscan-style three-story home in Coronado Cays. She was exactly as Lopez remembered her: slender and voluptuous at the same time, a mane of red hair many women would die for, long-lashed eyes the color of emeralds. She wore a long, low-cut white sweater over black leggings. When she greeted him and he held up his badge, her face turned white and she froze.

She recognizes me from when I interviewed her and her husband about Braxton Carrington's murder last summer, Lopez thought. Aloud he said, "May I come in, Mrs. Weston?"

"Yes, yes, of course." She led him into a living room full of expensively gaudy black and green furnishings and accessories. Lopez forced himself to look at an oversized Picasso-style painting on the far wall, away from the snug white sweater and swaying black leggings that looked like they'd been painted on Erika.

"Who's there?" a male voice called out.

"It-it's Detective Lopez from the Coronado Police Department." Erika's voice trembled as she spoke.

Stan Weston rushed into the room, his face as pale as Erika's, but he spoke cordially. "What can we do for you, Detective?"

"I have a few questions. Won't take long. Could we sit down?"

"Oh, sure," Erika gushed. "Come right over here." She led him to a black leather armchair trimmed in green.

When the three were settled, Lopez on the comfortable-looking but decidedly uncomfortable chair and the Westons seated across from him on a couch the color of Erika's eyes, he got right to the point, "I'm sure you've heard of the murder of Reese Sutherland, acting head of the law

266

department of Grant Lauder University."

"Everybody in Coronado's heard about it," Stan replied. "Tragic."

"Oh, yes. Tragic," Erika echoed, twisting a strand of her long red hair. "How well did the two of you know Sutherland?"

Stan shrugged. "Not that well. We were casual acquaintances."

"Oh yes. Really casual," Erika agreed, pushing her hair behind her ear.

Lopez was deliberately silent for a few moments. He knew this made them uncomfortable. Uncomfortable witnesses often made stupid mistakes. Finally he said, "Could I ask where you were between eleven a.m. and two p.m. on Monday?"

Stan answered first. "Well, let me think." He rubbed his hand over the top of his bald head. "Oh, I remember." He faced Erika. "Wasn't that the day we went to Costco to look at flat-screen TVs?"

"Yes! That's right," Erika said. "That's where we were. Costco. You see, we want a bigger TV."

Lopez made a point of looking toward the sixty-inch number on one wall. "Did you find one?"

Following his gaze, Erika's eyes got so big her lashes nearly touched her brows.

Speaking calmly, Stan answered again. "No. Didn't like anything we saw."

"Did anyone see you there?"

Erika let out a nervous giggle. "Lots of people always see you at Costco."

"Can you give me the name of anyone who saw you, maybe someone you talked with?"

"Not really," said Stan.

"What about a clerk?"

"No, we didn't talk with a clerk. We just wandered around looking."

"You spent three hours in Costco? Better you than me."

"Oh, we didn't leave right at eleven," Erika put in eagerly. Lopez saw Weston nudge her with his knee. "Um, but it was pretty soon after that. But it takes about thirty minutes to get to Costco, and, and..."

"Actually there was a back-up on the bridge," Stan explained. "It took more like forty-five minutes."

"That's right!" said Erika. "I forgot all about the traffic."

"And when we left Costco, we went out for lunch," said Stan.

"And did anyone see you *there*?"

"Hmmm. I doubt it. We went through a McDonald's drive-through, then took our food to the beach."

"Silver Strand," said Stan at the same time Erika answered with, "Mission Beach."

Lopez didn't know whether to swear or laugh. "Which was it?"

"Silver Strand," Stan clarified. "As you know, that's right across the causeway road from Coronado Cays." Erika beamed at the mention of the name of their exclusive housing development built between the Pacific Ocean and San Diego Bay. "Erika gets the names of the beaches mixed up. She likes them all."

"That's right. I like them all. Who cares what the name is? And it was beautiful that day!" Erika was gushing. "We had such a nice time." She tossed her hair back, gave Stan a loving look, and patted his hand.

Stan squeezed her fingers, a little tightly, Lopez thought. "And before you ask," Stan said, "no, we didn't talk with anyone there."

Erika piped up again. "Not a single soul." That got her fingers another tight squeeze.

Lopez looked back and forth from one to the other, again playing the silent game. Then he placed his palms on his knees and stood. The Westons followed suit. Lopez put out a hand to Stan and nodded to Erika. "Well, thank you both for your time."

"Of course," said Erika. "I'm sorry we weren't more help."

"That's okay. I'll be in touch."

Outside, Lopez looked out at the marina that ran between two rows of narrow, multi-storied houses in a variety of architectural styles. An obviously new, brilliant white catamaran, trimmed in black rocked gently in the slot before the Westons' home. The name "Erika" shone out in bright red letters from the side of the boat.

They're lying through their teeth, Lopez thought. *They don't know I have an eyewitness who saw them at Sutherland's house at noon.*

Lopez knew from the Carrington murder investigation that Stan Weston had moved to Coronado from Boston, Reese Sutherland's former residence. Lopez also knew that Weston's wife had died suddenly and Weston had married Erika soon afterwards. Was it too much of a leap to wonder if there was some connection crawling around in those facts? Was Weston's remark about his and Sutherland's "casual" relationship a bit too casual?

Another thing. The Westons weren't at all surprised to be questioned in connection with Sutherland's murder.

~~~

Inside, Stan Weston turned on his wife. Gripping her forearms, he shook her so hard her thick red hair fell across her face.

"You did it! You killed Reese Sutherland! He rejected you, didn't he? That's why you looked so unhappy in those Del Mar inn photos."

Erika jerked away. "N-no. Th-this is this your way of covering up the fact that *you* killed him!"

"Talk about covering up!" Stan shouted. "You were still there when I left."

Erika slumped down into a chair and covered her face. Her body shook with sobs.

Chapter Ninety-One

ᘓ

Kate didn't know whether to be excited or full of dread when her phone rang and she saw Gunnar's name on the Caller ID. Well, nothing to do but answer it.

"Hello, Gunnar," she told him, trying to sound calm.

"Hello, Kate. How are you?"

"Oh, I'm fine. How are you?"

"I'm fine."

Kate wanted to reach across the island and shake Gunnar. She kept silent.

After several awkward seconds, he said, "Look. I'm calling to see if you'd like to go out to dinner tonight."

"I'd like that, Gunnar," she replied softly, still not sure how he was feeling. "How about the Brigantine? It's right on Orange Street, not far from the Del. I'll call and make reservations. Seven?"

"Good. I'll come by and pick you up about six forty-five."

"Gunnar..." She stopped. "I'll see you at six forty-five."

Chapter Ninety-Two

❧

Justin Rhodes was sober now—not only in alcohol level, but in demeanor. He sat on a metal chair before a metal table in a metal-colored interview room. He had his elbows on the table and his unshaved face in his hands. He looked and smelled like he hadn't bathed for several days. From his own metal chair, Lopez stared at the young man.

As Lopez was about to begin his questioning, Justin lifted his head. "I'm sober now, Detective. Can I go? I don't know why you're keeping me here."

Lopez cut to the chase. "What do you know about Reese Sutherland, Rhodes?"

Justin's mouth turned down and his eyes became dark and glittery. He spat out a vile name for Sutherland, then said, "I know that the man *ruined* my life."

"How so?"

"He got me kicked out of law school. Suggested I go into landscaping instead. Can you believe it? After all those years of scraping and doing without and being so close to taking the bar—"

Lopez cut him off. "Why did Dr. Sutherland get you kicked out? Was there some kind of confrontation?"

"You could say that. I kind of lost my temper in his office one day. Took a poke at him."

"And?"

"He got me kicked out! I already said that." Triceps bulging, Justin brought his fists down on the metal table so hard it shook and caused a ringing in Lopez's ears.

"When was the last time you saw Dr. Sutherland?"

271

"Don't know exactly. Days ago. I went to his house and, uh, had it out with him."

"Threatened him, didn't you?"

"Maybe."

Though he knew the time frame was off, Lopez asked, "Is that when you killed him?"

"What!" If Justin wasn't stunned, he was making a good show of it, Lopez thought. Then a sly smile touched Justin's face. "Sutherland's dead? Couldn't happen to a better man. But, nah, I didn't kill him. Had to be somebody else."

Lopez changed directions. "Where have you been for the past week, Rhodes?"

Justin lifted his shoulders. "Don't know." He looked both defiant and shamefaced. "Can't remember."

"Humor me. Give it a try."

The bluster went out of the young man. He took a deep breath. "After I had it out with Sutherland at his fancy townhouse—and he treated me like the dirt on the bottom of his shoes—I went back to TJ. Spent a couple days there, then..."

"What did you do in Tijuana?"

"Hit the bars, I guess. It's all kind of fuzzy."

"How did you get back to the U.S.?"

Justin rubbed his hands over his face. "I don't remember."

"Do you remember getting into a fight?"

"Sort of."

"Sort of? What do you mean sort of?"

Justin turned belligerent again. "I mean *sort of*! I mean I don't know. I can't remember."

Lopez leaned forward until his face was nearly touching Justin's. "The arresting officer said you were mumbling something about hitting somebody on the head. Who was it, Rhodes? Sutherland? I think it was Sutherland."

"You can't prove that, and you know it. You don't even have fingerprints."

"And you know that how?"

"Look here, Lopez. I'm not answering any more questions until—"

"Right. You know enough about the law, Rhodes, to know you'd better get yourself an attorney."

Chapter Ninety-Three

❧

Dinner at the Brigantine had been awkward, despite the excellent shrimp and lobster Kate and Gunnar had enjoyed. Well, maybe Gunnar had enjoyed it. Kate had hardly tasted hers. All throughout the meal Gunnar had kept the conversation light and had not once brought up the subject that was uppermost in Kate's mind and heart—and surely in his, too.

Now, they walked side by side, not hand in hand, as Kate would have preferred, down Orange Street. Even on this cool late-November evening, a number of locals and tourists ambled about, simply enjoying the scent of the ocean breeze, the luxurious semi-tropical foliage in the median of the wide street, and the paradoxical cozy village/upscale town atmosphere. Talking little, Kate and Gunnar wandered several blocks in the direction away from the Del until at last, they arrived at a lovely park area.

Gunnar took Kate's hand—at last—making her heart flutter in delight. He led her along a flower-lined path to a bench overhung by the branches of a eucalyptus tree. The chilly air hadn't kept people inside, but it had kept them from stopping in the little park, so Gunnar and Kate had the place to themselves.

Gunnar pulled Kate onto the bench beside him and linked her arm into the crook of his elbow. Spreading his long legs out in front of him, he said, "Not much like Boston, is it, even though both are sea-side towns?"

"Um, no, I'd say it's quite unlike Boston."

Oh, no, another useless, get-us-nowhere conversation, Kate thought. Then...

"Do you miss Boston?" Gunnar kept looking straight ahead as he spoke.

Kate didn't need to consider her answer. "I do. Coronado is wonderful. The whole San Diego area is. The semi-tropical scenery is luscious, and the weather can't be beat. But..."

"But?"

Kate reached up to his face and turned it toward her. His expression was unreadable, but she knew she had to say what was in her heart, even if he felt differently. She knew that her love had to take that risk.

"But Gunnar Volstad doesn't live in San Diego. He lives across the country in Boston. And I want to be where he is."

"Oh, Kate. My sweet Kate." Gunnar gathered Kate into his arms, then brought his lips down on hers in a tender but passionate kiss. Several kisses later, Gunnar pulled away and reached into his jacket pocket.

Kate watched in delightful anticipation as he pulled out a small velvet box and opened the lid.

Chapter Ninety-Four

ℰℭ

"Lenae?"

Lenae looked up from her bed toward the door. Kate Elfmon! What a surprise. Cami Carrington had come to visit several times, but this was the first time Dr. Elfmon had come.

Lenae cleared her throat, but knew her voice sounded weak. "Dr.—"

"It's Kate, remember?"

"Oh, yes. Some things are still a little fuzzy. It's so good to see you, Kate."

"Please forgive me for not coming to visit sooner."

"That's okay. I was only barely aware of what was going on anyway. And I'm sure you've been busy."

Lenae couldn't help noticing how Kate flinched at the words. She thought she knew why.

"Well, yes, I have been busy. But..."

"Kate, I-I know about your going out with Reese Sutherland." She took in a deep, shuddering breath. "And I know about his murder. I've told the police that he was the one who tried to kill me, twice."

"Oh, Lenae, I'm so, so sorry."

"And I'm sorry that I didn't know the truth about him in time to warn *you* away from him." She paused. "You know, Kate, despite everything, I can't say I'm glad he's dead."

Kate looked away for a moment. When she turned back to Lenae, her eyes were moist and her voice soft. "I know."

"Yes, I guess you do."

Kate smiled. "On a pleasanter note, you say you were somewhat aware of what was going on while you were in a coma. That's truly amazing. What do you remember?"

"Bits, here and there. Reese's coming into the room and unplugging my oxygen machine is emblazoned in my memory. But, strange as it may seem, that's not what I keep remembering."

"Oh?"

"No. The main thing I remember is what Cami Carrington said when she was here the first time. And I remember that word for word."

Kate waited for Lenae to continue.

"She said, 'Lenae, I want you to know that God loves you, and He is here with you.' Then she prayed for me. Her words have played over and over in my mind." Lenae pressed her lips together, then turned a pleading look to Kate. "Is that true, Kate? Can it be true after the life I've led since I was a teenager? Can God really love me?"

Kate felt her whole countenance break into a beam. "It is oh-so-true, Lenae. God loves you. He always has and He always will. He loves you so much that He sacrificed His own Son for you. And for me." She reached into her purse and pulled out a small Bible. "I happen to have with me the very words He used to prove how much He loves us both."

Chapter Ninety-Five

ഉ

"You still think I murdered Reese, Detective Lopez?"

Raquel Wells' voice was edged with a panic that was not lost on Lopez. SDPD had not yet released Justin Rhodes and felt they had enough circumstantial evidence to charge him with Reese Sutherland's murder. Lopez had convinced the police chief not to do so until he did a bit more investigating of his own.

On that line, he had driven up to L.A. this morning to interview Ms. Wells again. She had let him into her one-room efficiency apartment in a seedy part of the city. She hadn't offered him one of the two chairs in the room, both of which were piled high with various items of skimpy-looking clothing. Her face was as much a mess as her apartment: eyes swollen, tear streaks on her cheeks, complexion nearly the color of her flaxen hair, which looked like it hadn't seen a brush since he'd interviewed her on Wednesday.

"I'm keeping an open mind, Ms. Wells. Your motive for getting rid of Sutherland was pretty strong."

Raquel kicked at a strappy silver sandal with heels at least four inches high. Her mouth turned down, and though her expression was bleak, Lopez reminded himself that she was an actress. In a quick change of mood, she raised her chin to a defiant angle. "You know what, Detective?"

"No, what, Ms. Wells?"

"I'm glad Reese Sutherland's dead. I wish I'd killed him a long time ago."

Lopez's brows shot up. "Then you did kill him."

Her mouth turned down even further. "No. I wish I had. When I headed back to his place—" She stopped.

"Go on. When you headed back to his place..."

"Um, that's not what I meant. I meant when I headed back *toward* his place. I had left my brush there. Cost me over two hundred dollars, and I wanted it back. But first I wanted to give Reese a piece of my mind, so I called his office."

"And that's how you knew he was at home sick. So you went there, and after you gave him a piece of your mind, you took a piece out of his head."

"No! It didn't happen that way. I decided the brush wasn't worth it. I never wanted to see Reese Sutherland again."

"The way I see it," said Lopez, "you did go to the house. You confronted Sutherland. He laughed at you. You couldn't take that. You picked up the first thing your hand rested on and brought it down on his head. Didn't mean to kill him, of course. But when you saw he was dead, you panicked and fled."

Her expression changed again, this time to one of disdain.

She's actually pretty good, Lopez thought.

"Oooh. You should be a script writer. That's quite a story. Would make a great movie."

"With you in the starring role?"

"Why not? But we're not talking about a movie; we're talking about a murder. And I didn't murder Reese Sutherland, may his soul rot in—No. That would be too good for him." She faced him squarely. "If you have some kind of proof, go ahead and arrest me, Detective." She held out her arms, wrists up. "Go ahead."

"Not yet, Ms. Wells. Not yet."

~~~

Raquel slammed the door behind Detective Lopez. She stood there and looked down at her wrists, the very ones she'd challenged him with.

That was one the most crucial performances in my life. And if Lopez didn't fall for it, if he finds out I did go back to Reese's house, it could be my last performance.

Chapter Ninety-Six

&

"You're sitting up!"

The delight in Mike's voice and face turned Lenae's impersonal hospital room into a cozy nook. A string of males—first teenaged boys, then grown men—had passed through her life over the past dozen or so years. Many had professed love for her, but never had she seen from any of them that light of pleasure that now shown from Mike Jenkins' rugged face. That, on top of the joy she'd found in Christ's love the day before, warmed her entire being.

"They let you go!" she exclaimed. "They know you didn't kill Reese!"

Mike gave her a wry grin as he bent over and kissed her forehead. She loved how he allowed his lips to linger there a moment. Rising, he said, "They let me go. But I'm not off the hook. And the only way I'm allowed to visit you is to keep your door wide open so the nurse can keep an eye on us. No guard anymore."

Lenae tilted her head at Mike. "Why do they think they need to watch you?" Then she understood. "They think you may try to harm me!"

"Since I'm still a suspect in Sutherland's murder, they know my every move. My lawyer wanted to stop them from harassing me, but I told him to let it be. I want them to see that my movements are ordinary and harmless." Mike settled back in his chair, an expression suddenly crossing his face that was as different from one he'd worn when he entered the room as bright noon to darkest midnight. The naked hardness—and yes, hatred—frightened Lenae.

"Th-that's because you *are* innocent." Lenae searched his face.

Mike's mouth tightened. "Once I figured out that Reese Sutherland was probably the father of your baby and therefore the one who tried to kill you, I was so mad I could hardly see straight. I wanted to take him by the throat the way he did to you and... I found out where he lived and went out to my car to head there."

"And?"

"Something stopped me. It hit me that I—and you—would be better off if I could learn more about Sutherland. The only so-called clues I had were two letters of the alphabet." Mike explained about how he'd found the letters G, for "the Glue" and R, for "Reese," to be significant. "I knew that wouldn't be enough to go to the police with."

"So what did you do?"

"I decided I'd let myself cool down and confront Sutherland the next day."

"But the next day Reese was dead."

"Right." Mike's mouth twisted to a satisfied grin. "Someone else took care of him. I was relieved. I might have lost my cool again if I'd actually met him face to face."

Lenae was silent, digesting what Mike had told her.

"The problem is," Mike went on, "I don't have an alibi, at least not one that can be verified."

"Time's up, Mr. Jenkins," the nurse called out, poking her head into the room.

Mike rose and kissed Lenae's forehead again. "They tell me you can probably go home tomorrow. I hope you'll let me pick you up." He caressed her cheek. "We have some important things to discuss."

Heaviness settled into Lenae's chest as Mike left. The warmth she'd felt when he first entered the room had turned to ice. The abrupt change in his face and body language when he spoke of Reese had been terrifying.

What if Mike is lying? she wondered. *He had plenty of opportunity; he said so himself. And that hatred I saw. I know I didn't imagine it. No. No! Mike is one of the most controlled people I know. He wouldn't let his anger get the better of him. He couldn't have built up his business the way he has if he was that kind of person.*

Just the same, that look on his face...

Shivering, Lenae let her gaze sweep the room that had again become impersonal. No, worse than impersonal. Like a prison. After a few moments, swamped with confusion, she did something she had only recently begun to do again. She looked upward and prayed.

Chapter Ninety-Seven

ॐ

"Hey, Dad, it's Dexter."

Dexter had talked with his father several times since Lenae's attack, each time drawing them a bit closer. Today, however, he was nervous about what he needed to say to Wayne Driscoll.

"Hey yourself, Son." Dexter still found it hard to believe when his father seemed happy to hear from him. "How's it going there in that paradise you're living in?"

Dexter let out a shaky chuckle. "It's great here, all right, but I wouldn't call it paradise."

Wayne was silent a moment before saying, "So, how is Lenae? You said she came out of her coma on Tuesday."

"She's still weak, but the doctors are pleased with how she's recovering. She went home today."

"That's great!"

Dexter didn't respond.

After a few seconds, Wayne asked, "Have you talked with her much?"

"Some."

"Some?"

"Well, yeah."

"Yeah?"

"Um, yeah. I've visited her every day but they only let me stay a few minutes at a time."

Silence reigned again for several seconds.

Finally... "What's going on, Dexter?"

At first Dexter didn't respond again.

"Dexter?"

Dexter's voice cracked. "I've got to talk with you, Dad. I've got to. I can't hold this in any longer."

Chapter Ninety-Eight

&

"You've got to be kidding!" Gunnar stood by Kate's side and eyed the Giant Dipper, the historic wooden, twister-style roller coaster at Belmont Park on Mission Beach. "You expect me to get on that thing?"

Kate tilted her head at him. "Why not? You're not scared, are you?"

"Out of my wits. Cami said it was built in what year? Seventeen ten?"

Kate poked Gunnar in the ribs. "Nineteen twenty-five, silly."

"And was condemned for how long?"

"Fifteen years or so. I don't remember. But they restored it quite some time ago. Besides, it's not that big. Its steepest drop is less than seventy-five feet."

"I'd feel safer on a five-hundred footer made of steel."

"Well, Cami says it's safe. She says she's ridden it dozens of times."

"I get the idea that Cami is a bit of daredevil beneath her ladylike Southern exterior."

"We don't want her to show us up, do we?"

"Well... If you put it that way, maybe I can scrounge up enough nerve."

"That's my brave hero. Besides, look how gorgeous it is today after all those cool days. Eighty degrees! Can you believe it?"

"I believe it all right. I'm sweltering. Never occurred to me to bring shorts in November. Don't forget, it was twenty-four when I left Boston."

"It's the Santa Ana breeze blowing in from the desert that heats things up now and then. But my point is, it's wonderful weather for riding a roller coaster."

"If you get past the danger you're putting yourself in," Gunnar grumbled. "Okay, come on." He grumbled beneath his breath some more. "Too bad we aren't married yet."

Looking back over her shoulder, Kate led the way toward the roller coaster. "What do you mean?"

"I would have already named you the beneficiary of my life insurance."

"You're impossible. You know that, don't you?"

Gunnar caught up to her, turned her to him, and planted a big kiss smack on her lips. "Yeah," he growled. "And you love it."

The ride lasted less than two minutes, during which Kate screamed like a wounded whale at every dip and sharp turn. When they stepped out of their seats, she stumbled, holding onto her head with one hand and clinging to Gunnar with the other.

"That was great!" he said.

"I feel sick," she said.

Gunnar guffawed. "And you're pale as a sheet, Miss Braveheart." He led her to a nearby bench, where she collapsed onto the hard seat and bent over to place her head on her knees. Beside her, he sat back and took in the sea of humanity taking advantage of the beautiful San Diego afternoon. People of all sizes, ages, and ethnic groups enjoyed the other rides at the park, swarmed the boardwalk, ordered ice cream or hot dogs at various concession stands, and splashed in the waves beyond. He couldn't help noticing, too, the long line waiting to board the roller coaster.

Gunnar envisioned himself telling his two sons about his "daring adventure"—not the Giant Dipper ride, but his engagement to Kate. He knew they'd be pleased. Almost five years since her death, they still missed their mother, but they had given their one-hundred-percent blessing to his pursuing Kate Elfmon.

Eventually Kate raised her head. Her face had returned to its normal light olive color, and she managed a weak smile. Despite the warm sun on her back, she snuggled up to him and joined him in his perusal of the scenes surrounding them. Occasionally they laughed or sighed or remarked on some beachgoer's scandalous attire. Little by little, their conversation turned to Reese Sutherland.

"You do believe me that I was never in love with Reese, don't you?" Kate asked, sounding anxious.

He cupped his hands around her face. "Kiss me," he commanded.

"Huh?"

"Kiss me."

She did. Soundly.

He released her. Eyes dark with emotion and voice husky, he said, "I believe you."

She let out a long, satisfied sigh and snuggled up to him again.

After a while, Gunnar said, "I hear Justin Rhodes is being held as a 'person of interest' in Sutherland's murder. I wonder when they'll make the charge official."

"Who knows? I still can't see Justin as a killer." She changed the subject. "I do know that the president of Grant Lauder has already named Albert Bainbridge head of the Law Department."

"What about the man Reese was filling in for—the one who's taking a sabbatical in Sweden?"

"Dr. Johannsen decided to stay in Sweden and live near some relatives," Kate explained. "The board had an emergency meeting and decided that, though it's unorthodox, under the circumstances they needed to move ahead right away. Partly for the school's reputation and partly for the students'sake."

"How do you feel about that?"

"Albert Bainbridge is not my favorite person, but I think he's well suited for the job. Not overburdened with people skills, but he's thorough and organized. And he's been with the university for several years, even has his office in one of the original buildings. That's a real plus—being with the university a long time, that is, not the location of his office."

Gunnar laughed. "Well, that should make for a smoother transition than bringing in a new man."

"That was their thinking," Kate said. "Months ago the school arranged a fund raiser banquet at the Del for Wednesday night, the day before Thanksgiving. The board considered cancelling or rescheduling, but that would be so challenging they decided to go ahead as planned. They'll include a low-key memorial for Reese and announce Dr. Bainbridge's appointment."

"Good plan."

Kate held out her left hand, admiring the exquisite ring Gunnar had given her.

"How did you know exactly what I'd want, Gunnar?"

"I know *you*, Kate. Straightforward but complicated. Practical but beautiful."

"Oh, Gunnar. I'm so happy. Or I would be if you weren't leaving tomorrow afternoon."

"I feel the same, honey. I'll be counting the days until you get home."

"Just in time for a Christmas Day wedding!"

"Just in time," he whispered and pulled her even closer.

Chapter Ninety-Nine

ॐ

"Are you sure you're okay?" Victor Carrington put one arm around Cami's shoulder and looked up at the magnificent arched, thirty-foot high sugar-pine ceiling of the Hotel del Coronado's Crown Room. Massive tiara-shaped chandeliers hung from the vaulted rafters and echoed the meaning of the name: "Hotel of the Crowned." Near the center of one window-lined wall, a jazz combo played low-key numbers, ideal background music for the Grant Lauder University fund raiser.

Cami knew her brother-in-law's simple question actually meant, "Is it okay being here at the hotel where your husband—my brother—was murdered?"

Cami had seen little of Victor since Braxton's death. First she'd been away for several weeks on her and Kate's motorhome venture. Since she returned to Coronado, both had been busy. He'd kept her informed about the company business and had called her after she found Lenae attacked, but he hadn't realized how important the incident was to her. Besides, he'd been extremely busy running Carrington Investments and its myriad subsidiaries, and doing a good job of it, to everyone's surprise.

"*Okay* is the right word," Cami answered Victor. "I'll admit some awful memories keep surfacing. But it had to be done sometime. I can't live in Coronado and never come to the Del." She looked up at the dark-haired, blue-eyed handsome man whose face was so similar to Braxton's, yet who had existed in his brother's powerful shadow and probably still did to some extent. "I'm glad the school board didn't choose the ballroom for this fund raiser," Cami told him. "I don't think I could have handled that."

Victor looked toward the door that led to the elegant Victorian lobby, then down the hall to the Oceanside Ballroom where Braxton met his death. Cami knew wrenching memories of his wife Ashley must be mixed with those of his brother. He dropped his arm from around Cami's shoulder. "As you say, Cami, we all—you and I and the twins—have to make our peace with this place."

As he excused himself, Kate walked up. She had been chatting with a pale but happy-looking Lenae Maddox, seated in a damask-covered chair at a round table spread with autumn gold linen. A low but luxurious arrangement of rust and yellow asters and chrysanthemums, tucked into red and gold autumn leaves provided a riot of color for the center.

Lenae was not fully recovered from her recent ordeals, but had been determined to attend the dinner. She had brought Mike Jenkins, who, upon Justin Rhodes' detainment, was no longer under suspicion of Reese Sutherland's murder. Cami knew Lenae had harbored serious doubts about Mike's innocence. He must have brought her around to his side.

Robin Byrd breezed up in her long red dress with its sequin-encrusted bodice. "Group hug!" Robin exclaimed, pulling Cami and Kate into an embrace. Cami laughed and joined in with the hugs.

"Look," Cami said as she drew away, forcing a bright pitch to her words. She spread her arms to include the host of Grant Lauder supporters. The women, arrayed in glittering jewels, glided about in stylish gowns or pants ensembles, while the men joined them in formal suits or tuxedos. A host of servers circled the room with pre-dinner appetizers. "It's a great evening for the school. They'll raise a ton of money tonight."

"There's Dr. Bainbridge," said Kate, inclining her head toward a group of guests who seemed to be offering premature congratulations to the professor.

"Look who else is here," said Robin, pursing her lips.

Not far away, tall, flame-haired Erika Weston, dressed more conservatively than usual, in a long, bronze-colored silk skirt and gold-colored turtleneck top with long sleeves, clung to Stan. No, it was he who was clinging to her, as though she may get away from him.

"I heard they were under suspicion, too, for a while," Robin commented.

"They were," Kate told her. "But now that Justin Rhodes is being held, everyone else is off the hook. I hear they're going to officially press charges soon." She looked thoughtful. "I still have the hardest time believing Justin would murder somebody. I hardly knew him, but it doesn't seem possible."

"Speaking of unlikely suspects, even Dexter Driscoll was on the list," said Cami. "Can you think of a *less* likely suspect?"

"No," said Robin. "I hear that murderers come in unlikely forms, but Dexter Driscoll? Not a chance."

~~~

Like Kate Elfmon, Carlos Lopez wasn't feeling satisfied about Justin Rhodes' guilt. He'd hoped he could find indisputable proof to make him feel confident about that fact before Justin was met with an official homicide charge. But today officials at SDPD had said they'd give Lopez until next Monday, no later, before charging Justin with murder. The charge would be elevated to first-degree murder if premeditation could be proved.

Maybe they're right, Lopez thought. *Maybe Rhodes really is the murderer.*

Not fully persuaded, tonight he had put on a black suit and bow tie and crashed this party in order to observe his mental file of suspects once more.

Raquel Wells was not present, of course, but the provocative starlet, with motive and opportunity, couldn't be discounted. Lopez had felt unsatisfied when he left her apartment. The woman was an actress. Was she putting on the performance of her life? She'd said she left an expensive brush at 'Sutherland's townhouse and didn't go back for it. However, an extensive search had not turned it up.

Young Dexter Driscoll wasn't present either. He'd gone home to Tucson to visit his parents for the Thanksgiving weekend. Lopez had a hard time keeping an open mind about Dexter's possible guilt. The boy simply didn't have it in him.

Ah, there was Mike Jenkins, practically glued to Lenae Maddox and clearly head over heels in love with her. Enough to kill Sutherland? Probably.

And there were the Westons. Imagining Dr. Weston as a supporter of higher education wasn't hard, but Erika? He doubted it. As for murder...

that was another thing regarding both Westons in Lopez's mind. *First thing tomorrow,* he thought, *I'm going to contact the Boston PD and get the details on Weston's first wife's death.*

Looking across the room, he saw Cami Carrington chatting with Kate Elfmon and Robin Byrd. Nearby stood craft-store mogul Kent Jacobs, his eyes devouring Cami in her flowing smoky blue gown. Cami seemed completely unaware. Lopez allowed himself a secret smile. With Braxton Carrington dead only four months, it was much too soon for Cami to consider another man, but there was none better than Kent Jacobs in Lopez's opinion.

Albert Bainbridge approached Cami and her friends, making Lopez wish for the hundredth time that the man didn't have an airtight alibi. His secretary had confirmed that he had not left his office during the time Reese was murdered. Bainbridge had been vocal about his resentment over being passed over by Sutherland as interim head of the law department. And he'd certainly benefited from Sutherland's death.

Lopez turned his attention back to Mike Jenkins, a man with a reputation of knowing what he wanted and doing whatever it took to get it.

~~~

"I'm so glad you're here, Dr. Elfmon," Albert Bainbridge told Kate. He had broken away from the people he'd been chatting with, and come to her side. "I know you and I didn't have the very best of beginnings, but I think you're the kind of person to let bygones be bygones."

With a quick prayer for patience and tolerance, Kate replied, "Looks like the fund raiser is a big success, doesn't it, Dr. Bainbridge?"

Dr. Bainbridge straightened his tuxedo jacket with one white-gloved hand and curved the other over an ornate gold-topped cane. He gave the cane two playful taps on the polished wood floor. "Please. Call me Albert."

Kate granted him a thin smile. "Albert. Of course." She added truthfully, "I've very happy for you, Albert. You deserve this promotion."

Albert bowed slightly. "Thank you. If only it hadn't come at such a cost. It's no secret that Reese Sutherland and I had our, um, differences, but the poor man didn't deserve to have his head crushed in."

Holding two goblets of water and heading toward the table where

Lenae still sat, Mike Jenkins paused, clearly having overheard Albert's remark. Mike stopped long enough to sneer and say, "The *poor man* deserved everything he got and more."

Just then, the band music tapered off to an end.

"Oh!" said Albert, looking toward the musicians leaving their places. "That means dinner is about to begin. I need to get to my place at the, er, head table." He lifted his chin high, thrust back his thin shoulders, and cane-tapped his way to the front of the raised platform and his important seat at the table.

Cami exchanged looks with Kate and Robin. The women waited until Albert was out of hearing to let loose their giggles.

Chapter One Hundred

ॐ

Cami was exhausted. Physically. Mentally. And especially emotion-ally. She had told Victor early in the evening that being at the Del was "okay." Eventually that changed, and not for the better. The later the evening became, the more her attention became fixed on the door from the Crown Room to the lobby. She imagined herself walking across that elegant Victorian room, down the hall, and into the Oceanfront Ballroom. In her mind she kept seeing herself just inside the ballroom and staring at the massive wall of windows that looked out to the Pacific. She could almost literally see the head table where she and Braxton had sat with Victor and Victor's wife Ashley, along with Debra and Durant. She'd had to close her eyes to shut out the pain of seeing Braxton taking a sip of pink champagne and falling onto the table.

Thank the Lord, the Grant Lauder fundraiser was over now. Cami was in the subtly elegant gold and white bedroom of her own home, where she'd learned not to think of Braxton every time she looked at the bed they'd shared. She stepped out of the smoky-blue party dress and slipped into a new pink nightgown. She'd given all the ones she used to wear when Braxton was alive to the Thrift Cottage run by Graham Presbyterian Church.

A few minutes later, she crawled into bed, fluffed up her pillow and lay down, thinking she'd be asleep by the time her head hit that pillow. However, despite her exhaustion, sleep eluded her. The myriad incidents of the evening, uneventful though they were, kept playing over and over in her mind.

A subdued and conservatively-dressed Erika clinging to Stan with one arm and rubbing the other one. Not once moving from his side.

Stan, tight lipped, glowering, holding onto Erika's arm in a vice-like grip.

Robin Byrd teasing serious-faced Carlos Lopez out of his obvious observation of the party-goers and into a grin.

Albert Bainbridge dressed to the nines and glowing like a bulb in one of the crown-shaped chandeliers, decrying Reese's death, and unsuccessfully trying to appear modest about his promotion.

Another glowing face—Lenae Maddox's. Cami wasn't sure if the glow came from a growing fondness for Mike Jenkins, from her recovering health, or from the commitment she'd made to Christ the day Kate visited her.

Mike, casting not-so-subtle glances at Detective Lopez while at the same time hovering over Lenae.

Cami tried to push the party from her mind with thoughts of tomorrow's Thanksgiving dinner. She was glad she wouldn't have to spend the first major holiday since Braxton's death alone. Even the twins would be missing, spending the American holiday in Scotland. Though there would be only herself and Kate and Robin, she'd decided to prepare a traditional Thanksgiving meal. Cami had prepared most of the food over the past two days. Edith and Edwin would have the day off,

"Thanksgiving Day," she murmured.

Thank you Lord, for Yourself, for Your Son, for Your Spirit. Thank You for Durant and Debra. Despite the heartaches, thank You for the years You gave me with Braxton. Thank You for my wonderful friend Kate. Thank You....

Cami fell asleep counting her blessings.

~~~

Like Cami Carrington, Detective Carlos Lopez was having trouble getting to sleep. Unlike her, he wasn't counting his blessings. He was playing over the events at the Grant Lauder fund raiser in his mind. When that seemed not to help at all, he returned to mulling over the arrest of Justin Rhodes for Reese Sutherland's murder. The circumstantial evidence pointed to Rhodes, but not in a straight line in Lopez's mind. Lopez liked straight lines.

Yes, because of his role as gardener, Rhodes had access to the gate code at the Cerca de Costa townhouses. He had taken advantage of that knowledge in order to confront Sutherland at least once. Sutherland's neighbor Stephanie Winslow had clued Lopez into that fact, and her husband had corroborated her story. Rhodes himself admitted that he did indeed go there and confront Sutherland on Saturday, November sixth, and even threatened him.

"But I didn't go back and kill him!" Rhodes had kept saying under intense questioning. At last, Lopez recalled, Rhodes had added the words that got him arrested: "At least I don't think I did."

"What do you mean?" Lopez had asked him.

A bleak expression had come over Rhodes' face. He hung his head and said in a hoarse whisper. "I don't remember. I was drunk for several days."

It didn't help that when a roaring drunk Rhodes was first picked up for disturbing the peace in a downtown bar, he had babbled about hitting somebody on the head.

Still, it didn't set right with Lopez, even though the charge that was about to come down on Rhodes was homicide rather than premeditated murder. Lopez's mind jumped back to some of the other suspects.

Sutherland's door was unlocked, indicating that he had probably known the murderer and let him—or her—in. That seemed to apply to most of Lopez's mental list of suspects.

Stan Weston: Sutherland knew the cosmetic surgeon from Boston.

Erika Weston: The voluptuous redhead had gone out with Sutherland at least once.

Raquel Wells: The would-be movie star had spent Saturday and Sunday nights with Sutherland and also admitted to knowing where he kept a spare key.

Dexter Driscoll: Still the least-likely suspect, the Grant Lauder student was probably a familiar face to Sutherland.

So was Dr. Albert Bainbridge with his airtight alibi.

Mike Jenkins: He was the only exception. The man claimed he had never met Sutherland. That could be a lie. Besides, who was to say that Jenkins hadn't somehow convinced Sutherland to let him in?

And what about fingerprints? Of course, Ms. Wells' prints were all over the place, including the bronze golfer. There would have been no need for her to clean them off. The only other recent prints were

Sutherland's. Lopez could picture any one of the suspects wiping away prints from the statuette and doorknob except for Rhodes. What drunk would think to stop and carefully destroy that vital evidence?

Maybe Rhodes *wasn't* drunk the whole time he was absent from home. Maybe he'd sobered up on Monday long enough to murder the man who had ruined his career.

But would Sutherland have let Rhodes in? Lopez didn't think so.

Muttering to himself, Lopez rolled out of bed, quietly so he wouldn't wake Ella, and shuffled his way to the kitchen. There he brought a cup of water to a boil in the microwave, then added two heaping teaspoons of instant coffee. He stirred it until it dissolved into a deep black mixture. He breathed in the strong aroma, took a sip, and went back to recounting his list of suspects.

Thursday, November 25

Chapter One Hundred One

ℬ

"Cami, why are you so fidgety?" Robin Byrd, holding a steaming sweet potato casserole topped with pecans, paused in the archway to Cami's elegant dining room.

Cami examined the table with a critical eye. The turkey was browned to perfection, but the platter was off center. She moved it. Then she picked up the dish of asparagus, beautiful beneath a creamy cheese sauce, and traded places with the salad of crispy lettuce and bright red cherry tomatoes. Next she fiddled with a place setting of her best Sevres china, heaviest silver flatware, and Waterford glasses. Finally she smoothed a non-existent wrinkle in the lace cloth.

"I'm not fidgety," she told Robin.

"You certainly are. What gives?"

"It took a long time to get to sleep last night, that's all." Though she'd fallen asleep "counting her blessings," the morning had brought its reminders of Braxton's and the twins' absence. She'd been fighting depression from the moment she woke up.

Kate came in, bringing a large bowl of corn with pimiento and placing it on the table.

Cami moved the bowl a little to the left.

"Cami, this is a regular feast," Robin said. "You've cooked enough to feed an army, for only three of us."

"She can't help herself," Kate said. "She loves to cook. Now when it comes to *my* culinary skills..."

Cami found herself able to grin and say, "Good thing Gunnar enjoys eating out."

"What's he doing today?" Robin asked.

"Having dinner with a family from our church. He called from Boston this morning."

Cami couldn't help a stab of melancholy envy that Kate had heard from the man she loved on Thanksgiving Day, when Cami would never again have that joy. She willed that thought away.

A few minutes later, Cami and her guests were settled before the overflowing table.

"Kate, would you ask the blessing, please?" Cami said.

"Of course."

"Make it short," Robin said. "I can hardly wait to dig in."

Honoring Robin's plea, Kate's prayer, though full of heartfelt gratitude, was short and to the point. As they ate, the conversation was more desultory than lively. Cami found herself wishing she'd never insisted on having Kate and Robin over.

I should have suggested that we go out to eat.

At last, when every serving dish on the table was almost empty, she put on a cheerful face and said, "Okay, who's for dessert?"

A duet of groans answered her.

"Oh, Cami, I couldn't hold another bite," said Kate.

Robin patted her tummy. "Me either."

"Not even Southern pecan pie?" Cami was already pushing her chair back.

"Maybe later," said Kate.

"Same for me," Robin said. "Anyway, as soon as we help you clean up, I've got to run. My parents, up in Burbank, will be expecting their regular Thanksgiving Day call from me. But I'll take a slice with me, if that's okay.

Somehow, Cami's Thanksgiving dinner had fallen flat.

~~~

It was hard for Kate to miss how glum Cami became after that wonderful dinner. A call from Debra and Durant helped for only as long as they were on the phone with her. As soon as the call was over, Cami sank into a funk again.

Finally, wanting to get her friend out of the house, Kate suggested the first thing that came to mind. "How would you like to drive out to the university with me? I left some papers there I need before Monday's class."

To her surprise, Cami said, "Good plan. Grant Lauder opened about a year after I moved to Coronado, almost twenty-three years ago. Braxton and I attended the dedication ceremonies. I haven't been there more than a few times since."

Both were silent for a few moments, remembering that the last time Cami had been at the school, Reese had rescued her from a fall.

Kate broke the silence. "Better get a jacket. There's a nip in the air today, almost like real fall weather," Kate said, thinking of cold autumn days in Boston and wishing she were there with Gunnar.

Cami ran up the stairs and came back with a white denim blazer that brought out the white swirls in her brown and white blouse, worn over brown linen pants.

~~~

After Kate picked up the papers she actually did need, she and Cami wandered around the campus. "That's the new gym over there." Kate nodded toward a large gymnasium that looked modern yet echoed the Spanish aura of the rest of the holiday-quiet college campus.

Cami surveyed the lovely grounds and buildings. "Look how ivy has grown up over the walls of the admin building. Reminds me of an east coast Ivy League school."

"I don't know that I'd go that far," said Kate, thinking of the thick foliage gracing the grounds of Boston U. She and Cami ambled around to the back of the admin building. "I'm told this was the first structure on the grounds."

"More ivy," said Cami, pointing to a wall covered with the twisting leafy vines that tucked round a door set back in an alcove.

"I never noticed that door before." Kate said. She pointed to the corner room. "Reese's office was right there, next to Bain—Albert's."

With Cami in front and laughing, they strolled on, picking their way through a couple of bushes that had grown part-way over the narrow path leading to the parking lot.

"You can see why this path rarely gets used," Kate said.

Tucking her hands into her jacket pocket as the two neared Kate's car, Cami told her friend, "This was a great idea, Kate. It's done me good to get out."

Monday, November 29

Chapter One Hundred Two

ℰℭ

Detective Lopez placed a thick folder in the metal file drawer in his office. The label on the file read "Reese Sutherland." Lopez had received word that Justin Rhodes had been officially charged with Sutherland's murder.

"So that's that," Lopez said.

With a sense of frustration mixed with unwilling acceptance, he shoved the file drawer shut.

~~~

"Well, do you like the dress?" Countenance aglow, Cami leaned both elbows on the table she and Kate were sharing at Miguel's Cocina, across the street from the Del. They were celebrating the end of four days of shopping for a wedding dress for Kate, and the server had taken away the beef flautas they'd split.

"For the four hundred and eighty-fifth time, I *love* the dress, Cami. And yes, I even love the color, even if I've never worn fuchsia in my life."

"Oh, Kate! The color is absolutely, positively fabulous with your dark hair. And I can hardly believe we found one for me in a pink shade that is the perfect complement for your dress. Light enough to be pretty without detracting attention from your dress." She reached for the check.

Kate clapped her hand over Cami's. "Oh, no. My treat this time. Consider it your wardrobe consultant fee."

"Okay. You win." Cami removed her hand and slipped it into one pocket of the white denim blazer she was wearing again today. It was quickly becoming her "go to" favorite. Her fingers touched the tip of a piece of paper. The pocket was large, and the crumbled-up paper was lodged into the forward corner her fingers rarely reached. She pulled it out.

"What is that?" Kate asked.

"Don't know," said Cami. "Oh, I remember. That day I fell at the school and Reese picked me up— As I was walking back to my car, I picked up a piece of trash and stuck it in my pocket. I'll throw it away when I get home." She laid the paper aside. "You know, Kate, I will always wonder how Reese Sutherland could afford his extravagant lifestyle. I mean, how many law professors can afford a luxury townhouse in La Jolla?"

"I never asked him, of course, but once I heard him say something about an inheritance of some kind."

"Oh well, it's not important. Ready to go?" Cami picked up the ball of paper and started to return it to her pocket. Wait, what was that? A bit of writing. With mild curiosity, she began to unfold the paper. "Looks like some kind of note." She spread it out on the table before her. As she read, she could feel her mouth dropping open.

"Cami, what is it? You look like you've seen a ghost."

Cami looked up. "Not a ghost. A note to a dead man."

~~~

"You have two visitors," the young woman at the Coronado Police Department front desk told Detective Lopez.

Lopez ran his fingers through his thick black hair. *Just what I need,* he thought. At noon he'd managed to put aside his frustration about the Sutherland case long enough to enjoy a pastrami panini at Café 1134. It hadn't helped.

"I wish you'd had them wait," he told the receptionist.

As he opened his door, it partially hid the leather-seated, iron-legged visitors' chairs in front of his desk. He almost dropped his coffee cup at the sound of a feminine voice with unmistakable Southern undertones.

"Detective Lopez!" Cami Carrington said, standing.

Lopez didn't try to hide his surprise, especially seeing that Kate Elfmon was with Cami. "What a pleasure, ladies. You've brightened my whole day. What can I do for you?" He took a seat behind his desk.

"I think Cami has something you'll be interested in," said Kate.

He took the note from Cami. He read in stunned silence. Finally he said, "Where did you get this?"

Cami explained how she'd first found the note and how she'd found it again a few minutes ago.

"It's time for me and Officer Pitt to make a visit," said Lopez.

Chapter One Hundred Three

☙

As Lopez and Pitt approached the door to Dr. Stanley Weston's cosmetic surgery, a face appeared at a window, then jerked back. Lopez entered the reception area and opened his mouth to tell the young woman at the desk to inform Weston he was there. Before he could speak, a gunshot rang out.

Epilogue
Two Weeks Later

∽

For the second time in two weeks, Detective Carlos Lopez, placed the file on Reese Sutherland's murder into his file cabinet. This time, a sense of satisfaction filled him as he gave the drawer an extra push of finality.

On the Sunday after Thanksgiving, he had gone to Grant Lauder University and wandered the campus. At the back of the admin building, he'd noticed an ivy-draped door that he realized led out of Albert Bainbridge's office, giving the man a way out without his secretary seeing him. On Monday he was about to go to the school again and question Bainbridge when Cami Carrington and Kate Elfmon showed up with a note that read:

> *FYI Sutherland, I received your recent demand for <u>another</u> payment. Well, my friend, your blackmailing days are over. You can forget your threats about tellingErika how Margo died. You have received the last dime you will ever get from me. You'll have to find another way to support your lavish lifestyle. <u>Never</u> contact me again if you know what's good for you. S.W.*

Though Lopez shuddered at the memory of finding Weston shot in the head by his own hand, he was glad to have this case closed. The note Weston had written to Sutherland would have been considered circumstantial evidence in a trial. The note, added to evidence the Boston police had uncovered concerning the death of Weston's wealthy first wife, was convincing enough to free Justin Rhodes and declare Weston the murderer.

This is the second time in less than six months I've investigated a murder case that involved Cami Carrington and Kate Elfmon. I sure hope those ladies have seen the last of the crime scene for a long, long time.

~~~

The Coronado Cays home that now belonged to Erika Weston exclusively had a "For Sale" sign out front. Standing at her door, Erika took a good, long look at the sign and the marina—now minus one white catamaran. Then she turned away and went inside, where she went straight to her phone and called a real estate agent in Boston.

After they'd greeted each other, the agent said, "I think I've found the perfect Beacon Hill penthouse apartment for you, Mrs. Weston."

~~~

"Pack that in the box with the other books on corporate law." Dr. Albert Bainbridge gave an authoritative nod to the student assigned to help him move into Reese Sutherland's former office. When the young man bent over to obey, Albert gave himself a congratulatory grin.

Moments later, back straight and steps precise, he tap-tapped his ornamental cane the short distance down the hall to his new domain.

~~~

Once again, Justin Rhodes had set his mother on a couch and placed himself before her to give her some news.

"I think I know what it is, Justin, but let me hear it from you."

"Well," he said, "you know how I love landscaping."

"Yes. And you have a real gift for it."

"In the past few weeks, I've thought long and hard about Reese Sutherland's suggestion that I give up law and eventually establish my own landscaping business."

"And?"

"He was right."

~~~

"I got in, Dad." Dexter Driscoll held up a letter as his father walked into the Driscolls' family room in Tucson, Arizona.

"What's that? Your acceptance into Tucson College?"

"Right. Too late to transfer to UAT," he said, referring to the University of Arizona at Tucson. "Besides, I'm not sure I still want to major in Political Science."

"Maybe by the end of the spring semester you'll have clear direction. I'll pray that happens. Meanwhile, you can't imagine how glad your mother and I are that you'll be going to school here and living at home with us."

For a moment, the memory of the day Dexter had made that frantic call home hung in the air. He'd felt a desperate need for "something more" in his life, a need brought on by his talks with Lenae Maddox after her conversion to Jesus Christ. Dexter still had questions and doubts galore, but he knew he'd come to the right place to find the answers.

Wayne Driscoll put his arms around his son. Dexter hesitated only a moment before returning his father's hug.

~~~

Tingling all over, Raquel Wells tore open a thick manila envelope she'd brought home from a low-budget film studio. Her quivering fingers pulled out a large sheaf of bound pages. Laying aside the envelope, she stared at the title on the cover.

"Torrid Nights in Nassau," she read aloud.

Raquel swept aside a pile of clothing from her sofa and settled herself down to dig into the lines for her leading role in the film. Beside her lay an expensive boar bristle brush.

~~~

"I'll miss this," said Lenae Maddox as she and Mike Jenkins stood at the window in her loft and took in the view of San Diego Bay and the Coronado Bridge sweeping over the sparkling blue water dotted with dozens of white sails.

Mike turned her to him and took her face in his hands. Over the past few weeks her color had improved, but she was still a little pale. He knew her strength had not returned in full. "I wish you wouldn't leave," he said, placing a tender kiss on her forehead. "I love you, Lenae. I want you to stay. I want you to marry me."

Lenae traced his rugged cheeks with her fingertips. "I love you, too, Mike." She held his gaze with her amazing eyes. "But this is something I have to do. I have to sort out these new feelings I've had ever since…"

"Ever since that spiritual commitment you made." He moved a few inches away and stared out at the scene below. Already "that spiritual commitment" of Lenae's had brought about changes in their relationship, the most evident being that she no longer allowed him to spend the night at her loft.

"That's right, Mike."

"But do you have to do it in Paris?"

A light shone in her eyes that made him know his case was hopeless. He remembered the young woman he'd seen painting by the Seine River a few weeks ago. The one who had reminded him of Lenae.

"Yes!" she said. "All my life I've dreamed of studying art in Paris. Finally I can afford it." She drew in a deep satisfying breath. "I can hardly believe how God has worked things out for me. First, that wealthy friend of Detective Lopez's wife sees my painting of the Talisman rose with the Hotel Del in the background. I had planned to burn it. Never wanted to see it again. Then she up and offers a huge sum of money for it and buys most of my other paintings as well."

"I think I'd like to strangle—" Horror swept over Mike as he realized what he was about to say to a woman who'd almost died of strangulation.

To his relief, Lenae smiled. "It's okay, Mike." She moved closer to him and tucked her arm into his. "It's only for six months, you know."

"Well, I can see that the mall project with Barbeau Architectes is going to require a lot of my personal attention. On-site attention, that is."

~~~

Kent Jacobs had been asked to chair Coronado's Fourth of July events next summer. The island's all-out celebration of the patriotic occasion required many months of planning. The committee always had a man and a woman as co-chairmen. Kent knew exactly which woman to suggest.

~~~

After several cool weeks (down to the fifties during the day), another Santa Ana wind was blowing through San Diego, this time taking the temperature to the high eighties inland and eighty-two at the beach on Coronado. In addition the "surf was up," and a number of die-hard souls were braving the cold waters.

"I bet Durant would be out there if he were here," Kate told Cami as the two strolled barefoot in the sand in the direction of the Del.

Cami laughed. "That would be too safe a bet to take you up on. Funny, though, as much as Debra loves this beach, she's never gotten into surfing." She hugged herself. "I can hardly wait for them to get home."

"And you're taking the company jet to Edinburgh tomorrow—a couple of hours after I fly back to Boston—to bring them back."

"Can you believe that Victor suggested that? I think he's so pleased with the way things have been going while he's been in charge, that he's feeling magnanimous."

"Not that you need his permission, of course."

"No, but it made me feel good for him to suggest it." She stepped closer to Kate and gave her friend a quick hug as they walked. "Oh, Kate, I could burst with happiness. The twins coming home and the three of us heading to Boston for your wedding!"

"With me wearing the dress you helped me find. You know, I almost wish Joel could see me in it."

"Maybe he will," said Cami. "Who knows what good things God allows the ones in Heaven to see?"

Appendix

Dear Reader,

We hope you enjoyed this second PICS (Partners in Crime Solving) book as much as we enjoyed writing it. As in the first book, *Storm over Coronado,* we aimed at a story that would entertain while inspiring you to walk closer with our Lord.

In chapter ninety-six, Kate presented the "Romans Road" plan of salvation to Lenae Maddox. Its name comes from the fact that all the verses are found in the book of Romans. You'll find that outline on the next page. For the most part, we have not written out the verses indicated. One reason is that a copy of this form is great to paste in the front or back cover of your Bible (feel free to make your own copy). Another is that it's good to open the Scriptures and let the person you're sharing the gospel with see the verses in their natural context.

Perhaps the Lord will allow you to lead someone to a saving knowledge of Jesus Christ using this simple outline. Perhaps you yourself will come to that wonderful knowledge. In either case, we'd love to hear about it.

God bless you every one!

Donna and Peggy